Totally Bound Publishing books by Maren Jenner

Sweet Nothings
The Cupcake Standard
The Jellybean Dilemma

I0652145

Sweet Nothings

THE JELLYBEAN DILEMMA

MAREN JENNER

The Jellybean Dilemma
ISBN # 978-1-80250-593-1
©Copyright Maren Jenner 2023
Cover Art by Erin Dameron-Hill ©Copyright December 2023
Interior text design by Claire Siemaszkiewicz
Totally Bound Publishing

THE JELLYBEAN DILEMMA

Dedication

To my best friends, Valerie and Abby.
I couldn't have done this without you.

Acknowledgements

First of all, I'd like to thank Totally Bound for helping this story reach its full potential and allowing me to realize my dream of becoming a published author. A huge thank-you to my editor, Nicki, for all her assistance and suggestions.

I couldn't have done this without my beta readers, specifically Lindsay and Heather. But the biggest thank-you goes to my CP Christine who is always available to toss ideas around or read another revision.

To all my friends and family who supported me on this journey, who believed in me, who never let me give up—thank you and I love you.

Lastly, a big thanks to you, my readers, because this wouldn't be possible without you.

Chapter One

I tapped the toe of my Jimmy Choo as I watched for Greg to pull the limo up. At last, his headlights flashed through the glass door, and I hurried into the frigid night. I didn't go far, though, since I'd promised Greg I'd wait for him to escort me to the car. Snow was my enemy when wearing heels.

Greg jumped out of the front seat as soon as he'd parked, striding toward me. His twinkling gray eyes met mine before he offered me his arm, and his mouth tipped up at one corner. "You actually waited for me."

With my chin high, I looped my hand to grip his forearm as we crossed the short distance. "I didn't want to risk spraining an ankle." Or making a fool of myself by falling into him as I'd done last month after my parents' gala. Though, the few moments in his strong embrace were almost worth my embarrassment.

"You're the one who decided to wear death-trap shoes."

As if to emphasize his words, one of my heels slipped, but I steadied myself against him. My heart raced as his peppermint and cedar scent enveloped me. I had to get control of myself. "These are Jimmy Choos." I sniffed. "I'll have you know this particular style isn't even available to the public yet." I looked up, way up, to see what he had to say about that. Even in my heels, he still had four inches on me, and it was more than annoying at times like this.

Greg scoffed. "Just cause they're pretty doesn't mean they're practical. Michigan doesn't give a damn about the latest fashion trend." He yanked open the back door of the limo with a chiding glare.

I transferred my grip to his gloved hand, feeling like a chastised puppy as I slid into the back seat. I couldn't do anything on my own, not even a simple walk to the car. A heavy fog of depression crept over me. Christmas was over. Tonight was the last of the parties I had to attend and the week until New Year loomed.

My brother Derek and his fiancée Avery had hosted tonight. Our friends Gina and Liam were there, too, along with their current significant others. Greg and I had been the only singles there.

Not that I minded being single. It was a huge improvement from being engaged to Kevin, my ex-fiancé I broke up with two months ago. But it was difficult to see Derek and Avery snuggled together, stealing touches or kisses every chance they got. My eye caught on Greg coming out with another armload of presents, and I sighed. It was especially hard when the man I wanted was always so close, yet so unattainable.

Greg shut the trunk with a thud that echoed through the limo, then he took his place in the front seat. The barrier between us was down, as usual. His gaze caught mine in the mirror, looking much less stormy than a few minutes ago. "Did you get your present?"

I frowned. We'd already exchanged gifts inside. My fingers grazed the soft cashmere scarf he'd given me. I'd gifted him a bottle of cologne, the same kind he always wore. It ensured I could have my fill of his delicious scent.

The light from a streetlamp glinted off a small package to my right. Excitement fluttered through me as I reached for it, a full smile blooming on my face when I felt the familiar weight. I held it up, giddy to see a whole bag of jellybeans wrapped in cellophane and tied with a lopsided red ribbon. I thought he'd forgotten. Warmth flooded me, a welcome change from the depressing bleakness that had cocooned me over the last few weeks.

"Merry Christmas, Jellybean," he said softly.

My throat grew tight at all the memories his gift brought to mind, and I had to swallow before I answered, "Merry Christmas, Just Greg." His face transformed with a genuine grin — the kind that made my stomach do all sorts of acrobatics.

"Home?"

I hated that word. It didn't come close to describing the house I lived in. Exhaustion, heavier than a weighted blanket, settled over me once more, but I nodded. As we started off, I pushed aside my bleak thoughts and let my mind drift to the origin of Greg's nickname.

Greg had hired on when he was nineteen as an apprentice to his uncle Harry, our main driver. Derek and I were thirteen, at the time, with too many activities for one driver to handle. My parents, owners of the vast Great Lakes Shipping empire, had wanted someone they knew and trusted. When Harry had recommended his nephew, that was that.

I smiled, calling to Greg, "How many nicknames did I try out on you?"

One side of his mouth ticked up, finding my eyes again in the mirror. "I didn't keep track."

Oh, how annoyed he'd been. There weren't many nicknames for Greg, so I'd pestered him for his full name, Gregory James Peterson, trying every combination in the book.

"What was so wrong with Greg anyway?"

Absolutely nothing. "I thought it was too formal." I shrugged. "Sorry." We both chuckled.

One day he'd had enough. As I'd exited the limo, he'd stopped me with a gentle, "Miss Rhonda?"

I'd haughtily paused, staring up at his face while also trying to look down my nose at him. Difficult to do with him so much taller than me. His six-foot-two frame had seemed even more gigantic back then.

"No more nicknames. It's just Greg."

And I'd smiled brightly. *"Fine, Just Greg."* Then I'd skipped off to my activity.

As the limo slowed to a stop in front of my too-big house, I grabbed my candy and waited for Greg to open the door. I took my time getting out, letting his steady hand guide me. At least my steps were clear so he wouldn't need to walk me all the way up.

I couldn't help glancing at his handsome face, a wave of longing crashing over me as I cradled my precious bag of jellybeans. This was the first time in two years he'd given me the gift in person. Shortly after I'd turned nineteen, Greg became my brother's driver. I didn't like to analyze why Greg had jumped ship. One specific incident stood out, but I shoved that aside, like always.

Lately, though, Greg had drifted back to me, but I wasn't sure why. It seemed like he had a good thing going with Derek and Avery, crossing over from mere employee to good friends with both of them. Since the gala, though, I'd seen more and more of him.

I studied him for another moment, wondering about those six years between us. Now that I was twenty-one, it felt like it shouldn't matter. My crush on him was as strong as the day it began two and a half years ago. Maybe even stronger.

But my feelings didn't seem to matter. He still never looked at me as anything other than an employer, at most a friend. I turned to make my way up the steps, dreading the emptiness of my huge, dark house.

"What should I do with the presents?"

The question halted me in my tracks, and I had to stop myself from wrinkling my nose. Just thinking of all the beautiful packages I'd ripped open, all labeled with my name, unsettled my stomach. I appreciated the thought our friends had put into picking out my gifts, but the idea of dealing with all the new stuff overwhelmed me. I sighed.

"Rhonda?" Concern laced Greg's voice.

Suddenly the steps seemed impossible to climb as the next week stretched before me, a depressing runway into another year. Just the thought of starting over made tears burn against my eyes. I turned to look at him as I asked, "What are you doing for New Year's?"

Frowning, he left his post by the car to stand in front of me. "What's going on, Jellybean? You're not yourself. Is it the breakup with Kevin, or is something else going on?" One gloved hand reached out, hovering in the space between us, stopping just shy of my arm.

I didn't pull away, but I didn't close the distance either as annoyance flashed through me. "I'm tired of people assuming my life ended when my relationship with Kevin did. Or apologizing for it. 'I'm so sorry to hear about your breakup!'" I rolled my eyes. "There's nothing to be sorry for. I knew exactly what I was doing then, and I haven't regretted it for a moment."

Truth rang through my statement, echoing in the silence between us. Yet my words fell short. I really didn't regret breaking up with Kevin, but it didn't change the fact that I was floundering.

My entire life I'd been raised for one job — to marry someone wealthy, and accept my place on that pedestal, visible for everyone's admiration and scrutiny. The thing about pedestals was they were only built for one. And it was hard to get down on your own.

Greg cleared his throat, looking like he might apologize.

But that was the opposite of what I needed, so I repeated my question, more firmly, "What are you doing for New Year's?"

He sighed. "I was thinking of going home. It's been a while, and my sister's having this big New Year's wedding…"

My jaw dropped. "Wait. You haven't said if you're going to your sister's wedding yet? It's only a week away!"

As he always did when he was uncomfortable, he adjusted his hat. "It's not that simple. I don't have a date, for one. And if I show up by myself, my family will try to set me up with every single girl there."

I practically felt him shudder, and my wheels started spinning. "Take me." The words tumbled out of my mouth before I could think twice.

"What?" His hat nearly flew off his head, the way his eyebrows shot up. He scoffed. "Yeah, right."

The more I thought about it, the more perfect the idea sounded. "Why not? No one knows me other than your uncle." I shrugged. "Sure, they've probably heard of me, but that just makes you sound better." My last name carried weight in all the right circles. "No one has to know you're my driver, unless you want them to. I've got nothing going on and I desperately need a change of scenery. Where is this wedding?" Images of warm, tropical places floated through my head.

"Marquette."

Those two syllables shut down any vacation fantasies I had. "In the middle of winter?" Michigan's Upper Peninsula was harsh at the best of times, but during the winter it was simply brutal. I frowned. "*That's* where you grew up? No wonder you're so grumpy."

A noise escaped from him, part snort, part grunt. "So, you *don't* want to go?" He folded his arms, staring at me with those unnerving gray eyes.

He was still taller than me, even though I stood on the step above him. "I didn't say that." The very thought of spending New Year's here threatened to send me into a panic.

"Then you want to come?"

This time I didn't hesitate. "Yes."

"And you'll go as my date?" Skepticism laced every word.

"Yes." My stomach flipped at the idea.

A slow smile spread across Greg's handsome face. "Rhonda Elgin going out with the chauffeur. What are you going to tell your parents?"

His words punctured a hole in the carefully erected barrier I'd placed my fantasies in. There had been a time when not a day went by without me dreaming of that very thing, but I'd ruined my chance of those dreams coming true in one short night.

I swallowed, fighting to keep the tremor out of my voice. "Unless you plan to announce it to them, I doubt they'll find out. Especially since they're out of the country." With a quick glance at the limo, I said, "Could you please put the presents on the dining room table? I'll sort through them later. Text me the details about the trip." I started up the steps, then I paused.

Greg was bent over the open trunk.

"And, Greg?"

That handsome head poked around the side.

"I mean it, I actually want details." Not vague suggestions. I needed actual concrete plans to figure out what I should bring. I waited until he nodded to finish climbing the steps.

Upstairs, I snitched a few jellybeans from the package before changing out of my dress. My shoes came off next as I rummaged for comfy clothes. It was a relief to let my hair down.

Then my phone started pinging. And it didn't stop. *What the hell?* I hurried over, wondering what the emergency was.

It was Greg, texting me every possible detail he had, mostly copies of messages from his sister. I trotted downstairs to find him leaning against the counter, behind the tower of presents on the dining room table.

His smirk grew as I scowled. "Was that enough details?"

"You seriously want to leave the day after tomorrow?"

When he shrugged, his uniform jacket bunched up around his waist, and he tugged it down with a sharp motion. "If we're doing this, we're all in. I haven't been home in a while, so it'll be a big to-do. I'll be in it for the whole nine yards — the bachelor party, rehearsal dinner, and, of course, the wedding." He paused. "All or nothing."

I digested the information, a far cry from the easy getaway I'd imagined.

He arched an eyebrow. "And, as you so politely pointed out, I should let my sister know sooner than later."

His challenging stare lingered on me, and I felt naked without my formal wear.

He stepped closer, an earnestness coming over him. "Rhonda, I know it's a lot. And it's short notice, but once I started thinking about going with you... I really want to. It'll be great to see everyone again. My sister will die outright of happiness, an Elgin attending her wedding!" His throat bobbed. "This might be overstepping, but I think it'd be good for you to get out of here."

Silence hung between us as I digested his words, the sincerity of his request taking me aback. *He wants me to go?* My heart skipped a beat.

"We're all worried about you, Avery and Derek especially. You've lost weight." He scanned my length, a frown tightening his mouth. "You hardly go anywhere. You don't talk to anyone."

Wow, I know Greg and Derek are close, but this is a whole new level. Is that Avery's doing? Unease sat in me that he was paying such close attention without me even knowing it. I didn't know what to do with his scrutiny. I swallowed hard, glancing at the floor.

"Come with me." His tone softened, almost begging me. "My family will love you, and I promise you won't be bored. What do you say, Jellybean?"

My eyes flicked back to his. When I took in that pleading smile, I simply couldn't say no.

* * * *

Two days later, a horn honked outside while I scrambled to find my other Jimmy Choo. *I just had it.* Three quick raps on the door let me know it was Greg. He always knocked the same way.

"It's open," I called, ducking under the table.

The annoying squeak of the front door sounded, once then twice. Countless repairmen had been fired and given bad Yelp reviews for not fixing that ridiculous noise.

"Your hinges are too tight."

My head slammed against the underside of the table, and I gritted my teeth against the pain as I backed out as gracefully as I could.

Greg grinned down at me, one black Jimmy Choo dangling from his finger. "Missing something?"

Rubbing my head wouldn't do anything except mess up my hair, and yelling at Greg wasn't going to make either of us feel any better. So, I choked back my annoyance, giving him a tight smile before biting out a clipped, "Thank you."

When I reached for my shoe, he offered his hand. I took it, my breath hitching at the warm touch. Usually his gloves formed a barrier between us, and I blurted out, "You're not wearing your uniform." The moment the words left my lips I wished I could take them back. I bit my lip. "I, um…"

I sagged into the nearest chair. "I'm sorry, that sounded idiotic. I haven't had the best morning and I'm running on no caffeine." Our gazes collided as I lifted my chin, relieved at the understanding in his.

Instead of handing me my shoe, he knelt in front of me. *What's he doing?* He gestured to my stocking-clad foot and softly asked, "May I?"

I nodded, still unsure.

One side of his mouth tipped up. His bare hand grasped my ankle ever so gently, reminding me of the night of the gala when he'd untangled me from my dress. Except now I couldn't breathe, each brush of his fingers sending jolts of electricity up my calf.

Then he slid my shoe onto my foot, buckling the dainty strap like he'd done it a million times. "All right, Jellybean, now you're ready to go to the ball."

When he offered me his hand, I wasn't positive I was steady enough to stand, especially in the wake of that dimpled grin.

Chapter Two

After I stood up, I kept hold of Greg's hand for an extra moment, to be sure my knees would actually work. I let go of him once I was confident in my stability. Needing a second to compose myself, I sauntered over to my stack of luggage. Which of course he commented on.

"How many times do you plan to change your clothes?" He arched an eyebrow. "We'll only be there for a week."

"Do you know how many events you want us to attend? I need an outfit for each." I rolled my eyes. What did he expect? As I strode outside, I balked when I took in the bulky, multi-colored SUV parked at the bottom of my steps. "What is that?"

He grinned proudly. "My baby."

I shook my head adamantly. "Nope. No way." I gestured to my high heels. "There is no way to get in and out of *that*"—I pointed as I glared at the monstrosity—"without killing myself. I'd have to repack all my outfits."

"If it means sensible shoes, then by all means." He stared at me as if waiting for me to trot off and do just that. When I didn't, he sighed. "Rhonda, we're going to the Upper Peninsula, what we locals like to call the U.P. Dressing up is Bog boots and flannel shirts. The goal is not to freeze and you…" His gaze trailed down my length under my unbuttoned pea coat, taking in my silk blouse, flared black skirt, stockings and open-toed Jimmy Choos. "You lose."

My ex-fiancé's parting words echoed through my head. *The only thing you're good for is arm candy. If you take away your clothes and makeup, what are you? Nothing.* The door slammed in my memory, making me flinch. I blinked, refocusing on Greg standing next to me, saying my name.

"You okay?"

I glared at him. "I'm fine. And the way I'm dressed is perfectly fine. You wanted a date — well this is what you get. But there is no way in hell I'm going anywhere in that rickety piece of crap. Town Car, limo, great. That?" I frowned at the rusted-out SUV, the body a splotchy green with a white hood and tires so tall I'd have to hop to get in. "No way."

He clenched his jaw, a muscle ticking in his cheek. "Be reasonable. We're talking about Marquette, in December. Those are snow tires."

"You already told your family I'm coming, right?" I lifted my chin a fraction of an inch as he nodded, miserably. "Good. Let me know when you have the proper transportation." I pivoted to go back inside. I couldn't believe Greg had the nerve to think that I, Rhonda Elgin, heiress to a shipping empire, setter of fashion trends, head of countless charities, would deign to set foot in that death trap. *Snow tires, my foot.*

Ten minutes later, a horn honked several times, short and snappy. I poked my head outside, satisfied to see my familiar Town Car in the driveway. I started to stalk down the steps as triumph had me preening. A clearing throat from the front seat stopped me in my tracks. "What?" I snapped.

He pointedly looked from me to my luggage, then smirked and pushed the trunk button. "Have fun in those shoes. Don't twist an ankle." He rolled up the window while he waited.

I would have stomped my foot, except he was right about my shoes...not that I'd admit it. Somehow, I managed to haul my things into the trunk, with all my nails intact, thank you. Out of habit, I almost climbed in the back seat. My hand hovered over the handle, but even I wasn't that cruel.

"Well?" I asked, smugly plopping into the front seat. "Let's go."

As my house grew smaller in the side mirror, the pressure in my chest lessened. Greg offered me a bottle of water, which I accepted with a quiet, "Thank you." Not too far down the road, I shed my coat and my shoes, tucking my stockinged feet to one side.

A restless energy filled me, and I didn't know what I was supposed to do. I had a cotillion under my belt. I could descend a staircase in four-inch heels without wobbling once. Fancy dinner settings, with several courses, multiple forks, spoons and knives? Wouldn't faze me. Waltzes, small talk, speeches, luncheons, charity events...all small potatoes.

Road trip? Seven and a half hours in the front seat next to Greg? My palms were already sweating, and it had only been fifteen minutes. Traffic grew heavy as we approached the highway. I'd just unscrewed the cap to my water bottle when some idiot swerved right into our lane, making Greg slam on the brakes. Water splashed down the front of me.

My blouse was as paper-thin as my bra. *Shit.* "Greg," I whispered hesitantly. I didn't want to startle him by the state I was in. I had to grab my coat, and reaching into the back seat would give him an inevitable eyeful.

He ignored me, too busy muttering under his breath at the inconsiderate driver. I tried once more, but he stayed focused on the road ahead. *Maybe if I'm quick.* I reached into the back seat, my torso near his shoulder as I grabbed my coat.

"Rhonda, what the hell?" he yelped, confronted with my see-through shirt. Turning his attention back to the road, he swerved, narrowly missing a car in the turn lane.

The motion jerked me back into my seat.

"A little warning would have been nice," he muttered.

My cheeks were hot as I hid beneath my coat. "I tried."

His knuckles were white, jaw clenched and shoulders tensed the entire time he fought traffic to turn into the Wal-Mart parking lot. He let out a long sigh. Giving me a tentative glance, he relaxed when he saw I was covered. "What happened?"

"I went to take a drink when you had to slam on the brakes." My chin quivered. I hated being yelled at, plus I was cold, damp and wearing a see-through shirt. Not to mention embarrassed as hell.

Those smooth fingers raked through his hair, which was longer on top and usually hidden by his cap. "Did you pack *anything* comfortable in all that luggage? It's a long trip and, don't get me wrong, you look good, but..." He trailed off as a big, fat tear rolled down my cheek.

How can I fail so completely at something millions of people do every day?

His jaw worked a few times, and he sighed. "Just wait here, all right? Climb in the back and keep your coat on. There's a blanket, too, if you're cold. I'll leave the car running." He stepped out of the door and shoved his hands in pockets, before dipping down to add, "I won't be long." Then he left.

I didn't even bother to get out. I hit the lock button and shimmied over the console to the back seat where I burrowed into the blanket. I flopped my head against the seat, frustrated at myself and my life. Every time a sliver of hope awakened inside me, an incident like this would snuff it out.

Since Kevin and I broke up, my days had been dull and empty. My life was meaningless. There was no point, and it had nothing to do with my ex.

He'd just been the icing on the cake. It was seeing Avery and my brother together that had made me realize that my relationship with Kevin was for all the wrong reasons. Avery stood up for my brother and made him feel worthwhile. They had just met a couple of months ago, but they brought out the best in each other.

I envied their synchronicity, as well as their individual sense of purpose. Derek had just launched an app which changed the shipping industry, making filling containers much more efficient. Avery was still studying for her degree in business.

Me? Until I'd seen the two of them together, I'd been content with my life. I thought I had it all—money, friends, the right fiancé. But after being around them, I saw my life as it really was—fake.

A rapping on the window startled me. I hurried to unlock the door, swiping at my wet cheeks as an afterthought. But I wasn't quick enough.

Greg's smile dimmed. "Oh, Jellybean." He set several bags on the seat next to me and sighed. Then he straightened, pulling his phone out of his pocket. The deep murmur of his voice continued for several moments before he reached in to unlock the front door. "Buckle up."

"Where are we going?" *He's not taking me home, is he?* I bit my lip as nerves twisted my gut.

He met my gaze in the mirror when he sat down, and he grinned before tipping his imaginary hat. "I know just the place."

A few minutes later, we pulled up to Derek and Avery's apartment complex. Greg hurried to open my door. "Avery's expecting you." He nodded when I hesitated, gifting me with a soft smile. "Go change. I'll find us some coffee."

Relief pulsed through me. He wasn't ditching me, and I not only had a safe space to change, I'd get to talk to Avery for a few minutes. I grabbed the bags, flying out of the door.

I braced myself as I stepped into the elevator. Small spaces were my nemesis. No one knew my deep dark secret—I was claustrophobic. I'd been expecting to change in some tiny restroom at a gas station, and I was happy to endure the elevator if it meant avoiding that horrible experience.

Knocking on the apartment door, I shifted from foot to foot. The door flung open, and my brother greeted me. His jet-black hair was tousled in his signature style. Our hair might be the same shade, but his eyes were a rich deep blue, while mine were pale. More like ice. I'd always been jealous of him for that, not to mention he'd gotten all the height.

He looked me over, concern etched on his face. "Rhonda, what's this about you going on a trip with Greg?"

Needing comfort more than anything, I stepped up to him and rested my head on his shoulder.

He immediately softened, shutting the door with one hand and patting my back with the other. "Hey, you okay?"

"Derek!" Avery squealed, running down the hall. "Did I hear the door? Is Rhonda here?" She skidded to a stop, her long, strawberry-blonde hair swinging around her. "Oh, good." She beamed.

"Geez, Ave. Chill." Liam's deep voice startled me.

I hadn't even seen him sitting on the couch. I squared my shoulders and moved away from Derek, unwilling to appear weak in front of my brother's oldest friend. "Hey, Liam."

He grinned, and I glimpsed why my friends always thought Liam was so hot. Not only was he rich—the guy was built, tall, and muscular. But he was too beefy for me, and a bit on the arrogant side. Plus, I'd grown up with him. He was our neighbor, and his mom was close friends with ours. But you'd never know he was two years older than us by the way he acted. Twenty-three to our twenty-one. When Derek skipped a grade, Liam had been right there to stand up for him.

I'd forgotten what that was like, to know someone always had your back. My brother and I were getting to that point once more. It hadn't been easy, and I had Avery to thank for it. But I still had difficulty remembering I wasn't alone anymore.

"So, you're running away with the chauffeur?" Liam chuckled. "About time you shook things up."

Derek glared at him.

I just sighed and turned to Avery. "I'm soaking wet under this coat. I managed to spill a bottle of water all over myself." My shoulders bobbed up in a self-deprecating shrug. "Is there some place I can change?" The sympathy in my friend's expression was almost my undoing, but I kept it together.

"Of course. C'mon." She led me to the spare room.

I hurried to change, wrinkling my nose at the too-big sweater and the jeans that bagged in weird places. There were no underthings either, so I kept my panties on but went braless. The sweater was baggy enough you couldn't tell.

Another bag contained thick socks and clunky boots. I stared at them for a long moment, loath to give up my Jimmy Choos. But Greg had been kind enough to pick them out, so I sat on the bed and put them on. Then I had to tamp down my makeup, for obvious reasons.

I stared at myself in the mirror for several moments wondering just who the person looking back was. With a deep breath, I bolstered myself before returning to the living room where three wide sets of eyes stared at me.

Avery was the first to smile. "I don't think I've ever seen you so casually dressed. Is that why Greg asked me what size you are?"

He did that? I nodded, crossing an arm over my waist.

A knock at the door took the attention off me, and Derek hurried to open it. Avery's best friend, Gina, peered in with a grin.

"Hey," she called with a cheery wave. The moment she noticed Liam, her face fell.

His expression twisted into a scowl. "They let just anyone in here."

Avery sighed. "Play nice, you two."

Gina walked in, shedding her coat then giving Avery a quick hug. I always marveled at how different they were. Avery was nearly six feet tall, while Gina was a couple of inches shorter than me. She was petite where Avery was curvy. Avery was fair, with strawberry-blonde hair that hung low on her back, and bright green eyes, always lit with her easy smile. Gina's olive skin complimented her dark hair and eyes. Her smiles were more difficult to come by, but you could always trust her to tell the hard truth.

Liam stood up, stretching wide and showing off a glimpse of taut abs. I noticed Gina snuck a peak before quickly turning away. Which surprised me. Liam looked nothing like her lanky, long-haired boyfriend, Josh.

"Well," Liam said. "I think I've stayed long enough." He glanced once more at Gina, who just stuck her nose in the air. Turning to Derek, Liam grinned. "If these girls get to be too much for you, let me know and we'll grab lunch."

Derek nodded. "I just might do that."

"Bye, Rhonda. Good luck with Greg." He smirked before he disappeared.

"Greg?" Gina asked.

I shook my head. "First, I want to know what's up with you and Liam. What happened to your truce? You guys were fine at Christmas."

Derek folded his arms. "Yeah, Gina, why don't you tell Rhonda what happened?"

Avery's lips twitched before she covered her mouth with her hand.

"I still maintain that I did just what was asked of me." Gina sniffed.

He lifted an eyebrow.

She sighed, her shoulders dropping slightly. "Liam was having problems with his girl."

I frowned. "The one he brought to Christmas?"

Gina nodded. "Yep. So, Derek invited them to have donuts and coffee with us. It was my turn to pick up the donuts." She shrugged before saying, "I simply brought everyone's favorite, but Liam has avoided me ever since."

"You bought him the biggest, pinkest donut I've ever seen!" Derek shook his head.

"It's not my fault no one specified what color frosting he wanted." One corner of her mouth tipped in a mischievous smirk.

I tried to picture Liam with his big, meaty hands closed around a pink, sprinkled donut and laughter burst out of me. "Gina, that's awful!"

"It was hilarious," Avery said, chuckling. When Derek didn't join in, she went over to nudge him. "Come on, Captain. You have to admit it *was* pretty funny watching him eat that donut."

Derek's mouth contorted until a bark of laughter escaped. Gina grinned in triumph, and he immediately looked guilty. "*Never* tell him I said anything."

When the amusement died off, Gina turned to me. "So, you and Greg?"

Spotlight's back on me. With a sigh, I began filling them in. "Greg's sister —"

"Wait," Avery interrupted. "Greg has a sister?"

"Evidently." I shrugged. He'd always been tight-lipped about his personal life, and it made me feel a little better that it wasn't just with me.

"And you're going as his date?" Her eyebrows shot up. "A *real* date? Or a 'just showing up so he doesn't have to go alone' date?"

Um. "The second one I think." We hadn't discussed it in precise terms. Speaking of dating, I desperately needed advice. I hesitated to say anything in front of my brother, but I needed their help more. "So, I've sort of had a crush on Greg since, well, a while now, and —"

"You've what?" My brother growled, stepping toward me.

Shit. I hid my face in my hand.

"Sorry, Rhonda," Avery said as she glared at Derek. "I'll handle this." She shoved Derek down the hall as he ranted about me crushing on Greg.

Yes, Greg had been our chauffeur growing up, but I'd never thought of him as anything more until the summer after I graduated high school. When he first started working for us, he'd been awkward and gangly. But always kind. I could count on him to be there when he said he would. He was the first constant in my life, although he'd always conducted himself perfectly.

Our lines were firm, him the employee, me the employer's daughter. Until I took matters into my own hands the fall after I'd graduated. And ruined everything.

I jolted back to the present as Derek's voice echoed back to me. Gina shifted next to me.

Avery interrupted my brother. "You can't say that! It's elitist. Greg's a good guy, and he's our friend."

Derek's response was muffled.

Avery said, "I don't care. They're both our friends first and foremost. So shut up if you want to stay here, or pout in the bedroom. Your choice."

When she huffed back into the living room, my shoulders sagged. "Is he really upset?"

"Nah, he'll be fine. I think he's just shocked to find out this has been going on for a while and he didn't know about it." She paused. "This isn't just some phase, right, Rhonda?"

I felt my cheeks heat as I shook my head. Over two years of wanting the guy was more than just a phase.

"Are you sure it's not just a reaction to getting over Kevin?" Gina asked.

A derisive snort escaped me, and I clamped my hand over my mouth. I hurried to answer. "No way. I was never into Kevin himself, just the idea of him." I sighed, trying to find the words to explain. "Kevin and I were my parents' ideal. He was the easy button. He's an asshole, and I knew it."

Derek started growling from the hallway. This time when Avery excused herself, the raised voices lasted for a few moments then all was quiet.

She grinned when she came back. "All right, your brother has been banished, and he knows the consequences if he comes out of that bedroom. Please continue."

I hesitated. "Kevin only cared about himself. He used me for my status, to make himself look better, and I used him for the same purpose. The sex was okay. But that's all it was." I shrugged.

They were both quiet for several long seconds before Avery said, "Wow, Rhonda, that sounds…awful."

"I didn't know how bad it was until you came around." The words came out as little more than a whisper. I was grateful my brother wasn't here for this part. "You and Derek showed me what it was to have more, to want more."

I paused for a long moment as the familiar ache opened in my chest. "Now, I can't go back." I sighed, crossing my arms. "But I can't seem to move forward either." The bleakness of my life threatened to overwhelm me, the emptiness of it like a gaping hole inside. "I thought maybe getting out of town would help, but I've already fucked that up, too."

"Tell us everything." Avery sat on the couch, patting the space beside her.

Gina nodded, perching on the arm of the chair across the room. So, I sat down and started from the beginning.

"Wait, you were crawling on your hands and knees when he came in the door?" There was mischief in Avery's tone. "Rhonda, has Greg ever given any indication he likes you, too?"

A flash of gray eyes filled with longing flooded my vision. His lips formed my name before I slammed my shields back into place. "Maybe once."

"I knew it!" She almost crowed in triumph. "And today you were practically ass in the air when he came in." She smirked, sharing a knowing look with Gina.

I thought of his soft hands on my ankle, sliding on my shoe. "Perhaps." That didn't explain his anger, though. I told her about the water incident, my shirt plastered to my chest and how he'd yelled at me. "Then he stomped into the store."

"Hmm. That doesn't sound like Greg. He's always so even-keeled." Her brow crinkled.

Tell me something I don't know. When she didn't say anything else, I prodded. "So, any advice?"

"Yeah, just relax," she said as if it were that easy. "I mean, it's Greg. You two have known each other forever, right? You were thirteen when he came around?" She paused, and I could practically see her mind working. "Wasn't he your driver for most of that? What made him switch to Derek?"

I clamped the lid over that memory and deflected. "Oh, that was about the time I got serious with Kevin. Derek needed a new driver when Greg's uncle retired."

I shrugged, trying to stay nonchalant. "Kevin already had one, so we just started sharing his."

"Really?" Her eyebrows jumped up. "You just broke up with Kevin, and now Greg's switching back to drive for you…"

She's reading more into this than there is. Honestly.

Chapter Three

Derek snuck back into the room and met my gaze. "Think about Greg's nickname for you," he said quietly.

"Derek!" Avery whipped around to glare at him, but her face softened before she turned back to me. "I didn't know you had a nickname. What is it?" She almost bounced on the couch in her eagerness.

"Jellybean," I whispered. They were my favorite candy, and Papa's, too.

The thought of him made my breath catch because I missed him so. Papa had always made Christmas special, and I put up with all the awful traditions — cheek pinching, mistletoe, itchy dresses, fancy food and shoes that hurt — just so I could end the night by sneaking into Papa's office with him.

Every year, I'd kick off my shoes, and my hair would come out of the bobby pins or ribbons, then I'd dance with Papa. He smelled of bourbon and cigars with a hint of mint. When it was time for me to go home, when I was so worn out I was practically asleep on my feet, my toes tucked back in my awful shoes, my bobby pins gathered up, Papa would slip me a bag of jellybeans, kiss my cheek, and tell me Merry Christmas.

Before I could elaborate further, my phone buzzed. I pulled it out to see a text from Greg letting me know he was back. I stood up. "Greg's waiting. If you guys think of any more advice, would you let me know?"

Avery bounded off the couch to wrap me in a fierce hug. "Of course. And text me if you need anything."

I nodded, glancing at Gina.

Gina smirked. "You got this, Rhonda. You're a badass, you just gotta figure out what you want, and go for it." She reached out to pat my shoulder.

Derek sauntered over. "I'll walk you out." A sheepish expression crossed his face as he slinked past Avery. She gave him a warning glare, and he held up his hands. "I'll behave, I promise." He waited for me to gather my bag and coat then escorted me to the hallway. We walked in silence for a few beats. "I know we've had our issues—"

"I've apologized for that, Derek. I know I was a bitch." I'd royally screwed up our relationship over the past few years, and it was just in the last several months we'd started to become comfortable with each other again. I didn't want to do anything to lose him.

"Would you let me talk?" He gave me a sidelong look until I nodded. "Good. I'm sorry I didn't realize how you felt about Greg before today. I feel like a good brother would have known."

He doesn't think he's a good brother? "Derek…"

"And I'm sorry I reacted the way I did. Greg is one of the best guys I know." We reached the elevator, and he pushed the down button. "I think you guys would be great together."

My lips tilted up. "Thanks." I stared at the floor while we waited. "There's a very real possibility that nothing will come of this, though. It might just be me."

The elevator arrived, and Derek put a hand on the doors to hold them open. "Then Greg is a fool." His soft words wound around me, warmth spreading through my chest as he wrapped me a huge hug. "Good luck."

"Thanks." I stepped into the elevator, and the doors closed with a quiet whoosh.

The tight space made me nervous, so I let the memory of that first Christmas without Papa resurface, playing out in my mind. He passed away right after my eighteenth birthday. It was a difficult time, of course, but I had managed.

Until I heard my first Christmas song.

Greg was driving me home from a charity fundraiser I'd helped Mom with. Not up for conversation, I asked Greg to turn on the radio. *Hark the Herald Angels Sing* began playing.

All my happy memories of Christmas had elation bubbling up, only for the devastating realization that Papa was gone to crash over me. No sneaking into his office to dance together, away from the stuffy expectations of the family. No classic rock to sing our hearts out to. And, worst of all, no bag of jellybeans.

Just as we pulled into our driveway, I started to cry, knowing Christmas would never be the same.

Greg noticed my tears right away. Pulling over, he turned in his seat to ask, "What's wrong, Rhonda?"

Through my tears and my hiccups, I explained. He shut off the radio, offering me comforting words, and he'd given my hand an extra squeeze when he helped me out of the car.

As expected, Christmas was exceptionally painful that year. Papa's absence felt like a huge hole, and nothing brought me the usual joy of the season. I'd put extra effort into my gifts, wanting something special to commemorate his absence. Papa had collected keychains, an absurd, unusual hobby according to my grandma.

So I'd made everyone a lanyard keychain, learning how to do intricate braids with the strips of plastic. My fingers cramped from all the weaving, and I meticulously found each of my family members' favorite colors. I passed out the little wrapped boxes, then had everyone open them at the same time. Their confused, dismayed expressions punched another hole in my stomach.

My parents decided to stay late with Grandma, so Greg drove me and Derek home. Derek's big gift was a new smart watch, and he focused on setting it up the entire way while I stewed. The limo just came to a stop before he raced into the house.

I hadn't given Greg his present yet and when he started to get out, I said, "Greg, wait." Then I handed him the box wrapped in shiny green paper.

I'd made him a lanyard too, with two shades of his favorite color—blue. As he peeled off the paper, I felt stupider by the second. No one else liked my gifts. Why would he?

He lifted the lid, and a smile tipped his lips as he lifted out the lanyard keychain. "Rhonda, did you make this?"

I stared down at the seat. "Yeah. Papa collected keychains, and I wanted everyone to have one to remember him by. Sorry. I know it's stupid."

"No." His firm tone had me looking up. He shook his head, kindness in his gaze. "No one has ever made me a gift before. This is special, not stupid. Thank you."

His grateful reaction caught me off guard and my throat thickened, but I managed to nod. He set the keychain back in the box, then stepped out to open my door. Massive snowflakes drifted down to cover the cement, and my shiny black shoes contrasted perfectly with the pristine snow as I slipped my hand into his gloved one.

I stood up, careful with my movements in my heels. Once I was confident in my stance, I grinned up at him. "Merry Christmas, Greg."

He removed his other hand from behind his back and presented me with a cellophane bag of multi-colored jellybeans tied with a lopsided red ribbon. "Merry Christmas, Rhonda."

My bottom lip quivered as I stared at the gift, disbelief coursing through me. Overwhelmed by the more than thoughtful surprise, I threw my arms around his waist, burying my face in his uniform and soaking it with my tears. Greg had awkwardly patted my back, murmuring soothing noises until at last I calmed down.

With a sniff and a step backward, I straightened my shoulders. "Thank you, Just Greg. *Now* it feels like Christmas." I managed a watery smile before I took my jellybeans up to my room, and I savored them for weeks to come.

My nickname had started soon after that, when he'd caught me snitching jellybeans out of my pocket.

The elevator door dinged, startling me out of my reverie.

As I walked across the lobby, I marveled at the stable presence Greg had been throughout my life. I'd always been able to count on him. My parents might show up for my science fair, dance recital or other events, but I always knew Greg would be there. He had always been someone I looked up to.

Growing up, I'd had my share of boyfriends. The summer after I graduated high school was when I actually noticed Greg, when I began wanting him as more than an employee. So many guys saw me as a dollar sign or arm candy, a stepping stone for prestige, or a trophy for their collection. Greg never made me feel that way, and he became my ideal.

Which is why I'd leapt at this chance to go on this trip with him.

I smiled when the doorman opened the door for me. Nerves tangled in my stomach, and I wondered just what Greg would think of me in this outfit. I took a deep breath, lifting my chin and squaring my shoulders.

Greg leaned against the car, not noticing me until I cleared my throat. His eyebrows shot up.

"Hot stuff, aren't I?"

To my disappointment, he didn't respond to my teasing. Instead, he asked, "All set? Did everything fit okay?"

Hiding my disappointment at his lack of reaction, I nodded. "The boots are a little big, but they'll do." Awkward silence descended again as he hit the trunk button, and I threw my bag in.

He opened the door wide as he grinned. "Your chariot, madam."

The familiar pose paired with his thoughtfulness eased some of the tension within me. "Thank you." My smile was genuine as I climbed in.

Greg slid into the driver's seat and began his familiar routine. Each time he sat behind the wheel, he went through the same motion. Sit, right hand on wheel, feet in, close door, left hand on wheel. Keys in ignition, start car. Rearview, check. Gas, check. Steering column, seat proper, side mirrors, seatbelt. Then he'd adjust his gloves and go.

When he reached for his non-existent gloves, I giggled. "Is something missing?"

His cheeks tinged pink as he cleared his throat.

I gave him an out, noticing the cups in the console. "What'd you get me from the coffee shop?"

"Oh, right." He put the car in park again and grabbed a bag from the back seat. "They had breakfast sandwiches, too. I wasn't sure if you'd eaten anything. I know you like ham and egg whites, so I had them make you one special."

He ordered me a special sandwich?

"And peppermint mocha." He gestured to the cup nearest me, a broad grin bringing out his dimple. "Your favorite." I stared long enough that his face fell. "That's right, isn't it? You haven't—"

"No. I mean, yes, those are still my favorites." I frowned, staring at the sandwich in my lap. "I'm just surprised you remembered."

This time he put the car in reverse, lightly resting a hand behind my head as he backed up. "Well, you ordered the same things for six years. Kind of hard to forget."

A smile played on my lips, and I waited until we merged onto the highway before I tried my coffee. "Mmm, it's delicious. It's like—"

He finished my sentence with me. "Winter in a cup." His eyes twinkled as I stared at him in surprise. "I haven't forgotten you, Jellybean."

The sweet words made my throat feel tight, but I hid it with a bite of my sandwich, which was also delicious. Avery's comments echoed in my head, and hope blossomed within me that maybe she was right. Maybe my attraction wasn't quite as one-sided as I'd thought. I'd have to be on the lookout for more signs.

As I took another bite of my sandwich, I thought about how much Greg knew about me. It made me realize how little I knew about him. He'd always been taciturn about his personal life, ignoring my pestering questions until I'd given up.

Now, though, I had the perfect excuse to get him to open up. "Okay, so tell me about your family. What am I getting myself into?"

"My family..." He took a bite of his sandwich, taking his time before he answered. "Well, not much to say about my dad. He's a businessman, in the lumber industry. Hard working, hard nosed. Just...hard."

I heard a lot in what he didn't say, in how his shoulders tensed, how each word was clipped. He and his dad had some issues, for sure.

"Mom is the backbone of our family. She works with Dad, just as hard, if not harder than him." A grin eased across his face, his grip on the steering wheel relaxing slightly. "I'm excited to see her again, but I'm most excited to see Mandy, my sister. We text a lot, FaceTime some, but it's been ages since we've been together." His expression grew wistful, and he quickly took a sip of coffee. "I haven't even met this guy she's marrying. Not in person."

I wonder what happened that kept him away for so long. "What's our story going to be?"

His frown created a furrow in his forehead. "What do you mean?"

I balled up my trash and threw it in the bag, then tucked a stray piece of hair behind my ear. "I mean, what are you telling your family about us? Are we just friends? Am I your girlfriend?" I shot him a teasing grin. "Did you kidnap your employer's daughter to drag her up here in the dead of winter just so you wouldn't have to be set up with your mom's friends' daughters?"

"Definitely the last one." His delivery was so matter-of-fact I couldn't help but laugh.

The boots made my feet too warm, so I kicked them off. I brought one leg up, resting my foot on the seat so my knee pressed against my chest. I propped my arm up on it and twirled a strand of hair around my finger. "Well, I think it's important to get our story straight. I don't want to go into this thinking I'm here for the week only to come out of it hearing I'm engaged," I teased. "I mean, I just got out of a crazy engagement, so I'm not at all ready for that." A hint of heavy truth weighted my tone, and Greg shot me a discerning look.

But he let it slide. "Damn. Guess I'd better tell Mom to put away the ring."

His comment caught me so off guard, the coffee I'd just sipped almost came out of my nose. I managed to swallow in between sputtering and coughing.

He chuckled at my reaction, and I gaped at him, taking in the adorable dimple in his right cheek. Flirtatious Greg — that was new.

And dangerous.

Greg drummed his fingers on the steering wheel as we worked on our mutual backstory. "Uncle Harry will know who you are, but he also knows I've been driving for your brother. How about we just tell him something close to the truth, that we met up again through a mutual friend?" He paused to glance over at me. "I'm thinking Avery."

I nodded.

"We started spending more time together. You happened to be free, so we decided this was going to be our first big trip together."

Wow, he's such a guy. I huffed as I shook my head. "What?"

"Do you really think your mom and sister are going to buy that?" I said dryly.

He frowned. "Well, I did until you said it like that."

My heel started to go numb, so I dropped my right foot to the floor and pulled my left one up. "Okay, think about telling Avery that you and I are dating. How would that conversation go?"

The sigh he let out almost blew us backward. "So many questions."

"Exactly. We need to discuss details. Sticking close to the truth is a great idea, because we'll remember it. But being vague?" I shook my head. "That won't do."

The car whined as he sped up to pass a semi, and the blinker clicked as he steered us back into the right lane. He snapped his fingers. "How about we tell them we met at the gala? You were leaving, got tangled up in your dress, and I caught you?"

The memory of his soft gloved hands on my ankle while my palms rested firmly on his broad shoulders flared in my mind, sending a thrill through me. I cleared my throat to hide my reaction. "That's good. But then what? Did we have dinner and start dating?"

He thought for another moment. "We've been taking it easy because of the holidays, but I talked you into coming home with me for this."

"That could work. We'll need more, though." I tapped my chin. "I guess we could use our real stories, starting with Derek's party, helping plan it, getting the two of them together."

His gaze slid to mine then back to the road. "Or after, like the day I came over to get Avery's stuff."

Oh, that had been a mess. Avery and Derek had just had a huge fight, ending in her running away with

Liam's help. I'd brought some of Avery's things to my house where Greg planned to pick them up. It just so happened that Kevin had stopped by — our first post-break up meeting.

"You'll regret this, Rhonda." He'd stood in the entryway, the box in his hands holding all the trinkets he'd left in my house.

Yes, it was my house, bought with my trust fund, furniture paid for by my investments, and decorated with my money. I'd had my lawyer go over everything, just to be sure. One single box was all he was entitled to.

He glared at me. "The only thing you're good for is arm candy. If you take away your clothes and makeup, what are you? Nothing."

Greg had walked through the open door and leaned ever so casually on the door jamb. "Am I interrupting?" He'd glanced my way, and I had forced myself to relax tense shoulders and pressed lips.

"Not at all. Kevin was just leaving."

Moving into the entryway, Greg had positioned himself between my ex-fiancé and me. "Well, don't let me stand in your way."

Kevin had glared at both of us, but Greg kept shifting so his glare never landed on me again. The door had slammed behind Kevin, echoing off the walls and the empty space in my heart.

Taking another sip of my peppermint mocha, I let the past fade. "Maybe we should keep that memory to ourselves," I said, unable to hide the tightness in my voice.

"Did he ever bother you again?"

Constantly. Should I tell Greg? Undecided. "Not like that." *Now, Kevin did it over text.* "Why'd we wait until the last minute to tell your sister we were coming? You know they'll ask, so it's gotta be good."

"Can I make it your fault?" He sounded so sheepish as he lifted one shoulder.

It was absolutely adorable, and I knew I'd never be able to say no to that look. I hoped he never found out, or I'd be in big trouble. "Of course." I thought for a moment before saying, "What if a big charity event that I was in charge of was moved at the last minute, freeing us up?"

"Perfect." His boyish grin made my stomach flip.

My coffee was getting down to the end, so I took the lid off and drained it, lapping up the whipped cream. When Greg glanced at me again, he chuckled.

"What?"

"You've got something, right here." He tapped the end of his nose.

I darted my tongue out and found some whipped cream.

"What was that?" His eyebrows shot up.

Now my nose was wet on top of everything. Digging out a napkin, I wiped it off. "You didn't know I could do that?"

He shook his head.

"Some people can fly. I can lick my nose." I shrugged. "Not the best as far as superpowers go, but not the worst either."

His forehead crinkled as he slowed down for another semi. "What's worse?"

"I don't know. I think telepathy would be pretty awful. Hearing voices all the time, never being able to shut off the noise?" I shuddered at the thought.

"And if you could have any superpower?"

"That's tough." I paused, twirling another strand of hair around my finger as I thought. "Flying is definitely up there, but I'd have to say teleporting because it'd be amazing to get from one place to another just like that." I snapped my fingers. And if I was ever stuck inside a tight spot like that closet again, I could *poof*, be gone. "What about you? If you could have any superpower, what would it be?"

He didn't even hesitate. "To go back in time." He didn't elaborate.

His words were so firm and final I decided I better not pry. At least for now.

Chapter Four

Traffic grew heavier, so I left Greg to his thoughts. My mind drifted to Kevin. Our breakup had brought several issues to light, ones he'd been counting on our marriage to hide.

His exorbitant spending, for example. He came from a family with wealth and status, as did I, so it made sense to combine our resources. Once we'd split, and I'd gone over my expenditures with my accountant, I couldn't believe the ridiculous things he'd spent money on. Especially the flamboyant outings with his guy friends, where they'd given the ladies who had accompanied them whatever they wanted.

Those women were another issue. He'd been more discreet in our time together, but we'd both known we were headed for a marriage of convenience. Though I was by no means a prude, sex had never been very enjoyable for me, so I didn't expect Kevin to suffer because of my preferences.

Now, however, he seemed to be on a mission to prove to me just how much women enjoyed sex with him. Almost daily, I received texts with pictures of him with a different woman. Very lewd pictures of them in every known position—sometimes with a note attached.

Don't you wish you were here? See what you're missing? I bet you regret breaking up with me now.

I'd sigh, save the text in a confidential folder for evidence of his continued harassment, then delete it from my main messages, and block him. I couldn't very well change my number. I was Rhonda Elgin after all, heiress to a shipping empire. How many charities had me on speed dial? My number was practically tattooed to me, and Kevin knew it. So he'd just get a new phone, or use his latest conquest's.

My family had a team of lawyers at their disposal. I could get a restraining order, but then I'd have to tell my parents. They were so proud of how 'adult' our breakup had been, so 'scandal free'. I hadn't had the heart to fill them in on Kevin's true nature.

Not to mention my embarrassment that I had allowed someone like him in my life at all. I'd gotten myself into this mess, and I was determined to dig myself out. On my own.

"You're awfully quiet over there." Greg glanced my way, tightening his mouth in concern.

I forced a yawn that became real halfway through. My words this morning had been true, last night was rough. Kevin had texted me just before bed, which triggered something in me. My sleep was fraught with nightmares of Kevin trying to force me to have sex then shoving me into a dark closet afterward.

"Just tired," I murmured. "The coffee hasn't kicked in yet, and I didn't sleep great last night."

Several long seconds passed before he responded. "How about some music? You can close your eyes if you want. We've still got a long way to go."

I bit my lip. I'd never been great at sleeping in the car. "I guess I can try."

He flipped through the stations, finding one that claimed to play everything. His fingers tapped to the fast beat as I curled my legs up on the seat beneath me, leaning against the headrest. I didn't shut my eyes right away as I watched Greg drive, listening to him hum along to the music.

My eyelids grew heavy, but I still wasn't comfortable. I shifted several times in a row until Greg tilted his head toward me. I sighed, feeling like I should explain. "Sorry. I've never been one for sleeping in the car."

"I get it. Not the most comfortable place." He frowned then said, "What if we…?" One hand reached down, and he fumbled to lift the armrest up. "That should give you a little more room."

My heart beat faster as I stared in disbelief at the upright divider, at the empty space now between us. *But what will keep me from bumping into you? Where's my buffer?*

"You could use my shoulder." The words came out hesitantly, a pause between each one. "For a pillow…if you want."

I focused on breathing as I fixated on his shoulder. Greg had given permission to lie on him *and* taken away the barrier between us? *I thought Christmas was last week.*

"It's okay if you don't." He paused again. When I didn't respond, he sighed. "Just, never mind." His hand reached for the armrest, and mine shot out to stop him, our fingers colliding.

"No!" His startled gaze flew to mine. *Way to make that more awkward, Rhonda.* "I mean, I'd really like that. Thank you."

Biting my lip, I let go of his hand and edged toward him. *Where do I put my head?* His arm still hovered in mid-air, and his chest beckoned. I took a deep breath then swooped in to snuggle against his warm, firm torso. His muscles tensed beneath me.

Several moments passed before the tension left his body, and he brought his hand down to rest on my side. I relaxed into him, crossing my arms over my middle to grip my biceps. It seemed safer than letting my hands dangle. I didn't want to grope him in my sleep.

His bare hand shifted slightly, and his pinky grazed mine as I drifted off, his comforting scent of cedar and peppermint chasing away any hint of nightmares.

When I woke up, the steering wheel greeted me. I blinked, realizing I wasn't where I had been. One hand was under my cheek, cupped firmly around...Greg's muscular thigh. *Oh. My. Word.* It took everything in me not to shoot upright, but I didn't want to make him swerve again. Like he had when I'd spilled water down my front.

"Hey, you're awake."

Yep, and using your lap as a pillow, thank you very much. My cheeks warmed as I started to move.

"While you're down there"—he paused, and my mind raced, absolutely raced to a million dirty things—"could you grab my pack of gum? I dropped it while you were sleeping."

My heart skittered back into a normal rhythm while I chastised myself. *What am I thinking? Did I honestly think that Greg, who couldn't even bear to look at my shirt plastered to my chest, would casually ask me to suck his dick?* I chuckled at the idea.

The pack of gum rested between his feet, within easy reach. All I had to do was anchor my hand on his thigh and reach down with my other. Except, as I started to lean, he slammed on the brakes again.

I jolted forward, my head smacking into the steering column. His hand darted from my shoulder to keep me from flying off the seat, my lap belt holding my lower half in place. I managed to brace myself against the floor, but my hand on his thigh slipped. We skidded to a stop. All around I heard screeching tires, horns and squealing brakes. At least there wasn't any crunching metal or crashes.

After a few deep breaths, I assessed myself and my position, realizing I was okay. Other than my hand now rested on Greg's dick while his cupped my left breast. We hurried to let go at the same time, awkward silence hovering between as I sat up.

"Brings a new meaning to tit for tat, huh?" I couldn't help but joke.

He raised an eyebrow, glancing at his lap. "Is that what they're calling it now?"

My cheeks were hot, but it was better than never addressing the incident by shoving it under the proverbial rug. "Yep. I think we'll start a new trend." We both chuckled, though it sounded a little stilted. Then I held out the package I'd retrieved from the floor. "Gum?"

Genuine laughter erupted from him, and I couldn't help joining in. After taking a piece, he slid it into his mouth, stuffing the wrapper into his pocket. "How's your head?"

I gingerly touched the spot I'd hit, just above my hairline. "Tender, but no lumps. I'll live, thanks to my live-action seat belt." I added a teasing grin, warmth spreading through me when he smiled back. "What happened anyway?"

Greg shrugged. "Not sure. I saw brake lights and realized everyone was stopping." He shifted in his seat, trying to peer around the large semi-truck in front of us.

Traffic began inching forward with the steady pace of a determined snail. Greg frowned. "Can you see any mile markers or exit signs?"

We were in the right lane, so I rolled down the window, wincing at the cold wind blowing in my face as I stuck my head out. "There's an exit too far up, but I can't tell what it says."

He pulled out his phone, bringing up the map. "How do you feel about stopping for lunch?"

* * * *

The gum snapping hostess trailed a long, red nail over her seating chart. I surveyed the crowded diner, realizing everyone must have had the same idea of avoiding traffic with a late lunch. The hostess tilted her blonde head for us to follow her. She led us to a table that jutted against the wall with a one-sided booth facing it. Her eyebrows lifted, as if daring us to complain.

Greg glanced at me. "Is this all right?"

I almost hyperventilated as I pictured being crowded against that wall. "If you don't mind sitting inside."

He nodded, scooching along the hard plastic booth. His forehead furrowed as he waited for me to follow.

"I'm going to hit the bathroom first." I hurried off.

It wasn't much, smaller than most closets. I opened the door, dreading the tight space. But nature called, so I gritted my teeth, pulling the door shut behind me. I pretended I was home, in my own bathroom with its wide-open floorplan and big windows.

The narrow walls didn't give me much room to maneuver. As I washed my hands, the room closed in. Squeezing my eyes shut, I pictured being anywhere else while I struggled to keep my breathing normal.

I hurried to dry my clean hands on a rough paper towel then reached for the door handle. But it didn't open immediately. A similar memory of a tighter closet and a darker space threatened to overwhelm me as I jiggled the handle, desperate to get out. The walls zoomed in, my heart raced, and all moisture left my mouth.

When the lock gave way, I stumbled into the hallway where I leaned against the wall for several moments. I looked anywhere but at the bathroom as I sucked in deep, gulping breaths.

What had my therapist said to do? *Count backward from ten.* I tried that, twice. Then I focused on my surroundings, using my other senses of smell and sound to ground me. I was okay, I told myself over and over.

My heart at last began returning to a normal rhythm. Greg would be wondering what had happened to me, so I shoved the remains of the panic aside. Shaky legs carried me down the hall, as I walked back to the table.

Greg glanced up at me over his menu, then he did a double take. "You all right?"

It was all I could do not to collapse into the booth, but I managed to keep my distance, perching on the edge. My palms were damp as I rested my hands on the cool table.

"You'll fall off, if you're not careful."

I slipped, starting to do just that, but he caught my arm just in time, yanking me toward him.

He frowned. "Jellybean, what's wrong?"

I automatically shook my head. The secret had been mine for so long that sharing it now just felt wrong. Not to mention it would ruin the perfect image I strived to maintain.

I reached for my water. "Just thirsty." My forehead felt as clammy as my hands, and I sucked down the liquid. Then I opened my menu for something to do, but it might have been in Swedish for all I understood it.

"Any idea what you're going to get?"

Another head-shake. My straw hit bottom, loud noises erupting as my glass emptied.

Greg slid his full glass over to me. "You should eat something."

I put my straw in his glass and sucked the water down, pleased to feel my temperature returning to normal.

He sighed, exasperated with my silence. "How about I order for you, and you promise to try it?"

Nodding, I snapped my menu shut, relieved to have the decision out of my hands. When the waitress came, I paid no attention to what Greg ordered, focusing on keeping my wits about me. Another glass of water emptied. Then I realized what would happen if I kept sucking down liquid—no way in hell was I going back into that bathroom. I frantically shoved the empty glass away.

Greg shifted on the seat beside me, seeming quite uncomfortable.

"You got ants in your pants?" The words marched out of my mouth before I could stop them.

He stared at me, amusement in every line of his face. "How old are you?"

I played with the paper holding my silverware together as a bittersweet voice echoed in my mind. "Papa used to say that when I couldn't sit still. It just slipped out."

"I do that sometimes, quote people I don't mean to." He shifted again as the waitress came back and refilled our waters. He gave her a full-dimpled smile before returning his attention to me. "We've just been sitting awhile, and I'd hoped for a decent booth to stretch out in."

I assessed the situation with a frown. His six-foot-two frame was nowhere near able to relax in this small space. Hell, my five-foot-eight ass could barely make it without kicking the wall. And after being crammed in the car for hours before this, I understood all too well.

I peered under the table. "What if we—?" I swung my legs onto his lap as he froze. "Now you can spread out," I said triumphantly. I didn't have a great back rest, but I angled my body toward him, resting my shoulder against the booth.

He shifted again, his muscular thighs tensing beneath my calves as he stretched his legs. Then he let out a relieved sigh.

"Better?" My smile grew as I watched him relax.

He nodded. "Thanks."

I leaned my elbow on the table, but the sticky surface offered no safe space. I gave up, then nibbled on my lip, debating if I should ask him what was on my mind.

"What?" Greg arched an eyebrow.

So, I just spit it out. "Will people actually believe we're a couple?" His frown had me racing to explain. "We're not exactly comfortable with each other." I gestured to my legs on his lap. "Take this for example." My mind flicked to earlier in the car when he'd raised the armrest, and I'd almost hyperventilated. "Maybe we should just say I'm a friend or something."

He swirled his straw in his water, the ice clinking in his glass. "Maybe that would be easier." His tone was dull, no emotion on his face.

A wave of longing washed over me. I was on a road trip with Greg, the man of my dreams. My legs were in his lap. What better time to take another chance? I hadn't had the courage since the incident. Maybe it was time to try again, especially if Avery was right.

"What if we took our time getting there?" I shrugged, feigning nonchalance. "Maybe stay tonight in a hotel and practice the whole girlfriend-boyfriend thing a little more."

He chuckled derisively. "Yeah, right. Good one, Rhonda." He shook his head then turned to study the artwork on the wall.

Disappointment coursed through me, but our food arrived. The waitress slid a huge burger with a pile of fries to Greg, then set a matching plate in front of me. A chocolate shake was set between us, piled high with whipped cream and a cherry on top.

My hope rallied at the sight of that one shake. Complete with two straws.

"Thanks," I told the waitress, then turned to Greg, who stared at his plate. "What's with the shake?"

With a sullen expression on his face, he shoved my legs off his. "Just eat, Rhonda." He bit into his burger, ripping off a piece.

I surveyed the food in front of me, then the shake between us. Gritting my teeth, I decided to try once more. "Why one shake?" I wanted the answer, needed something to cling to.

He shook his head. "Forget it. It was stupid." His words came out harsh, almost angry, and he shifted further into the corner. Away from me.

The distance between us lengthened, until I couldn't stand it anymore. *At least I tried.* My appetite gone, I clenched my jaw and stood up. "Give me the keys."

"What?" His head snapped up.

Fury hit me at his confused expression. "The keys. Now."

He let out an exasperated sigh but handed them over. "We had a deal," he called as I strode out of the diner.

His words rolled off me as I stormed over to start the car. Then I tumbled into the back seat where I stared at the ceiling. What a trip it had been so far.

His reactions had been all over the place, his mood swings more than I could keep up with. I'd done my part. But every one of my ideas made him withdraw and shut me out. If he wanted us to act like a real couple then the ball was in his court.

I heard the front door open, saw Greg shut the car off in my periphery, but I refused to acknowledge him. Until my door opened. A cold blast of air whipped in as two strong hands yanked me out of the car, and I yelped as Greg set me on my feet.

"Are you done sulking?" He scowled.

Indignation flared at the accusation. "Me?" My hands flew to my hips. "You're the one with the brooding antihero act, shoving me off your lap and not giving me the time of day. You'd give Batman a run for his money."

His glare turned icy, and I fought the urge to flinch when his tone matched. "We had a deal. I'd order, and you'd at least try it."

Determination straightened my shoulders. *No, I'm not letting him guilt me into giving in.* "Forgive me if I didn't have an appetite after being turned down," I shot back.

Shit, I said too much. I bit my lip, waiting for his reaction to my unintended confession.

"What do you mean?" Silence stretched between us, but he didn't let me off the hook. He stared at me, silently demanding an explanation.

I sighed, tucking my cold hands under my arms. "When I said we should get a hotel because we'd never pass for a couple, you just laughed at me. Then you shoved me off your lap like you were mad I even suggested it."

The frigid breeze whipped between us, emphasizing our distance as he searched me. "You were serious?"

I pressed my lips together, taking a beat before answering. "Yeah, Greg." I lifted my chin slightly, trying to hide my hurt even as I whispered, "I'm always serious when it comes to you."

He shifted closer then stopped, as if fighting a war I couldn't see. He swallowed hard. "You're asking me to break through years of ironclad boundaries and firm lines I drew for myself." He swiped a hand down his face before adding, "But I'm trying, Jellybean."

I gaped at him, at this first ever acknowledgment that he wanted to take a next step. That he wanted to become more.

But I couldn't keep being shut down, couldn't be the only one trying to bridge this gap. I opened my mouth to tell him so when he made a gesture so sweet my doubts halted in their tracks.

He held out his hand. "Come eat with me?"

Chapter Five

Hope blossomed in me as I stared at Greg's offered hand. It was a good start, but I pressed him to give me a little more. "Will you let me sit with my legs on yours, so you can spread out?"

His cheeks tinged with pink, but he nodded.

A grin split my face as I slipped my hand into his. His long, calloused fingers wrapped around mine, sending electricity skittering up my arm. When we fell into step together, I tried to place the heady emotion I felt.

Elation.

Pure, undiluted elation coursed through me as we walked toward the diner hand in hand.

"This isn't so bad," he said, opening the door for me. "Maybe we have a chance after all." His teasing smile brought out his dimple, and he didn't let go until we settled into our booth. He even lifted my legs on top of his before I had time to do it myself. "Good?"

I nodded — too overcome to speak.

The waitress appeared with our plates, sliding them in front of us. "Anything else?" With a shake of my head, I waited till she left before turning to Greg for an explanation.

He chuckled. "Nobody likes cold fries." He snitched a few off my plate with a grin before popping them in his mouth. "I know you don't love beef, so I wanted to mention that yours is a turkey burger. You seemed preoccupied when I was ordering."

"Thanks." I put the toppings back on my burger, stacking everything as neatly as possible. "How am I supposed to fit this in my mouth?"

"That's what she said." Greg clapped a hand over his lips, his cheeks turning a deep shade of red.

"Did you just—?" I burst out laughing, setting the burger back onto my plate. The laughter compounded as Greg folded his arms on the table and hid his face. My sides ached but I couldn't stop.

Finally, I could breathe again. "Greg." I grabbed his shoulder, but he shook his head.

His muffled voice sounded from under his arms. "Greg's not here. He died of embarrassment."

"Oh stop." I rolled my eyes. "That's not any worse than copping a feel when you pretended to be my seatbelt earlier. Or when I basically napped with my face in your lap. How about my see-through T-shirt at the beginning of the trip?"

He peeked out.

His embarrassment couldn't hold a candle to mine, and I wasn't going to let him hide. "I'm going to ignore you and take a mouthful of this nice, big, juicy, piece of meat now." His groan made me giggle. Then the milkshake caught my attention, and I realized I'd never received an answer. "Greg. Why'd you only order one shake?"

His non-response confirmed my suspicions.

Happiness swelled up, knowing Greg wanted to share the sweet treat with me. Just the thought of one shake and two straws had me beaming. I wasn't about to let him back out now. "Okay, sit up, get your straw over here and smile like you mean it. I want to see that dimple." I tucked my straw into the whipped cream, scooting the shake to the edge of the table.

Despite his reluctant movements, he followed my instructions and his straw plunged in next to mine. He leaned close, putting his arm behind my shoulders. I savored his warmth, inhaling his scent.

This was exactly what I'd always wanted. Sitting side by side with him, I got lost in his gray eyes and forgot to breathe. Until the loud clatter of someone dropping silverware broke the spell he held over me. I sucked air into my lungs, trying to reorient myself.

I didn't want to scare Greg off. Not when he was closer than ever.

"Drink up." I held up my phone, snapping several pics of us in various poses. "Perfect. My turkey burger is amazing. My fries are delicious. And the shake is just right." I smirked. "Now I think I'll finish off this piece of meat."

Half an hour later, we headed back to the car. When Greg did a quick walk around as he always did, I took advantage, using the time to update Avery and Gina. I had to share my giddiness, and I knew they'd be just as thrilled as I was. Even if it was just a bit of hand-holding and sharing a milkshake.

I compared them to my previous friends, Yolanda and Fawnda. We'd called ourselves the Three

Musketeers, and the irony wasn't lost on me. The worst part was they'd dropped me as soon as I'd broken up with Kevin. Last I'd heard, Fawnda had even made a play for him.

And that had been the end of our trio.

Gina's abrasiveness had shocked me at first, especially after the false flattery of Yolanda and Fawnda. But it didn't take me long to realize I preferred Gina's direct approach to their backstabbing and cattiness. *Not much of a trade-off.*

Greg hopped into the car, then maneuvered us into the flow of traffic. He'd already checked his phone to make sure the highway wasn't at a standstill. I waited until we were up to speed before I started a conversation.

"Do you have any friends?" *Wow, that came out wrong.* "Um, I mean, uh." I studied my lap. "Please don't stop talking to me. It's just the only people I see you around are Derek, Avery, Gina and Liam."

He chuckled, reaching over to rest his hand on top of mine for the briefest of moments, and the quick graze had my stomach flipping. He settled his elbow onto the armrest, his long fingers resting on top of the gear shift. "It's okay. I don't have a lot of friends down here. By choice. I had you and Derek and Uncle Harry." He shrugged. "I've always been a bit of a loner, plus I was kind of on call. Now, with Avery and Gina in the mix, it's a full-time job."

I had never thought about him putting his life on hold so I could be carted around all the time.

"Stop." He read me like a book. "Don't you dare feel guilty. Driving you and your brother was just what I needed. You two have always been more than a job to me." He paused. "Especially you, Jellybean."

He was always more than just a driver to me, too. My constant, my friend. And he'd kept his professional stance even after I'd begun crushing on him.

A torrent of questions longed to pour out. Why had he stopped working for Derek? Why hadn't he told me earlier that I meant something to him? And why, oh why wasn't he holding my hand right this very second?

But we were just getting into comfortable territory, and I didn't want to stir up the past.

Maybe I could rectify one of the issues. I looked down, deciding at least half the armrest was mine, and I laid claim to it. Our forearms rested side by side, mine short enough that there was no way my fingers could reach the gear shift. I was quite comfortable with them resting off the edge of the console, thank you very much.

The rest of our trip was spent arguing over music and reminiscing. The time flew by and before I knew it, I saw a sign welcoming us to Marquette. We drove through the picturesque town, catching glimpses of the colossal Lake Superior. I couldn't see any of the Great Lakes without thinking of my parents. Our livelihood came from those lakes, the source of our money and reputation.

My thoughts drifted to Greg's parents. I let myself daydream about the quaint house they lived in, something normal, like a two-story farmhouse with a wraparound porch. Nothing ostentatious like the massive house I'd grown up in. I winced remembering the echoing, cavernous walls and the museum-quality feel of it. Mother's reprimand echoed in my head from every time we were too loud or rambunctious. *How dare we run or play or be kids.*

I doubted Greg's mom was like that. I imagined her as warm and caring, with a big welcoming smile.

Someone who baked cookies with her kids, read them stories before bed, and made chicken noodle soup when they were sick.

The closer we got to arriving, the more excited I became. I was with a normal guy, not someone who wanted me for my money or status. Not some rich, spoiled brat with a full staff waiting on him hand and foot.

If I could make this work with Greg, maybe I could have what Avery and Derek had. Even if it meant I had to wear baggy sweaters and off-brand jeans occasionally. I might even admit I was a tad more comfortable — if someone tortured it out of me.

Greg put on his turn signal by a driveway that wound up a huge hill, and I held my breath in anticipation. When I saw the big, arching gates, I frowned. The moment he pulled through them, and I got my first glimpse of a house as massive as mine, my fantasies began crashing down around me like an unstable stack of blocks.

Surely this was a mistake. Greg wasn't like the others — he was different, normal…right?

The idea of appearing in the ratty clothes and little makeup had my teeth on edge as my mother's voice echoed in my head. *"You only get one chance to make a first impression."*

Greg grinned, shutting off the engine, turning to me with excitement etched into every nook of his face. "What do you think?"

"*This* is your house?" A burst of panic flared in my chest.

He nodded, as if I were supposed to be thrilled. A familiar iciness coated my heart as I re-evaluated the reason Greg had brought me. *Arm candy, indeed.*

I glanced down at my Wal-Mart clothes and slip-on boots. My skin felt greasy from travel, and my makeup had to be smudged. *So much for flannel shirts and Bog boots.* Devastated, I watched the last of my stupid dreams slide down the drain with a sinking feeling in my stomach.

For one second, I wallowed. Then I pulled my heiress cloak back on and put my foot down. "There is no way I am walking into a house of that caliber like this. Not when you clearly brought me here to impress your family."

His forehead furrowed in confusion. "Rhonda, what—?"

"No." I lifted my chin. "I won't step out of this car until you find me somewhere to change and do my makeup." This was one fight I wouldn't lose. "Are we staying here?"

"Probably. I mean, I know other family will be in town, but my folks have plenty of room." Greg stared at me for a long minute. "I thought you'd be impressed. I don't understand what the big deal is."

"Of course you don't." I pressed a finger to my temple, trying to rub away the beginning of a stress headache. "I can't make a first impression twice. Your family is expecting Rhonda fucking Elgin, so that's who they're going to get." I dropped my hand and folded my arms as I demanded, "Now, find me a place to change."

Ignoring the hurt that flickered across Greg's face, I went through my wardrobe in my mind. Even as I tried to tell myself it didn't matter that he'd brought me up here to show me off. It didn't matter that he was just like every other guy I'd ever met. It didn't matter that I was back to being dollar signs, a status symbol, and a way to pretty up the scenery.

And the pain in my chest is just heartburn.

Greg pulled into a truck stop a few miles up the road.

"I won't be long."

He huffed out a muttered, "Yeah, right."

My blood boiled at his skepticism. "Look, Greg." I let his name drip with all the acid I felt at the moment. "You want arm candy—it doesn't happen with the wave of a magic wand. But when I say fifteen minutes, I mean fifteen minutes. It's not like this is my first time." I slammed the door behind me.

Sixteen minutes later, I walked out of the spacious bathroom, not a hair out of place, makeup absolutely perfect. I was every inch the version of Rhonda Elgin his family would want, right down to my Jimmy Choos.

"All set?" Greg asked tightly when I sat down in the car.

I clicked the seat belt into place, feeling the small noise echo between us as if it sealed my fate. "Yes." I focused on shoving every thought, every daydream into a little box to be examined or tossed out later. When we pulled into the driveway this time, Rhonda Elgin, heiress, was ready.

When Greg offered me his arm on the steps, my fantasies of strolling hand in hand as equals obliterated. I pasted on my charitable smile, so familiar it was like a second skin.

"Greg!" A tall woman in black slacks, a long-sleeved blouse, and perfect ombre hair greeted him happily, pulling him into an exuberant embrace.

I forced my smile to stay in place as they broke apart and turned to me.

"Mom, this is Rhonda Elgin." His dimple appeared, though his expression dimmed as he took in my practiced smile. He always could tell the difference. "Rhonda, this is Julie Peterson, my mom."

I stuck out my hand. "Mrs. Peterson, it's a pleasure to meet you. What a lovely home you have."

"Why thank you, Rhonda, but please, call me Julie. Come in, come in. Where's all your stuff?" She seemed borderline insulted, so I stepped closer to Greg, patting his arm.

"Oh, Greg here just couldn't wait to see everyone and introduce me. We'll get the bags later."

She nodded in understanding, and Greg shot me a grateful look as we followed her into the house. I ignored him.

Thundering footsteps raced down the stairs. "Greg!"

A beaming, lithe girl almost as tall as he was raced toward us. She skipped the bottom two steps to launch herself at him. Greg caught her, wrapping both arms around her waist in a hug so tight he lifted her clear off the floor.

When he set her down, his grin stretched ear to ear. "Hi, Mandy."

The frown she gave him was murderous, then she punched in him the arm hard enough to make him yelp. "Why didn't you RSVP earlier??"

Intervention was definitely needed, and I cleared my throat. "I'm afraid that was my fault. Greg's been talking about coming since we started dating a little over a month ago. But I had this huge holiday charity event I'd already committed to running."

I gave Greg my best doe-eyed look and sighed. "This sweet guy didn't want to leave me alone for New Year. Anyway, due to an inept employee, our venue was double-booked. I knew how much Greg wanted to come up here, so I offered to reschedule our event, and I let him know right away." I glanced from mother to daughter, pleased they were buying this hook, line and sinker. At five foot eight, I was used to feeling tall, especially in my heels, but these ladies towered over me. Next to them, I felt like a child. "My apologies for the late notice."

"Y-you're—?" Mandy stammered. "You're *the* Rhonda Elgin!"

I nodded, wincing when Greg got another punch. His sister was a pistol.

"You said your date was named Rhonda, but you didn't warn me that *the* Rhonda Elgin would be at my wedding!" Her hands flew to her cheeks, then her hair. "I'm a mess!"

Quickly, I touched her arm. "Mandy, don't even worry about it. I'm sure I'm a mess from traveling." *As if.* "But I came here to meet Greg's family and congratulate the bride-to-be. I'm so excited for you. I wish you every happiness, and I'm thrilled we're able to attend your wedding."

Still looking a little starstruck, Mandy lowered her hands. "Really? That's so sweet. I heard you broke up with Kevin. I'm sorry, that must have been awful."

Then why bring it up? Somehow, I managed to keep my smile in place. "Actually, it was for the best. I think I got the better end of the deal." I sent another sappy look Greg's way.

But it was true. Even annoyed at Greg, he was a freaking Jimmy Choo compared to the worn out, off-the-rack heel Kevin was.

I changed the subject. "When do I get to meet this fiancé of yours? Peter, right?"

She gaped at me, showing how thrilled she was I knew his name. "He'll be here for dinner in forty-five minutes." She froze then let out a panicked shriek. "I still have to change!" Without so much as a goodbye, she spun around to race back upstairs.

Greg nudged me to mouth a heartfelt thank you. I steeled myself against the flutter in my stomach, giving a closed-off nod in return. He frowned at my obvious distance. Luckily, his mother didn't seem to notice.

I turned to her with a sugary smile, one that almost guaranteed I'd get my way. "Would I be able to see my room before dinner? I'm afraid traveling wore me out, and I'd love to rest a little if possible."

"Oh, of course. Maybe Greg could bring your things." She shot him a pointed look, and he hurried toward the door. "You and Greg will be upstairs."

The possibility of staying with Greg in one room hadn't even crossed my mind, and my heart hammered the entire way up.

Julie opened a set of solid oak French doors with a flourish. "This is what we call The Suite. I wasn't sure what your sleeping arrangements were, and this way you have options." We stood in a small sitting room. "There are two bedrooms and one bathroom. You get first pick since you're here and Greg's not." She gave me a wink, pointing to the right. "That's my favorite because it stays darker longer."

I headed straight for the room. The muted cream tones and artsy wall-hangings set me at ease. A queen-sized bed sat in the middle of the room while a balcony overlooking Lake Superior stretched behind. I turned to thank Julie, but she was gone. Instead, Greg came in with my bags.

"What's with the cold shoulder?" he grunted as he set down the luggage.

"I'm being friendly and talkative to everyone, including you." I sniffed.

His lips pressed together before he said, "You know what I mean. Something happened."

Oh, like me thinking you actually wanted me here only to find out you're just like every other guy in my life and using me as a status symbol? I stared out at the lake, at the frozen waves jutting against the dull, cloudy sky. "I'm just tired from traveling." My throat was tight, and I knew it wouldn't be long before I lost my fragile hold on my control.

"It's more than that." His words were soft, pleading. "Talk to me, Jellybean."

You're not who I thought you were. I clenched my hands into fists just to grip something, desperately needing him to leave. "Please. Just let me rest."

Silence reigned for several long moments, then his footsteps faded. I waited another minute to be sure I was alone before sitting down on my lonely pedestal and giving into my tears.

Chapter Six

I managed to not be splotchy by the time Greg tapped on my door, telling me dinner was ready. The clothes I'd arrived in were suitable, but I'd changed out my earrings and touched up my makeup. He greeted me with a tentative smile. I returned it with a closed lipped one of my own, keeping my demeanor cool. A flash of disappointment flew across his face, gone so quickly I doubted I'd even seen it.

When he offered me his arm at the top of the stairs, I didn't want to reject him. We still had a show to put on. So I looped my hand through, resting my hand on top of his forearm as we descended. His family waited at the bottom of the stairs, the chatter quieting as we drew near. I donned my familiar charitable smile, feeling it turn genuine when Mandy grinned back in giddy excitement.

As soon as my foot touched the main floor, she raced over. "Rhonda, this is my fiancé, Peter. Peter, this is Rhonda Elgin. Her family owns the Great Lakes

Shipping Company. She's practically Michigan royalty, and not only is she coming to our wedding, she's dating my brother!"

I was surprised she didn't bounce up and down with the excitement exuding from her. I turned, holding out my hand to Peter. "A pleasure to meet you."

He clasped my hand and gave a polite nod. "The pleasure's all mine."

Julie touched Mandy's shoulder, calming her daughter instantly. Gesturing to the man next to her, Julie said, "And this is my husband, Daniel Peterson."

The stiff, gruff man who stood before me was like night and day compared to his excited puppy of a daughter. My smile almost faltered in his domineering presence, but I held it, and my chin, in place. "Thank you for having me, sir."

He just dipped his head in my direction then arched an eyebrow at his wife.

Julie swept out an arm toward the dining room. "Dinner is ready, so let's be seated, shall we?"

Her more formal manner grated on me, and I knew her behavior had changed because of Greg's dad. He seemed like a stickler for formality and routine. I wondered how it had been growing up with him as a father, marveling that Greg turned out as decent as he had.

The table was all set. We took our seats with Mr. Peterson at the head, of course. The cook brought out dish after dish of heavenly smelling food fit for a feast—a whole turkey, its skin golden brown, and already carved, a heaping bowl of mashed potatoes with a carafe of gravy, a steaming bowl of winter veggies and a basket of fluffy rolls. My mouth watered.

I watched Peter and Mandy as we passed around the dishes of food. They could barely keep their hands off each other, and I loved the way his midnight skin contrasted with her tanned tones when their fingers entwined on the table. His grin lit up the room, a contagious joy emanating from him.

Conversation ebbed and flowed. Mr. Peterson grunted when asked a direct question, otherwise, Julie steered the topics to include everyone. Even me.

"What's the agenda for the rest of the week?" I asked Mandy after our plates were cleared, and we waited for dessert. "Of course, the wedding is Saturday. Greg told me of other events, but we were unsure of specifics."

Uncertainty drenched Mandy's face as she nibbled at her lip. "Well, I'm having a bridal shower two days from now, but I wasn't positive you'd want to come."

My eyebrows shot up. "I'd love to, if it's not an inconvenience."

She beamed before giving Greg a dirty look. "See," she hissed, "I told you she'd want to come." Then she focused back on me. "Friday night is the bachelorette party, which of course you're welcome at. And yes, Saturday is the wedding."

She gave Peter's hand a squeeze. As she turned, I studied her profile, comparing her to Greg. Her eyes were bluer, and her sandy brown hair was longer, but the same color. I saw similarities in their face structure. Both their parents were tall, but thankfully they'd inherited their mother's nose. It would've been a whole different picture if Mr. Peterson's beak had been the dominant feature.

I started yawning way too soon. My nap had lasted me this long, but I was fading fast. I stood, making my excuses for my early departure. "My apologies. I think

I need to retire for the evening. Feel free to stay, though, I know you have some catching up to do."

With a smirk telling me he knew exactly what he was doing, Greg tilted his chin up for a kiss as I walked by his armchair. I couldn't ignore him without looking like a dick. I hesitated, steeling myself before I leaned down, my lips brushing his stubbled cheek.

His eyes locked on mine, intense and heated. "Good night," he whispered.

I walked upstairs to the amused murmurs of his family, disgusted I hadn't found a way out of the kiss. A hint of peppermint lingered in my nose, just from being so close to him.

What would it be like to really kiss him?

I chided myself, reminding my body Greg wanted us for status and nothing more. There would be no kissing for the foreseeable future.

* * * *

Sleep came right away, and I slept hard, safe in the glow from the sitting room light that peeked in through my cracked door. Sometime later, I woke up, needing to use the bathroom. When I opened my eyes, absolute darkness surrounded me. No sitting room light, no alarm clock. Not even a hint of moonlight gave me reprieve from the total blackness.

Frantic, I reached for the end table. I always plugged my phone in, just in case the lights went out.

But it wasn't there.

I searched in a wider circle, my movements becoming more panicked when I still came up empty. My hand knocked into a lamp, which crashed to the floor, but I barely heard it as the panic overwhelmed me. My breaths came in short gasps, and the blood roared in my ears. I knew the walls were closing in.

Then the light flicked on. The sweet, sweet light. The walls retreated to their normal places, and my fisted hands loosened a fraction where I clutched the sheets.

Tears of relief poured down my cheeks, and I started shaking. Greg's deep voice rumbled from far away. It wasn't until I felt the bed dip, until my lungs filled with his blend of cedar and peppermint, that I realized he was there.

He pulled me to his bare torso. I curled against him, soaking up his warmth as he cradled me in his arms. The nonsensical words he murmured rumbled through his chest to vibrate against my ear.

My upper half cuddled right up to his chest, my cheek resting just below his collarbone. One of his large hands stroked my hair, the other splayed across my lower back. My legs were curled up on his lap, his spooned around me. Eventually I became aware of how much of my bare skin was pressed against his. I slept in a silky spaghetti strap tank with matching shorts while he had on boxers.

That was it.

Even though I'd never felt safer, never come out of a full-blown attack faster, I'd never felt more embarrassed when I realized what had happened. I stiffened against him. Ignoring his exasperated sigh, I disentangled myself from his embrace to reclaim my dignity as I scrambled to put my walls back into place.

Greg swiped a hand over his face. "Jellybean, it's three in the morning. Please, just talk to me. I want to help. Won't you tell me what's going on?" He reached for me, trying to bridge the distance I was so desperately trying to put between us. "Rhonda."

My name was the softest whisper, a butterfly's wing of a caress that slipped through my defenses, and I admitted, "I'm claustrophobic. At one of my friends' sixteenth birthday parties, we played sardines. It was my turn to hide, and I'd never been there before. I went into a closet, shutting the door behind me without checking it out fully."

I shuddered at the memory, gripping the blanket to ground me. "The door was supposed to be locked already, so it locked behind me. The light switch was on the outside, and there was no room." I recalled the moment I realized I was trapped. My breaths came faster as I remembered how narrow the space was, barely big enough for me to turn around in. "My phone was in my purse, nowhere near me. It took hours before my friends found me. Then they had to get help because they didn't know where the key was."

Greg's hand covered mine, his thumb rubbing my skin in a soothing motion.

Might as well get it all out. "I hate using public bathrooms because they're so small. At the diner today, the bathroom door stuck for a minute, and I freaked out. That's why I looked so awful when I came back to the table."

His hand squeezed mine.

One more shaky breath in and out. "I hate the dark. The light was on in the sitting room when I went to sleep, so I didn't think about it. But when I woke up…"

His face fell. "I turned off the light." His thumb continued its hypnotic motion. "I'm sorry."

I shook my head, hating the guilt on his face. "You didn't know." I added in a chagrined whisper, "No one does."

"Why?" This time his voice held a myriad of hurt. "Why didn't you tell us? Tell me? Did you think I would judge you? Make fun of you?"

Each word stabbed at me. "I saw a therapist for a while, and it got better. It never disappeared completely, but I figured out how to cope." I shrugged. "With my reputation, my status, I didn't want to appear imperfect. I just hoped it'd go away, I guess."

Greg released my hand to cup my cheek, wiping away the remnants of moisture. "Are you okay now? Right now?"

I nodded. "I want to use the bathroom, then I'll plug in my phone so it's here." I swung my legs over to stand up.

"Wait!"

I managed to freeze mid-swing.

"Just—" He stood to peer over the end table at the floor. "The crash woke me. The lamp shattered, and I don't want you to cut yourself. Don't go that way?"

The last part was a question, more like a favor. I listened, not wanting to get cut, but also wanting to please him. I took his outstretched hand, letting him help me to my feet, then followed in his footsteps into the sitting room.

"Where's your phone and charger?"

I told him as he slipped some shoes on.

He returned a few minutes later with my things. "Okay, come on then."

When he turned toward his room, I studied his bare, muscular back. And gasped. "You have a tattoo!"

It was unique, daring, and, most of all, unexpected. A black dragon curved its way from just below his neck over his right shoulder blade, ending near his rib cage. As I studied it, I realized it was more of the idea of a dragon. Carefully placed black lines formed an abstract outline, but none of them connected. I loved it.

Before I could stop myself, my fingers ran over the ink on his back, and his muscles tensed under my touch. "Sorry." I made myself step away. "It took me by surprise. I didn't think you were the tattoo type."

"I didn't think you were the type who liked tattoos," he murmured over his shoulder.

Not sure what else to say, I followed him to his bedroom. He plugged my phone in on the side near the door, then folded back the covers and gestured to the bed.

My mouth went dry as a whole different set of tension gripped me, and my bladder reminded me it had never been emptied. "Um, be right back."

I rushed to the bathroom where I took care of business, then stood in front of the mirror as I racked my brain for some option that didn't involve me sleeping with Greg.

Next to Greg, I corrected. *Not with.*

I didn't trust myself to sleep beside that gorgeous man all night without exploring him. And I was supposed to be mad at him, still. This wouldn't do at all.

A knock sounded on the door. "You all right?" Concern laced Greg's words.

I eased open the door and said meekly, "Maybe I should sleep on the couch."

He set his jaw, staring at me with more determination than I'd ever seen in him, before he pointed to his bedroom.

I shuffled in, then perched on the edge of the bed before I tried again. "What if — ?"

"Rhonda." He loomed over me, making me look up. Way up. "I *need* some sleep. If you're right here, I won't worry about you. Your floor is covered with sharp things. I promise we'll fix it tomorrow. I promise I won't try to ravage you in the night." A hint of humor mixed with exasperation as he ran a hand through his hair. "Please, just lay down?"

I searched his face, and, seeing the truth combined with his exhaustion, decided to give in. It was just for one night, and it didn't change anything. Even if I was annoyed at him, he was still Greg. I trusted him enough to keep his word, despite his shady motives for bringing me here.

He breathed a sigh of relief as he watched me settle in. "Is it okay if I turn off this light? The one in the sitting room is still on." He waited for my tentative nod before flicking off the switch. A moment later, his weight dipped the other side of the bed.

It took several long moments for me to adjust to the dark. I lay rigid on my side, staring at the crack in the door as I waited to discern the sliver of light. My breaths came quicker, my heart pounding as the fear trickled in.

"Hey, Jellybean." Greg's sweet voice cut through the flutters of panic beginning in me. "My shoulder's here if you need it."

I didn't think twice, just rolled over to curl up against him. He slid his arm under me, and I felt safe. Cocooned in his embrace with his firm chest as my pillow, I finally went to sleep.

The next time I woke up, it was light outside. Greg's mom hadn't been kidding when she said the sun hit this room, but I was grateful for it. I tilted my head up to see Greg frowning. "What?"

"Just wondering which Rhonda I'm getting today." His voice was wary.

The morning stubble on his chin was the same sandy brown as his hair, and I itched to run my fingers over it.

When I didn't offer any information, he asked, "Care to fill me in?"

I sighed. I felt like I should move off him, but I was comfortable. My head fit so well in the crook of his shoulder. "I get tired of only being arm candy all the time." My fingers traced a line through his small patch of chest hair.

He shifted, his frown deepening the furrow between his eyebrows. "What do you mean?"

I tried to keep the pain out of my voice. "All my life, guys have looked at me and not seen me. They see dollar signs, a step up in the social ladder, a way to the top." I took a breath, bracing myself for the reminder of the wound Greg had inflicted on me yesterday. "I'd pictured things so differently on our drive up here, and when we pulled in…" I trailed off, feeling the depth of that hurt all over again.

In one swift motion, he flipped us over, putting himself on top, his indignant expression inches from mine. I gasped, thrilling at the delicious weight of him resting on me until he fired off a barrage of questions.

"What are you saying? You shut down because my family has money?" Disbelief and exasperation coated every word. "You forgot everything you and I have ever said or done, everything you know about me, because you saw a big house?"

Anger flared in me, burning out the flickers of desire in my quest for the truth. "Why did you bring me, Greg? Why haven't you come back here in years? Why now, when you have Rhonda Elgin to show off to everyone and cover your ass?" My voice rose with each demand, and I was almost yelling by the time I finished. "Why didn't you tell me?"

The muscles in his neck stood out. His jaw clenched, and his face turned red. "I thought you'd be happy! I thought it'd be a nice surprise. That maybe if we were the same status, you wouldn't have to be drunk to kiss me. Or feel the need to fuck someone else in the back seat while I sat there. Dammit, Rhonda." He pushed off the bed with such force the mattress bounced for several seconds. Grabbing some clothes, he stormed into the bathroom and slammed the door.

Anger had me grinding my teeth as I let out a growl. I flopped onto my side, punching a pillow. He had no idea what I'd been through that night, and him throwing it in my face only made me madder. The memory surfaced in my mind, and I couldn't stop it from replaying.

The summer after I graduated high school, I'd tried everything to get Greg to notice me. But it hadn't worked. He'd remained the same friendly, professional driver I'd always known.

I'd turned nineteen that fall, and my parents' annual gala was held a month later. My parents were going straight there after a meeting. Derek insisted on driving himself. Which meant that Greg would be driving me, and only me.

And I had a plan.

I spent hours finding the right dress, wanting to look as enticing as possible. I settled on a short, strapless one with a swishy skirt. The icy blue fabric matched my eyes and contrasted with my dark hair. When at last the night arrived, I was so nervous that I snuck a shot of tequila before I went outside, for liquid courage.

Greg stood next to the limo in front of my parents' house, wearing his dimpled smile that made my knees go weak. He opened the door with a flourish, but I didn't get in right away.

I ran my hands down my dress. "What do you think, Greg?" I made sure to lower my wrap and turn slowly in front of him. "Do you like it?" Nerves fluttered in me as hope poked her head out.

His words held a tightness I didn't understand. "You look very nice."

The compliment bolstered me, and it took all my courage, but I closed the distance between us. Grabbing his uniform, I stood on tiptoe and pressed my lips to his.

He reared back, flinching as if I'd hit him. "Rhonda! What are you doing?"

His glare had me feeling like an absolute idiot, and I ducked my head, whispering, "I wanted a kiss."

"Have you been drinking?" At my nod, he said dryly, "Well, I'm flattered, but I don't cross that line with my clients. Especially with my employer's daughter, and definitely not when you've been drinking."

Each word infuriated me. I stamped my foot, my hands clenching into fists at my side. "I am not a child, Greg. I'm nineteen."

He scoffed. "Then act like it."

I'd seethed the entire way to the gala. He was only six years older than me, not that much in the scheme of things. And we were both adults.

I stewed throughout the event. My parents hosted the damn thing, so I had to do my duty, sitting on stage while they gave speeches and handed out awards to deserving employees. My cheeks hurt from the fake smile I'd cemented in place, while reliving my humiliation over and over.

As soon as the ceremony had finished, I sought the refuge of my friends along with the oblivion of alcohol.

Chapter Seven

That night I met Kevin. An arrogant snob from a well-known family, he wasn't at all my usual type. Before I knew it, we were making out, passing a bottle of tequila between us whenever we stopped to come up for air.

What I'd needed most right then was validation, and Kevin wanted me. Every time I'd crossed my legs, his eyes were glued to the movement. If I bent down, his gaze locked on my cleavage. And I had soaked up every minute.

So when his hand slid up my thigh to trace my panty line, I didn't stop him. When he suggested we go somewhere more private, I said I knew a place. Then I led him to my limo.

I'd had sex before, and I didn't see what all the hype was about, but I wasn't about to ruin my attention high. Kevin's mouth smashed into mine, pushing me against the limo as he fumbled for the handle. He managed to pry it open, and we tumbled in, a tangle of limbs. I ended up on his lap in the rear facing seat, upending the too-light bottle of tequila while he struggled with his zipper followed by a condom.

Then he was inside me. Kevin yanked down my top, baring my breasts with a greedy chuckle, but then he found his rhythm and didn't pay them much attention. To be honest, I was already growing bored. I contemplated taking another drink when a slight movement caught my attention.

The divider was down several inches, which I hadn't noticed until then. My gaze slid up over the reflective barrier and slammed into Greg's wide, gray eyes.

The sight of him in my drunken state started a reaction that every other guy had failed to achieve. A ripple went through me. Suddenly it wasn't Kevin beneath me, it wasn't his thumb on my clit. I was riding Greg. His length slid into my most sensitive part, and I moaned, my breaths coming faster. I felt the pressure building, increasing under Greg's disbelieving stare that never wavered. Like he couldn't look away.

Kevin groaned beneath me, and Greg jerked back like I'd struck him. I didn't have time to wonder about it, though, as Kevin took my nipple in his mouth. I closed my eyes. All I could see were Greg's lips clamping over my breast, and I came, hard, mouthing Greg's name. When I opened my eyes, Greg was gone, and Kevin had passed out beneath me.

I leapt off him, pulling up my bodice and stumbling out of the door, but Greg was nowhere to be seen. So I climbed back into the limo, on the other seat this time, and I replayed the moment in my head, the way I'd imagined it. Eventually I got cold enough that I decided to kick Kevin out, find my driver and demand to go home.

Except Greg had disappeared. I told the valet I was ready to go, then went back inside the building to wait. The scene played on repeat in my mind until my limo pulled up. My stomach turned from nerves or too much tequila, I wasn't sure, but I braced myself for whatever I'd see in Greg's expression as I walked down the steps.

It wasn't him. A different person, a complete stranger in a similar uniform, waited for me. "Miss Elgin?"

I nodded, keeping several feet between us.

"Hi, I'm Barry. I drove your brother tonight. Your driver, Greg, went home ill, but he wanted to be sure you had a ride. I believe your brother texted you as well."

Sure enough, I'd dug out my phone to find a text from Derek explaining. I had deflated like a balloon, feeling hollow and bereft. "Thank you, Barry. I'd like to go home now."

"Of course, Miss Elgin." He'd opened the door for me, tipping his hat as I climbed in.

The back seat smelled like tequila and sex, making my stomach roll once more. I opened one of the panels in the wall, finding some mints we kept on hand. Popping one in my mouth, I breathed it in. The peppermint scent reminded me of Greg, punching me in my gut like an iron fist. I flopped onto the seat, my hand resting under my cheek as I stared into the darkness.

I hadn't heard a word from Greg that whole weekend, and on Monday morning an envelope had been delivered to me with his resignation. Effective immediately.

The noise of the shower turning off pulled me back to the present. I didn't want Greg to find me lazing about in bed, so I jumped up to get dressed. Only to remember that all my things were still in the other room.

Dammit. Maybe if I watch where I step?

Getting a splinter seemed like a better option than facing Greg at the moment, so I hurried to my room. Of course, my suitcases lay behind several feet of shards. *That must've been one hell of a lamp.*

I turned on the main light, gingerly picking my way through the debris field. The lamp was a lighter color than the carpet, making it easy to spot the pieces. I'd just slip on a pair of my shoes for the way back. I grinned at my resourcefulness, focusing once more on where to step. Halfway across, I heard a bellow that made me cringe.

"What are you doing?" Greg's angry face appeared in the doorway, even madder than it had been before taking a shower.

I pictured his face frozen that way and giggled to myself before resuming my tedious trek.

"Rhonda, stop."

His pleading words meant nothing to me. After all, what was he going to do?

A few seconds later, I found out. In just a pair of black sweatpants and tennis shoes, he stomped in, threw me over his shoulder and carried me from the room.

"I was almost there!" I couldn't ignore his warm arm clamped across the back of my thighs or the bare, muscled expanse beneath me, still dotted with bits of moisture from his shower. My stomach thrilled as I failed to look away. *He could've at least put on a shirt.*

I flew back over his naked shoulder, frantically grabbing the hem of my tank so it stayed put. The last thing I wanted was to give him a show on top of everything. He set me down hard enough that I winced, and it was a testament to how angry he was that he didn't notice. Adrenaline coursed through my entire body.

"What was so important that you were walking over broken glass barefoot?" he demanded, keeping his hands on my waist as if afraid I'd run right back over to do it again.

Desire rolled through me as I took in his rigid stance. I wanted to thread my finger through his hair and yank his mouth to mine. Instead, I flipped my hair over my shoulder to make sure he saw every inch of my skimpy pajamas. "I didn't think you'd appreciate me tromping around your house half-naked. I need my clothes." I added in my most snarky tone, "I would have worn my shoes back."

Those magnificent eyes turned stormy as they surveyed my few scraps of clothing as if seeing them for the first time. His face turned an odd shade of purple. With a peculiar choking noise, he spun away from me to huff out of the room.

Why did my bare body always piss him off so much? I remembered how he'd yelled at the sight of my water-drenched shirt in the car, and I fought the urge to cross my arms over myself. We were both adults here—he could deal with it. When he returned a few moments later with my suitcases, he lifted an eyebrow as if to ask if I were happy.

"My shoes." I paused, then added a reluctant, "Please." His jaw tightened once more, and I could tell he was trying to keep a lid on his fury. But if he didn't want me going in there, what was I supposed to do? I threw him a bone as he stalked out the door. "Just the black pair."

When he reappeared, he tossed them on the bed. "Will that be all, Miss Elgin?"

I glared. "Yes, thank you. You're dismissed." My icy tone delivered each word with frigid precision.

Before he shut the door, his gaze slid down my body one more time, as if against his will. I wasn't sure if it was him or the door that groaned.

When I made it downstairs, barefoot and wearing a fitted tee with yoga pants, I was surprised that Greg was the only other person around despite it being close to eight a.m. He lounged on the couch, reading a newspaper. *At least he put a shirt on.*

"C'mon. You can help me make breakfast." He snapped the paper closed, striding toward the kitchen and giving me an excellent view of what those sweatpants did for his tight ass.

At that moment, I was happy to follow him anywhere. Then confusion set in. "Wait, don't you guys have a cook?" I knew someone else had made dinner last night.

The derisive glance over his shoulder and the curled upper lip set me on edge before the words even left his mouth. "Is the heiress afraid of getting her hands dirty?"

My hands flew to my hips as I took offense. "I know how to cook, thank you very much. I was just curious."

His voice was a little softer when he responded. "Her name is Myrna, but she doesn't work Mondays. I thought I'd make omelets for everyone."

We didn't speak again until after we were in the state of the art kitchen. Almost every surface was stainless steel and sparkling clean. It was a bit eerie seeing my face everywhere.

Greg started a pot of coffee, then went to the fridge to pull out omelet ingredients, setting them on the massive island. "The skillets are in the lower cupboard over there. Find me the one with the blue handle?"

It gave me something to do, at least. The cupboards themselves were black, and I crouched before the one Greg had indicated, glancing back to make sure it was the right one. He nodded, so I opened the door. *Holy pans.* There were so many that I opened the other side of the cupboard, resting on my heels just to gawk at them. *Their cook must love pans.*

How many do my parents own? I pursed my lips as I scanned the cupboard, searching for a blue handled skillet. Not seeing it right away, I shifted onto my knees to peer into the cupboard better.

"Morning, Greg." Mandy's voice almost made me jump out of my skin. "Are you actually going to cook, or are you just planning to stare at Rhonda's ass all morning?"

I glanced over my shoulder as Greg fixed a murderous glare on Mandy. It was cute seeing him flustered. She shrugged, the picture of innocence until she winked in my direction. When I turned back to the cupboard, a blue handled pan caught my attention, and I pulled it out triumphantly. I set it on the stove with a clang, next to Greg who focused on the counter.

The remaining hint of anger I'd held on to drained out of me as I replayed our morning. His angry words accusing me of forgetting everything we'd said and done because his family had money. How affronted he'd been at the very thought. His fury at me risking injury to myself. And just now, he'd been caught red-handed checking out my ass.

My lips tipped up as I remembered how sweet he was after my panic attack and how safe I'd felt in his arms. Could I really be mad after all that?

Plus, Mandy was still watching. So, I wrapped one of my hands around his strong forearm, using it to balance as I stood on tiptoe and brushed my lips against his cheek.

While I was there, I whispered, "No worries about checking out my ass, turnabout's fair play after all. Those sweatpants should be illegal." With an audacity I hadn't realized I possessed, I pinched his ass before I walked away, his cheek firmer than I'd imagined. My action was an olive branch, a peace offering.

"Rhonda," he croaked on my name, making me pause in my exit. Clearing his throat, he tried again. "What do you want in your omelet?"

I smiled at him, sweet as pie. "Surprise me. You know what I like." I let my tone hold enough suggestion that his nostrils flared at the double entendre, and I purposefully raked my gaze down him before I left.

Except I didn't know what to do with myself once I was out of the kitchen. A cold shower was the smart choice, but I didn't want him thinking I was running away. Mandy saved me, appearing through the swinging door a few minutes later with two piping hot cups of coffee in her hand.

She offered me one. "Greg said for you to try a sip before you judge it. He found some special creamer he thought you'd like, even if it's not your specialty froufrou drink." She shook her head. "His words, not mine."

Curiosity got the better of me, and I lifted the mug to my lips. "Peppermint!" My delight faded as I tried to reconcile the Greg who made sure my coffee was perfect and made omelets for everyone, with the Greg I'd fought with this morning.

"What?" Mandy sat down at the dining room table, propping her chin on her hand.

I frowned. "Your brother. He confuses me."

Her laughter echoed around the room. "I'd be worried if he didn't. Was that him I heard stomping down the stairs this morning?" She shook her head at my nod. "Figures. I thought I'd come down here to him slamming around in the kitchen, banging pots and pans, muttering to himself." A soft smile spread over her face. "But he was just standing there, gawking at you like a lovesick schoolboy. It was so cute." She chuckled. "I knew then whatever he was annoyed about wasn't that big of a deal."

I hoped it was true. Thankfully, Greg was no longer scowling when he brought out three omelets. And he slid mine over first.

Mandy smirked when he grinned before sitting next to me. "Told you so," she said, catching the plate he slid to her.

He looked from me to her in confusion. "Who told you what?"

I took a quick bite to keep from answering, immediately glad I had. "Holy shit, this is good." I winced at my language, grateful his mom wasn't around to hear my slip.

Mandy paused with her fork halfway to her mouth. "This is the first time he's made you an omelet?" At my nod, her fork hit her plate with a clang. "What is wrong with you? Haven't I told you to lead with that?"

A giggle escaped my lips at the absurd image of Greg arriving to pick me up, rolling down the divider and offering me an omelet. The more I thought about it, the more ridiculous the picture was. Soon, I couldn't breathe.

Mandy's phone rang, and she excused herself while shooting me a mystified look. Greg waited till she was out of earshot, then faced me with a quizzical frown.

I struggled to get the words out. "All I could think about was you coming to pick me up. I get in, you roll down the divider, and hold out a steaming plate to me." I schooled my face into a hopeful expression. "Omelet?"

His laughter mingled with mine, the rich deep tones underlining my higher ones. Our hilarity danced together, into a joyous crescendo where we were both left breathless and holding our stomachs.

Mandy returned glancing at me then her brother. She took her seat once more, waiting for us to calm down before saying, "So that was Peter. We're invited to a sledding party today."

"Sledding?" I asked.

She nodded.

Greg shrugged when I didn't have more of a reaction. "There's nothing else on the agenda today. What do you say? Wanna find out how real yoopers do it?"

I frowned. "Yoopers?"

Mandy said, "Yeah, that's what we natives call ourselves here in the Upper Peninsula or the U.P." She used a funny accent for the last part. "But you forgot the 'eh'." They both snickered at some joke I didn't get.

I chewed another bite of my omelet before admitting, "I've never been sledding before."

Both their jaws dropped. Mandy was the first to respond with, "Never?"

I shook my head.

"Well, then you have to come!" Her smile was genuine, and she turned to Greg, waiting for him to agree.

He smiled too, identical to hers except for his adorable dimple. "Yes, we will."

A thrill went through my abdomen when he turned back to me, lit up with excitement. Sledding sounded fun, though hours outdoors was not my usual thing. I'd put up with it if it meant more time with Greg.

After we'd finished breakfast, we went upstairs to get ready. Mandy dropped off some of her warmer clothes that she thought I might be able to use. Even if they'd be on the tall side. I bit my lip, glancing from the pile of clothes to the closed bathroom door where Greg was changing. I didn't have a clue about how to begin.

The bathroom door opened, Greg frowning when he saw me still standing there. "Aren't you going to get dressed?"

My cheeks grew hot as I studied the floor, feeling dumber by the second. "I'm not sure where to start."

"Oh." A wealth of emotion laced that one syllable, but not judgment.

Thank goodness. I heard him cross the room, felt his body heat as he stood next to me.

His tone was incredulous as he asked, "You never went out and played in the snow?"

I frowned. "Yeah, sure. But it's been years, and it's so much colder up here. I want to make sure I do it right."

He flipped through the pile Mandy had brought, handing me a soft, thin pair of pants. "Start with these, then put the pants I bought you yesterday over them." Next he gave me a shirt of similar material. "Wear this under your sweater. And I'll find you some socks. You said the boots were a little big, right?" When I nodded, he grinned. "Good."

I hesitated, preferring to change in the bedroom than the bathroom.

"Change wherever you're most comfortable, Rhonda." One hand settled on my shoulder for the briefest of caresses.

I had goosebumps as I walked away. When I came out, I already felt toasty. The under layers seemed to insulate me, holding in my heat. I couldn't imagine being cold in them.

"Think fast!"

Something flew through the air at me, and I barely managed to catch the thick pair of socks.

"Nice." The dimple made another appearance. "Put those on over a pair of your regular socks and meet me downstairs." He paused. "Might want to pull your hair back. And use the bathroom now. There aren't any close by, and I doubt you'll want to go in the woods."

I balked at the thought, doing as he suggested, then met him and Mandy downstairs. They both had on nylon insulated overalls and were stuffing their feet into boots.

Greg tossed me a similar pair of the overalls. "These are the shortest snow pants we have, but we'll make them work."

Mandy was already done, bundled up in her coat with a cute hat complete with a pompom on top of her head. She carried mittens under one arm. "I'll go load up the sleds."

I shoved my legs into the too long pants, pulling the straps up over my shoulders, then zipping up the middle section. I felt pathetic. My feet weren't even visible, and the straps wouldn't stay up.

Greg chuckled. "C'mere, Jellybean."

I shuffled over. His touch was gentle as he adjusted first one strap, then the other, tightening them as far as they would go. My stomach flipped as his arm brushed my chest. My toes were visible by the time he stepped back, and the straps stayed put. I grinned.

"That's better." He tapped my chin. "You'll have fun, you'll see."

Next came a cute stocking cap like Mandy's, this one in a bright purple with two braids hanging down. Once I'd put on my boots, I reached for my coat.

But he shook his head. "That's not going to cut it." He handed me a heavy, thick thing that said Carhartt on one side, helping me get my arms through. Once I was zipped, he gave me a pair of gloves. "And I have mittens for when we get there."

I felt like someone had wrapped me in a foam mat. "I'm supposed to move in all this?"

He laughed as he zipped up his own coat, tugging a black hat over his ears. "Come on."

Chapter Eight

Mandy had a big SUV that fit the large wooden sleds she called toboggans in the back, and we all crammed in the front. It wasn't a long drive, but it was pretty. The sun sparkled off the layer of snow, and I had to squint to see anything.

"We'll be in the woods most of the time, so it won't be as bright there," Mandy said.

The spot she turned into was little more than a path between trees. If I hadn't seen tire tracks leading into the distance, I would have been more worried. A clearing opened around the bend with several other vehicles parked in it.

Mandy and Greg leapt out first while I struggled to even get upright. Greg grabbed one toboggan, Mandy the other. Then we took off, our footsteps crunching through the crusted top layer of the snow as we walked toward the woods. Mandy raced ahead to see her friends as I dropped further behind.

Greg slowed, letting me catch up. "Maybe I should call you Shorty instead," he teased.

"I'm only short compared to your family of giants! Five eight is a perfectly respectable height, thank you very much." But I smiled, letting him know I was just playing. "Besides, I like Jellybean."

His mouth tipped up in a crooked grin. "So do I." His voice was husky, the words heavy.

My stomach flipped, and I had to look away. *Does he mean my nickname? Or me?*

As we neared the tree line, the sound of laughter and voices carried to us. It took a moment to adjust to the lower light of the shaded area. Finally I made out the group of ten people near Mandy. Several of them piled onto the toboggan she'd brought, then disappeared out of sight.

I drew closer, gasping at the huge, steep hill. "We're going down that?" Trepidation raced through me. I'd pictured a normal hill like we had back home, but this was a freaking mountain.

Greg nudged me with his elbow. "It'll be fun, I promise."

"Do I have to go alone?" I turned, staring up at him.

He shook his head before brushing my cheek with his gloved hand. "Never."

I breathed a sigh of relief, the word echoing through me and easing some of the tension. When we reached the others, Mandy introduced us, telling everyone that I was a sledding virgin. I turned to Greg for help, but he rocked back on his heels, shaking with silent laughter at the fuss they made. I couldn't be mad, though, because it was all in fun.

Until they insisted we go next.

"Let her watch a couple times," Greg said. "Plus, she needs to get her mittens on."

I could have kissed him, welcoming the excuse for a delay. Though, once the image of kissing Greg was in my head, it wouldn't leave, and my gaze dipped to his lips, imagining what they'd feel like pressed against mine. My many layers suddenly seemed like too much, as if someone had turned up the heat.

Mandy and Peter went down the hill next, letting out loud whoops that echoed through the trees. Other sleds sat off to one side in a heap, but the toboggans seemed to be the favorite. Someone else had brought one too, so there were three in total.

Greg pulled me away from the group and showed me the mittens. "I'll help you put them on." At my indignant frown, he chuckled. "Trust me, it's easier this way. Hold your hand out, straight and stiff."

I did my best, and he tugged the mitten over my glove. It took a moment to get my thumb in the right spot, then he yanked the cuff of the mitten over my coat sleeve.

"Keeps the snow out." Then he did the other one.

He frowned when finished, reaching over to pull my zipper all the way up. His gloved hand hovered very close to my chest, and I didn't breathe until he let go.

"Ready?"

I almost asked for what but caught myself just in time. Instead, I nodded, trying to gather my courage. We approached the edge of the slope, a toboggan waiting for us.

Greg held it steady. "Climb on."

I'd seen enough to know that the front person should sit cross-legged. I tried but my normal flexibility was hindered by the extra padding. It took a minute.

Once I'd stopped shifting, Greg sat down behind me. His long legs needed to fit on the sled too, so I lifted my knees letting him stretch out on either side of me. My knees rested on his thighs, and despite the umpteen layers between us, I swore I felt his body heat.

Another quick scoot and Greg's front pressed firmly against my back. *Um.* My heart stopped as he reached around me, one hand grabbing the rope then settling at my waist. "All set?"

There were no handles. "What do I hang onto?"

His husky voice sounded low in my ear. "Me."

I swallowed hard, unable to react right away. Tentatively, I glanced at his thighs, covered by the thick snow pants. *I grabbed more than that just yesterday.* I gulped, then wrapped my mittened hands under his muscular legs. A thrill leapt through me as he tensed at my touch, and I pictured his muscles bunching beneath all the layers. My breathing was shallow as I adjusted my grip, wondering if I would survive this.

"Ready, Jellybean?" The huskiness amplified.

I didn't trust my voice, so I nodded.

"I can steer, okay? So make sure you keep your arms and legs inside the sled all the time."

I nodded again, letting out a little gasp as he gripped me tighter to him, his breath warm on my cheek.

"Here we go." He shoved us off, and we flew.

The hill itself was free of trees, a wide swath that ended in a clearing. I couldn't even scream because my breath disappeared, and I held on to Greg, needing something solid to clutch. The trees flew past on either side, snow and wind stinging my eyes, but it was beyond exhilarating.

I couldn't stop grinning. My stomach dipped when we hit a bump, sailing high enough to catch some air.

The ground finally evened out, and we slowed to a stop.

I sat still, beyond overwhelmed.

"What'd you think?" Greg's voice sounded next to my ear, filled with all the adrenaline I was feeling.

I whipped my head around, a wide grin stretching my cheeks. "Let's do it again!"

His laughter echoed around us, and his hand tightened on my waist in the briefest of hugs. "I was hoping you'd say that." He stood first then helped me up. "We need to get off the path, so others can use it. Sledding etiquette one-o-one."

The trek back up wasn't nearly as fun. Greg didn't leave me behind, though, and insisted on pulling the toboggan. We watched others whip by. One pair zoomed down on plastic sleds, seeing who could reach the bottom first.

At the top, I sat for several minutes as I caught my breath, happy to let others have their turn. When I'd rallied, we went again. The morning flew by in a rush of adrenaline and excitement.

Every time I sat with Greg on the sled, a thrill went through me, even before we started down the hill. As his body pressed against mine, my heart beat faster, my pulse thrumming in my ears. Each time I wrapped my hands around his thighs, he tensed, showing me I wasn't the only one affected. Every time he asked, "Are you ready, Jellybean?" I wanted to reply with an ardent, "Yes."

Just after one o'clock, Peter and the others decided to go get lunch. Mandy decided to go with them.

"We'll get the toboggans, no worries," Greg offered after he'd agreed to drive her SUV home.

She hugged him, waved at me, then hurried to catch up with her friends. I watched them go.

When I turned back to him, Greg asked, "Ready to head to the house?"

I bit my lip. "One more time?" It was a long shot, but I wasn't going to pass up an opportunity to have Greg all to myself in the woods.

His grin was reward enough. He positioned the toboggan at the top of the slope, and I sat down, holding my knees up as he slid under them. We'd done this so many times today, I'd have thought it would be easier by now. My breath caught as his front settled against my back, seeming closer than before.

He took an extra second to push my ponytail aside, his mitten brushing my cheek before his warm breath cascaded over my skin. "Gotta be able to see."

I swallowed against the dryness in my mouth, my palms damp in my gloves. Then he shifted again, reaching for the rope as his hand settled on my waist. I rested my mittened hands for an extra beat on his thighs, feeling brave as I slid them down to hold on. I waited, anticipating his next words.

"Ready, Jellybean?" His voice was low and husky.

My stomach flipped as his lips brushed my ear. "Yes," I breathed, leaning into him.

He launched us down the hill, this time aiming for the divots and jumps. We flew through the air at least twice, me jostling him on the landing. One last bump near the bottom of the hill dislodged me enough that my leg flew out. It didn't hurt, but our sled went careening off the path and tipped us over. We rolled over and over in the snow.

Greg landed solidly on top of me with a quiet *oomph*. His weight just made my heart race more as he looked down at me in concern. "Are you all right?"

I nodded. I was aware of every bit of him pressing me into the snow. One of his legs nestled between mine, and our torsos touched. His arms framed my shoulders. My gaze drifted to his oh-so-kissable lips, so close to mine.

Somehow, I managed to ask, "You?"

His nod was distracted, his attention all on my mouth. I shifted beneath him, a thrill zipping through me as he drew even closer. Our lips met tentatively, as if he were asking permission. They touched for the briefest of moments before Greg pulled back. His wide eyes were stormy and his breathing ragged.

But I was done waiting. I'd been waiting all day, I'd been waiting for years, and I could wait no more. I surged up to meet him, one mitten clasping the back of his head, the other gripping his shoulder. He froze for a moment before his lips moved on mine. Then he slanted his mouth, deepening the kiss, as if he couldn't hold back either. His arms tightened around me, devouring me with a passionate hunger.

I'd dreamed of kissing him, so many times, but this surpassed every single one of my daydreams. My chest felt like it would explode, desire coursed through me and I cursed every single layer between us. I had to wrench away, needing oxygen, and he rolled off, into the snow beside me. Our chests heaved as I stared up at the sky.

As far as first kisses went, he'd just ruined me for all other men. *Talk about a dream come true.* The feeling of his lips lingered, as if his essence were still there, and I savored every second. He stood up, brushing himself off, then he offered me a hand.

I shook my head, not ready to move yet.

He frowned. "You're going to freeze."

I stuck my tongue out. "Maybe I want to make a snow angel." I moved my arms and legs back and forth the way I'd done so many years before.

Greg watched me with his head tilted to one side, pure amusement on his face.

"What's so funny?"

He shook his head. "You'll see."

This time I took his offered hand up, studying my snow angel. Then I burst into laughter. "My snow angel got some action!"

A jumbled mess in the snow led up to where we'd landed. Greg's knees, feet and arms dug in beside my imprint, but his footprints walking away sealed the impression that my snow angel really had gotten laid. Greg chuckled once more before turning to head up the hill.

I looked over my ridiculous creation once more, shaking my head. *Snow angel's getting more action than me. Sigh.*

Greg's back was to me when I began trudging after him, and it proved too tempting a target. I paused to ball up some snow, aiming carefully. When it hit his shoulder, he yelped, whirling around as I threw another one. Which smacked him square in the chest.

I laughed at his indignant expression, but it turned to a squeal as he tore after me, bending down to scoop up snow on the run. His shot hit my leg, just before I ducked behind a tree. I peeked out to find him gaining on me, so I raced around the tree the opposite way, tossing another snowball over my shoulder. This one missed completely.

I didn't even make it to the next tree before he tackled me, both of us landing back in the snow, shaking with laughter. I squealed and squirmed, trying to get away.

"No way. You're mine now."

As much as I liked the sound of that, I had one more trick up my sleeve. I grabbed a fistful of snow and smashed it over my shoulder, into his face.

He hollered at the cold but didn't loosen his grip. "Oh, you're going to pay for that." He gripped me tightly, pinning me down with his knees on either side of me.

All sorts of wonderful images of what we could do in that position sprang to my mind. I felt his hands on my neck. Then something cold and wet slid inside the collar of my shirt, down my back. I yelped as the melted snow dripped down my spine.

He leapt off me. "Don't fight dirty, unless you can handle the consequences."

I begrudgingly took his offered hand, only to squeal when he hauled me up on my feet and flush against him. He didn't hesitate this time as his mouth crashed down onto mine, and my hum of pleasure was swallowed by him. My mittens rested on his shoulders as his arms tightened around me.

He broke away, stepping back with a smirk. I gaped after him as he started up the hill once more. *I'll take those consequences any day.* As I followed after him, my wet shirt plastered to my back, but it didn't even faze me. Not when my lips still tingled from his touch.

Thoughts of Greg's kiss warmed me all the way to the house. We unloaded the toboggans, and I was about to go inside when he stopped me with a hand on my arm.

A serious furrow creased his forehead. "You're not just arm candy, Rhonda, you know that, right? Not to me."

I froze, desperate to hear the words of reassurance, especially from him.

"I let you invite yourself along because I needed a friend with me to even consider coming back here." He yanked off his hat, running his hand through his disheveled hair. "Having you along gave me the courage to do that."

Warmth shot through me at the admission.

"I wanted to surprise you, with the house and my family. Not hurt you. I never want to hurt you or use you. That's not who I am and"—he stopped to swallow—"I hope you know that."

Guilt hit me then, low and hard, right in the gut. What I'd accused him of, thought him capable of, was despicable. I laid a hand on his chest, waiting for him to look at me. "I do know that, Greg. I've just been with so many assholes that I forget everyone isn't like that. I'm sorry." I thought about the rest of what he'd said. "And I'm here, as your friend, ally. Whatever you need."

I left it there, wanting to be so much more to him, but knowing we'd just started scratching the surface. We hadn't named this new, tentative thing between us, and I didn't want to push. Didn't want to give Greg any reason to run away. I'd waited so long for him, and he had his own timetable, needing to take things slow. I wasn't going to ruin it by pushing.

"Thank you. That means a lot to me." He stepped back, clearing his throat. "Come on, let's go get warm and dry."

* * * *

An amazing aroma greeted us when we stepped into the entryway. Julie greeted us from the dining room table where she'd been reading on her tablet.

Greg inhaled deeply, his face lighting up. "Is that what I think it is?"

Julie nodded. "Myrna had some in the freezer. Thought it'd be a good day for it."

I stood there, waiting for someone to clue me in.

Greg took pity on me. "Myrna makes the best potato soup I've ever had, and she always made it for us after we went sledding." His grin held a wicked glint as he turned back to his mom. "Mandy's going to be so mad when she hears she missed out."

She chuckled as we trudged past. "Make sure to hang up your wet things!"

The way Greg heaved an annoyed sigh before hollering his agreement sent a pang of longing through me. My mom had never done that. Jealousy pricked me at the ease of their relationship and the familiarity of this conversation. Even though he muttered on about how he was a grown man and was smart enough to hang up his damn clothes, I knew he loved his mom.

It took forever to peel off all my soggy layers. After hanging our wet things on a clothes rack, we traipsed upstairs. My dry, comfy clothes felt like heaven. Greg waited for me in the sitting room, wearing those ass hugging sweatpants again. *Oh darn.*

The potato soup was as delicious as they'd claimed, plus it warmed me inside and out. My cheeks stayed flushed from the time spent outdoors, but I didn't regret a moment of it. Especially since something had shifted between me and Greg. An obstacle removed.

We settled on the couch to watch a movie, and he sat right next to me, no prompting, no maneuvering. We were really doing this. *Whatever this is.*

One question burned within me, and now was as good a time as any. Glancing around to be sure his mom wasn't in earshot, I asked quietly, "Greg, why didn't you RSVP to the wedding?"

His arm tensed next to mine, and his mouth tightened. He stared down at his lap then sighed. "What I said outside is part of it. I needed someone to come with me, and I just kept putting it off, hoping I'd find that person." He glanced at me. "The other part was you. I knew you weren't in a good place, and I didn't want to leave you alone, especially for a holiday. You had me worried."

My heart twisted at the thought of Greg being that concerned for me, but then his admission sank in, and I gaped at him. I felt like someone had just told me grass was purple and proven it. "You care that much?"

Maybe it wasn't me against the world. Maybe Greg really was in my corner. And grass really was purple.

His brow furrowed together. "Jellybean, I've always cared."

A crack formed in the ice coating my heart, and I grinned. I shifted on the couch so our shoulders touched, thrilling even more when he didn't pull away. We stayed like that for the rest of the movie. The credits had just started rolling when a door slammed, and Mandy stormed in.

We hurried over to see what was wrong, arriving just in time to watch her plop onto the stairs, drop her head in her hands and start sobbing.

Chapter Nine

We exchanged concerned looks before Greg asked, "What's wrong?"

Mandy choked out, "Erin's stuck in Minneapolis," between sobs. Her phone slipped to the floor with a dull thud.

Greg's lips pressed together. He flew to her side and kneeled next to her, wrapping his arms around her.

Afraid I knew the answer, I asked quietly, "Who's Erin?"

He responded, "Mandy's best friend since kindergarten. And her maid of honor."

"What happened, Mandy?" Maybe I could help fix it.

The muffled answer came from somewhere in the vicinity of Greg's shoulder. "Her flight got canceled due to a snowstorm."

My mind raced to all we needed to do — check the weather, see who else would be affected, and what other arrangements needed to be made. "What was she responsible for?"

Her tear-streaked face appeared for a second before crumpling once more. "Everything!"

Not the smartest choice. Always better to have a local in charge because of circumstances like this. But we'd make it work. "Mandy." I touched her shoulder. "I know this seems like the end of the world, but it's not. I've dealt with worse situations and tighter deadlines. I'm a pro at pulling together last-minute details, and I'd be happy to help in any way I can. Could you give me Erin's number, maybe let her know I'll be calling?"

Her blotchy face appeared once more, and she sniffed. "For real, Rhonda? You'd do that?"

I nodded, with a gentle smile. "Of cour—"

She flung herself at me, nearly knocking me over. "Thank you!"

I managed to sink onto the stairs instead, patting her back. "You're welcome."

When at last she stood up, she dialed Erin. "I'll fill her in. I've already sent you her number," she said to me as the phone rang. "Erin? You're not going to believe this!" And she walked upstairs, chatting away as if she hadn't just had a complete breakdown.

I felt Greg staring at me. "What?"

He stood up, holding out his hand. "I'll drive you around." His warm palm slid against mine, his fingers wrapping around my hand as he pulled me up. But he didn't let go. He just stood there with our arms entwined between us. "Thank you, Jellybean. You saved the day."

I swallowed, hoping the butterflies would stay put. "Well, I haven't done anything yet." With a quick glance at my comfy outfit, I sighed. "Tomorrow I'll have to glam up a bit. Not all heroes wear capes, you know," I said, grinning up at him. "This one wears Jimmy Choos."

"Yeah, she does." He touched my cheek and anticipation fluttered in me. But he stepped back, and the moment was gone.

After a quick discussion with Erin, I was amazed at the amount of tasks that still needed to be done. And now it all rested on my shoulders. Mandy had one other bridesmaid, but she was seven months pregnant. The only thing she could do was show up at the events.

I felt better once I made a plan. I coordinated with Greg, mapping out the next day. And found myself eager to spend more time with him. Just us.

That night we went upstairs early since we knew we had to clean up the mess from the lamp in my room.

"Ready to kick me out already?" I half-teased to cover the disappointment of giving up my excuse to sleep next to Greg.

He stilled, turning his piercing gaze on me. "Never. I'd never kick you out, Jellybean."

His words made my mouth go dry, and I studied the carpet. He went back to picking up the big pieces as I vacuumed up the smaller shards, going over every inch of the space. I wondered if he had any idea how much that simple declaration affected me. I played it over and over, searing the words into my heart while a small smile danced on my lips.

When it came time for sleep, I climbed in next to him. "Just so you don't have to worry about me."

He smirked knowingly. "I think you're addicted to your new pillow."

The teasing lilt in his voice sent a thrill through me. *More flirting, and in bed.* "Maybe." I focused on his bare shoulder, pursing my lips before I said as lightly as I could, "Maybe I should try it out, one more time. Just to see."

A pleased smile crossed his face as he stretched out his arm, and I snuggled into him, humming with pleasure at his warmth.

His lips brushed my forehead. "Good night, Jellybean."

"Good night, Just Greg."

* * * *

Our first stop the next morning was the bakery, to double check the cake order for the shower. The array of cupcakes formed the skirt of a wedding dress. The bodice was made of cake as well, with beads and tulle draped over one shoulder. The tops of each cupcake were swirled high with white frosting, some with pearly sprinkles on them. The overall effect was breathtaking. I'd never seen such an elegant display, and I told the baker so.

After confirming payment, as well as delivery place and time, I checked one item off my list. At this rate, we'd be done in no time.

Mandy and Julie were contacting guests about coming in sooner to beat the storm. So, our next stop was the local hotel to see about arranging rooms for this evening. I could've called but I knew from experience that in-person contact yielded better results.

Greg escorted me up the slippery sidewalk. Once inside, I put on my game face. I strode up to the counter, smiling at the young lady waiting to help me. "Hi, I'm Rhonda Elgin. I'd like to speak to your manager, please. Nothing is wrong," I reassured her. "I just have several business questions that I need addressed and would like to go straight to the source."

She straightened at my name. "Of course, Miss Elgin. I'll see if she's available."

"Thank you so much." I waited as she disappeared into the back, though it was an effort not to drum my fingers on the counter.

Greg stood to the side. It was clear he was with me, but not close enough that anyone would direct their questions to him.

A gorgeous lady with rich, dark skin and sharp eyes strode from the back, her heels echoing off the tile. "Ms. Elgin, my name is Simone. What can I help you with today?"

I explained our dilemma with the storm and the wedding. I assured her that price was not an object, and I'd be happy to upgrade rooms if necessary, even paying in advance.

"No trouble at all, Ms. Elgin. In fact, we've had several cancellations due to the weather, so you're doing us a favor. I'll see to it personally all the guests under your reservation get upgraded and have a later check out. If any of them need an extra night, please tell them to let us know right away. And to see me if they have any questions or concerns."

I smiled gratefully. "Oh, thank you so much, Simone. That is more than generous. It's nice working with an understanding and capable woman like yourself."

She stood taller under my praise. "I hope you will consider us for your future stays, Miss Elgin."

"Greg," I said, glancing at him for confirmation. "The wedding itself is here as well, right?"

He nodded.

Once more I faced Simone, leaning in. "I know it's New Year's Eve, but I do hope you're working the event?"

"Oh!" Simone's hand went to her chest, a broad grin on her face. "Yes, I am. I've been working with our event coordinator, Desiree, to make sure everything is in order. And Erin. I was expecting to see her today."

"Sadly, Erin is stuck in Minneapolis for the time being, so I'm helping out. This is Greg, the bride's brother, and I'm his girlfriend." It took a lot to get the g word out smoothly, but I managed. Though Greg's lips twitched with amusement, and all I wanted to do was jab an elbow in his side.

But that would ruin my image, so I refrained.

"Here's my card." I dug two out. "One for you, and one for Desiree. Please don't hesitate to contact me if you need anything between now and the wedding." We shook hands, and I left, excited to check another box off my list.

Greg and I climbed back into the freezing car, wishing I had some sort of protection between my bare legs and the icy leather seats. As soon as Greg started the engine, I pressed the button for the heated seats, grateful when the warmth began seeping through.

"Do you always get what you want?"

My head snapped toward him, not quite sure how to take his question. Because obviously I didn't always get what I wanted—one exception sat next to me.

"In a business deal like that," he clarified. "I saw the change in you, the way you walked up to the front desk. It was like you already knew you'd won."

Oh, that old trick. "That's just a tool of the trade," I said, waving him off. "I've been doing this for a while. Long enough that I've learned what works and what doesn't. Confidence is key. You also need to know what you want and what you'll settle for. Always have a bottom line. Start by being kind."

He stared at me for a long moment, curiosity and admiration in his assessing gaze. "You amaze me, Rhonda. I'm so glad you came on this trip with me."

Warmth spread through me as we pulled out of the parking lot. I was glad Greg had brought me on this trip, too. This new shift in our relationship was exciting but he was still my friend. Still the one I could depend on. It was like having a new accessory with an already perfect outfit.

My mind drifted back, wondering what would have happened if the night of the gala had gone differently. If the last two years would have brought us closer together. The memory of popped into my mind, me in the back of the limo, how I'd locked eyes with Greg and —

"Penny for your thoughts?"

My cheeks gave me away almost instantly, and I ducked my head.

Greg chuckled, low and deep. "I'd say those thoughts are worth more than a penny."

Yeah, that night cost me two years without my friend and chauffeur. Not to mention I wasted my time on that asshole Kevin. I rubbed a couple of fingers against my temple, but I couldn't think of how to respond. So I opted not to say anything.

He cleared his throat, taking the hint. "What's next on the list?"

Back in safe territory, thank goodness. I pulled out my phone, finding my text from Erin. "Okay, cake — check. Hotel — check. Plus, an extra check for meeting staff and getting my card to their event coordinator." I shot him a self-satisfied grin before I continued.

"Decorations and goodie bags are the next stop. That's for the shower, bachelorette party and wedding." Most of the decorations for the wedding were at Greg's parents' house, but this order contained a few last-minute things. "Then we have to swing by Raymond's since they're catering the shower, rehearsal dinner and the wedding."

He flipped on his turn signal and nodded. "Good. We can grab lunch too. I'm starving."

I wasn't hungry yet, but probably would be by then. We pulled into the D & R Party Store, where Greg parked as close to the entrance as he could. I opened my door, slipping on an iced over puddle, and clinging to the door for dear life.

Greg rushed to my side, wrapping a steadying arm around my waist. "What did I tell you about waiting for me?"

Once I'd transferred my grip from the door to him, I parroted, "Yeah, yeah. 'If you insist on wearing ridiculous shoes, at least have the sense to stay put till I get over there.'"

His admonishing stare drilled into me as we shuffled across the parking lot, and I knew he was waiting for me to admit he was right.

"Fine. I won't get out until you're here. Happy?"

"I'd be happier if you wore something with decent traction," he growled before opening the door.

"But then you'd miss looking at my delicate ankles and stellar calves," I teased as I sauntered inside. "And wouldn't that be a pity?"

He didn't follow immediately.

I turned to find his attention locked on my lower half. Amusement crept in as I asked, "Coming?"

He startled at my voice, ducking his head as he hurried to catch up. *How cute.* From the store front, I'd expected a small space with a limited selection. The front door led down a narrow hallway which opened into a massive warehouse with rows and rows of invitations, decorations, fake flowers and all sorts of odds and ends.

"Wow." My voice echoed in the large space.

"Surprising, isn't it?"

I nodded.

A stranger's voice boomed from the register. "How in the world are ya stayin' warm in an outfit like that? You let your woman walk around in those shoes in the middle of winter? What are you thinkin', eh?" The guy behind the counter had frizzy silver hair, pulled back into a long ponytail despite being bald on top. A toothpick dangled from one corner of his mouth, an untrimmed beard bushed from his chin in every direction and his flannel shirt was buttoned wrong.

My expression turned menacing as I sized him up. I'd eaten lesser men for breakfast. My heels sounded steadily on the cement floor, beating out his death knoll.

"Hello. I assume you were talking to me since we're the only two in here, and I assure you I am more than capable of speaking for myself. Just as I am more than capable of dressing myself. I'm Rhonda Elgin, and I believe you have an order for Erin Dougherty. She was supposed to let you know I'd be picking it up." I delivered each word with the precision of a surgeon's scalpel and just as sharply.

The man gawked before stuttering out, "Oh, I'll just check on that for you." And he disappeared.

Greg barely contained his laughter until the guy was out of earshot. "Wow, that was harsh."

I turned my icy glare on him. "He directed every comment to you, implying you were in charge of me. You didn't have a problem with that?"

With his hands held up in surrender, he took a few steps back. "No, you're right. He got exactly what he deserved."

"Thank you."

We both hid our smiles. I drummed my nails against the counter, running through my to-do list once more in my head while I waited. A gentle brush against my neck made me shiver, and I whirled around.

Greg's hand hovered over my shoulder. "Your tag is sticking out." He searched my face, as if asking for permission.

I relaxed, turning my back to him once more. His fingers grazed my skin, but their heat seared me as if I'd collided with a branding iron. I shivered again, this time from the delicious warmth rushing through me.

"There." His breath was hot on my cheek.

I sensed his nearness, knew if I leaned back even an inch, I'd be flush against his firm body. Somehow having that space between us was more erotic than if we'd been touching. We were in a dangerous dance, him and I, orbiting each other like planets around the sun. We kept coming close, our paths bringing us nearer and nearer, but never quite crossing. I felt him shift behind me, and I held my breath in anticipation.

A door slammed, making me jump. When Greg stepped away, the space between us once again felt as big as a canyon. Footsteps sounded — the guy's balding head barely visible over the two boxes he carried. Greg rushed to help.

Once the boxes landed on the counter, I peered inside, matching the contents with the list on my phone. Almost everything was there. "And the favor bags?"

The man frowned, taking the box from me. He shoved a few things aside, then pulled out a flimsy bag. "There you go."

The bag tipped over, as if it were too ashamed to even try to stand on its own. I peered inside, confirming my suspicions. Erin had ordered thirty pre-filled, favor bags for the shower guests. I'd admit it was a neat service, but their idea of a favor bag differed greatly from mine.

The bags were full of cheaply made items, and the man had charged Erin over fifteen dollars apiece. It took all my willpower not to just walk away.

Instead, I pinched the bridge of my nose, taking several deep breaths. "I'm sorry, but these just won't do. Please take them off our order."

He frowned. "She ordered favor bags. And these are favor bags."

I tried to keep my tone civil. "This is dollar store crap that won't impress anyone. You're overcharging us for cheap shit that took no effort to put together. The service advertised *unique* favor bags for every occasion, and there is not one unique thing in this, including the bag itself. I'm *not* paying for them." I crossed my arms and gave him my fiercest glare.

His face turned a deep red, and he looked ready to blow.

"Excuse me." Greg stepped up to the counter. "Does Darla still work here? I'm an old friend. Is there any way we could talk to her?"

The man stared at Greg for a long moment before huffing out an annoyed breath. He bit out, "I'll go get her." And he disappeared.

I glared at the employee's back as long as it was visible, then turned to Greg to scold him for interfering. But he spoke first.

"Let me handle this, okay?" Greg said. When I started to protest, he continued, "Just let me give it a shot? If it doesn't work, you can pick right back up where you left off." I didn't agree right away, and he sighed. "How about we bet on it?"

I scoffed, folding my arms. "You've been hanging out with Gina too much." But I was intrigued. "What'd you have in mind?"

"Whoever gets this settled gets to pick three songs the other person has to dance to at the wedding." He arched an eyebrow, waiting for my reaction. "Deal?"

I nodded. He stuck out his hand, and we shook on it just as a short, stocky woman marched up to the counter. She had the dead eyes of a person who had worked too long in customer service, her mouth pressed into a thin tight line. I smirked to myself. *This'll be fun to watch.*

Chapter Ten

The woman's gaze narrowed as she glanced at me, her voice robotic as she asked, "What seems to be the problem?"

Greg leaned forward ever so slightly, and I didn't recognize his expression. His lips tipped up in an enticing smile, confidence in every bit of his movement. If I had to name it, I'd have said he was trying to be charming. And damn, did it look good on him. If he ever used that on me, I wasn't sure my knees would hold me upright.

"Darla?"

Her head swiveled so fast I was surprised she didn't get whiplash, and recognition dawned. "Greg? Is that you? Oh my word! What in the world are you doing here?"

He grinned smugly in my direction. "My sister's getting married Friday, so we're picking up some supplies, and I wanted to say hi. How are things?"

With pink cheeks, she rushed to tell him day to day details. He nodded along, buttering her up until the next break in the conversation.

"So just about everything seems to be great with the order. One of Mandy's friends put this all together, you see. The only problem is with the favor bags. Mandy had something else in mind, and she'd just be devastated if she didn't get her way." He practically batted his eyelashes at her. "I know you put some time and effort into these, but is there any way we could take the favor bags off our order? Pretty please?"

She looked like she was about to swoon. "Of course. I wouldn't want to upset the bride." Out came the flimsy bags. She stacked them on the counter, punched in a few buttons on her computer, and gave Greg a sunny smile. "All taken care of." She handed him a new receipt.

"Oh, Darla, thanks so much. It was great to catch up." Greg picked up the heavier box, leaving me the lighter one. With one more grin, he strode away.

I hurried after him, not sure if I was annoyed he'd gotten off so easily or happy the problem was solved. *Well, maybe solved is too tidy a word.* Sure, we hadn't been charged for the favor bags, but Mandy and Erin were still expecting them.

Greg pushed open the door with his back, taking in my frustrated expression. "Next stop, Raymond's. We can figure this out over food, okay?"

I had to smile that he'd read my mind. "Okay."

"Wait here. I'll bring the car to you." Then he winked and went out of the door.

I almost dropped the box. By the time he pulled the car up, my heart beat at a normal pace once more. Until he took the box out of my hands and his fingers brushed mine in the process. *So much for a normal heart rate.*

Just thinking of gripping his arm and sidling up to him had my head reeling. I needed a break from all the flutters, and my poor heart agreed with me. With the car this close, surely I could make the few steps on my own.

Greg shut the trunk as I found out just how wrong I was. Luckily, I went sliding in his direction. I slammed into his solid chest and his arms wrapped around me. I clung to his broad shoulders as his scent washed over me, desire pooling low in my abdomen. His face hovered inches from mine, and I couldn't help focusing on his lips as I replayed yesterday's delicious kisses.

"I should be mad you didn't wait for me, but it's not every day a beautiful lady throws herself at me." His voice was huskier than normal. "Doesn't seem like something I should complain about." The words were light, belying the tension in his grip and how hard he swallowed when he'd finished speaking.

Also, he was wrong. It *was* practically every day I threw myself at him, or at least thought about it. I wasn't sure who moved first, but our lips touched, gentle and tenuous. This shift between us was still so new and fragile, anything more intense might shatter it into a million pieces.

Greg pulled back, searching me as if looking for an answer, but I didn't know the question. One side of his mouth ticked up. "Better get you out of this cold before you freeze."

Cold? Nothing on me is cold. I basked in the delicious heat that spread through my body in the aftermath of his kiss. Freezing wasn't an option, but I let him guide me into the car anyway. We made it to Raymond's in a dazed silence.

Finally, a business with a decent parking lot. I still waited for Greg, threading my arm through his. Just in case. When we were safely inside, he hung up his coat. I studied the pictures lining the entryway and startled when he touched my shoulder.

"Can I hang up your coat?" he asked in a husky tone.

I nodded, and his fingers slipped under the edges, gliding the coat over my shoulders then down my arms as I stepped back. Images of him undressing me flashed through my imagination, and I hungrily followed his movements. He placed my coat on the rack, then spun around. But he looked past me and froze.

"What?" I asked, all kinds of scenarios running through my mind.

His throat bobbed before he answered. "My ex-girlfriend, Carrie, is Raymond's daughter, and she's here. I didn't know she was back in town." His panicked gaze landed on me, begging me for help. "She's the main reason I left, why I took the job with your family."

"Hey, it's all right." She must have done a number on him if he was this shaken after being gone for so many years. Indignation flared in me at the very thought of anyone hurting Greg. I stepped closer to him, wanting his focus on me. "We'll just play pretend some more." In one confident move, I reached up to cup his cheek. Then I stood on my tiptoes to brush my lips against his, splaying the fingers of my other hand against his chest for balance. "The girlfriend game, round two?"

A tentative smile appeared on his lips as some of his panic disappeared. Emboldened by his reaction, I not so subtly undid one more button on my blouse. I smirked when he went rigid once more.

"Rhonda?" His focus stayed on my chest.

Perfect. "I just want to be sure I have your full attention." The button hovered on the line between sexy and too much, but it was for Greg, so I didn't care. I leaned forward, just a little.

With his height, he definitely got an eyeful, and he sucked in a startled breath. "I don't think that'll be a problem."

A woman behind me called his name, but his focus stayed glued to that open space at the top of my cleavage. I couldn't stop my grin, even as my stomach flipped. This time, I leaned into him, sliding my palms up his chest and tilting my chin. I wanted him to come to me.

I didn't have to wait long.

His lips crashed onto mine, nothing fragile or unsure about this kiss. Sparks flew between us. Hints of the flames that could erupt if we'd stop dancing about and take that leap.

When I broke it off, I murmured, "We should probably behave. We are in a public place."

He muttered back, "I don't wanna."

My grin widened. This time when I heard his name, I started to turn, but Greg still watched me. He wrapped a possessive arm around my waist, tugging me against him. *I could get used to this.*

A pretty brunette strode toward us. She was tall and athletic, a beautiful smile lighting her face while her ponytail swung behind her with each step. "Greg Peterson, is that you?"

Greg shifted to the side of me, his voice flat. "Carrie, hi. I didn't realize you were back."

She glanced my way. "Oh, and who do we have here?" The sneer in her voice couldn't have been mistaken for anything else. I was surprised she didn't just flat out say, "Oh, guess what the cat dragged in."

I plastered on my best social smile, holding out my hand, fingers down in a way that baffled all women. A man would take my hand, thinking I wanted a kiss pressed to it. But a female? It couldn't be turned into a handshake. She just had to grip my fingers awkwardly. A perfect power move.

"Hi. I'm Rhonda, Greg's girlfriend. You must be one of his little friends from high school. He's been showing me around his old stomping grounds all day." I frowned, tilting my head up toward Greg. "I don't remember you mentioning a Carrie, though." With a dismissive shrug, I glanced back at her, happy to see her jaw clenching. "Must have slipped his mind."

Then I noticed a familiar face on the wall behind her caught my eye and cried, "Oh, Greg, look! There's a picture of Daddy. I knew he did a lot of his business meetings here, but how cool is that?" I grabbed Greg's hand, pulling him along as I rushed over.

Carrie gasped when I stopped in front of my father's picture. "I'll just let Dad know that Malcolm Elgin's daughter is here. Excuse me." She hurried away.

I stared at the picture of my dad shaking hands with Raymond himself.

Greg's low chuckle rumbled through me as he pressed against my back. "That was something else. I don't think I've seen her scurry before." He kissed my cheek. "Thank you."

The two whispered words against my skin had me melting. "You're welcome," I murmured back. His hand rested on my hip, and I covered it with mine, feeling content, safe and way happier that I had been in months.

"Ms. Elgin?" A booming voice startled me from the trance Greg held me in.

When I turned, there was Raymond, the restaurant's owner, a man I recognized from more than his picture. He'd attended several of my parents' galas, various business meetings, plus charity events and fundraisers. His full dark head of hair, bushy eyebrows and sparkling black eyes could not be mistaken for anyone else, especially combined with the voice that could be heard from any corner of the world. He clasped my shoulders, air-kissing both my cheeks.

"Raymond, how are you?" I smiled. "And it's Rhonda, please."

He beamed. "Rhonda, you are exquisite. I cannot believe how you have grown! Why, the last time I saw you, you were just a teenager. Now look at you." With both my hands in his, he turned me one way then the other. "Beautiful, just like your mother." His attention shifted to Greg behind me. "And there's no way this strapping young man could be Greg Peterson."

The broad grin grew even wider, which I hadn't thought possible. Raymond released me, moving to grip Greg's shoulders before slapping him on the back. "My boy, it seems you've done rather well for yourself, eh? Landing an Elgin?" He gave Greg a knowing wink. "In town for your sister's wedding? You know, we're catering all her events."

His volume made me wince, but I tried to hide it as I nodded. "That's part of why we're here." I explained about Erin. "So, we thought we'd come for lunch and check on the catering for Mandy's shower tomorrow.

Just to confirm that everything's all set, that you don't need any more details from us."

"Ah, mixing business with pleasure, I see. Of course, let me get my schedule book." He came right back, and we went over the menu, for my benefit. Everything seemed to be well in hand.

I gave him my sweetest smile. "Any way you could add in a few extra servings of everything? With this snowstorm, we've had several people arrive early, and I won't be surprised if we have a few shower crashers."

He straightened his shoulders and nodded. "For the daughter of Malcolm Elgin, anything."

I patted his arm gratefully. "Thank you so much, Raymond. I can't wait to eat some of the delicious food my father always raves about. It's the highlight of his trips up here."

Raymond took my hand and kissed the back of it. "You have just bestowed upon me the greatest compliment a chef can receive." He called once more for his daughter. "Give them our best table."

Carrie held her chin high as she cradled two leather bound menus in the crook of her arm. "This way."

I couldn't believe Raymond was making his daughter seat her ex-boyfriend. Even my oblivious father would never be so cruel, though I didn't focus on that for long. Greg walked behind me, touching the small of my back. It felt like his very fingerprints engraved into my skin when he removed his hand to pull out my chair. I wanted to run to the bathroom, to see if he'd actually left a mark.

"Our specials today are homemade lasagna and roasted duck with a cranberry sauce. Kelly will be your server. She'll be with you shortly," Carrie said in a strained voice. "It was nice to meet you. I hope you enjoy your meal."

It was a relief when she left, and I watched the tension drain out of Greg. I wanted to ask him more about Carrie, about what had happened between them. But he was so private about the details of his life, I just didn't want to push. *Someday, if all goes well.*

I flipped open the menu, glancing through the varied list of entrees. A chicken pasta dish sounded too good to pass up, with a creamy white sauce, artichokes, mushrooms and spinach. That settled, I scanned the décor.

The atmosphere was elegant and quiet, just the way I liked my restaurants. Linen tablecloths covered each round table. Cloth napkins, water goblets and wine glasses stood at the ready while candles flickered in glass vases. The plush, dark green carpet was tastefully muted, a perfect contrast with the mint walls. Beautiful artwork hung throughout, but the focal point was the view of Lake Superior. I imagined summers here would have the deck crowded, the clinking of glasses and silverware carried off on the breeze wafting in from the crashing surf.

"We have to come back when it's warm." I paused, holding on to the fantasy in my mind, with Greg across from me. "Their deck would be an amazing place to have dinner."

He nodded. "It books up fast, so we'd want to make reservations now."

I pursed my lips. "How's the third Friday in June look for you?" A pang of longing hit me low in my gut.

But he just shook his head as if I were teasing, then he focused once more on his menu. My words hadn't even been considered, not for one second. *Will he ever take me seriously? Will this ever stop being a game of pretend? Will I ever have Greg for real?*

The waitress came to take our order, interrupting my bleak thoughts.

"And a glass of pinot grigio," I said after ordering my pasta with a side salad.

Greg decided on the chicken fettuccine Alfredo and side salad. "I'll take a pinot grigio, too."

After the waitress left, I turned to him. "I didn't know that you drank wine."

His dimple appeared. "Good, I haven't given away all my secrets."

All his secrets? If he's given away half his secrets, I'm a monkey's uncle. I frowned as I played with my napkin.

"What?" he asked, taking a sip of his water.

"You really think you're an open book?" I rested my chin on my hand, studying his reaction. My gesture must have done interesting things to my cleavage because his attention was below my chin again. "Greg?" I couldn't keep the laughter out of my voice.

He started. "What?" He took in my smirk, and his lower lip jutted out as his face shut down again. His words came out tight and heated. "It's your own fault. You and that stupid button."

The laughter died within me as I was yet again faced with his anger at seeing my skin. What was his deal anyway? We both studied the tablecloth. I glanced around the sparsely occupied room, then slipped the offending white circle back through its hole.

Greg's shoulders dropped several inches, and his hands released from their fists. A ragged sigh escaped his lips. "What was your question?"

Why does the sight of my skin piss you off? "You think you're an open book?"

His forehead crinkled. "Yeah, I do."

It was all I could do not to snort.

"You don't agree?"

I shook my head. "I've known you for" — I paused to count — "eight years now and last week was the first I'd heard of your sister. It wasn't until you saw Carrie that you thought to mention her. Hell, I didn't even know you grew up here until a couple days ago."

The waitress showed up with our glasses of wine, and I thanked her. After she left, I lifted my glass. "Another detail I just learned."

One corner of his mouth tipped up. "Your mom actually got me into wine."

Liquid almost spewed back out of my mouth, but I managed to swallow it. It'd be a shame to waste good wine. "What?"

He brought his glass of pinot grigio under his nose, inhaling the bouquet before taking a minuscule sip. "Not bad."

The man knew how to taste wine. All he was missing was the aerating swirl before the taste, but I was surprised he'd done that much.

"You probably remember when I lived in the carriage house at your parents' for a couple years?"

I nodded. He'd move in there when I was sixteen, so of course I remembered. My friends were all jealous that I had a hot chauffeur at my disposal, but I didn't see it at the time. He was gangly and awkward. Plus, he was my friend and way too old for my taste.

"I was in the kitchen while your mom hosted a wine tasting for one of her events, and I got roped into giving my opinion." His mouth quirked up in a fond smile. "I'd never tasted wine before, but I was told I had an innate sense for what paired with what." Greg lowered his voice as if sharing classified information. "I became her secret weapon, and a wine connoisseur to boot." He took another sip of wine. "Pinot grigio is one of my favorites."

"Mine, too," I said eagerly. "Though a dry riesling has been right up there lately. Have you been wine tasting in Michigan at all?" He'd driven me and my friends all over the countryside on our various excursions, but had he ever experienced it himself?

He shook his head, his smile dimming a bit. "It's not something I wanted to do alone. My family is more into beer."

Oh. "Maybe…" *Did I dare put myself out there again?"* "Maybe we could go sometime. When you could taste, too."

He studied me for a long minute before he simply said, "Maybe."

It was better than a hard no. Tension uncoiled in my chest, tension I hadn't realized was there.

"You three musketeers were quite the crew on those trips." He chuckled. "Do you see much of Yolanda or Fawnda anymore?"

A pang shot through me at the thought of my former best friends, and I took a big drink of my wine as if I could wash it away. "Nope. Once I broke up with Kevin, well, Fawnda made a play for him and Yolanda…" I trailed off thinking of her harsh words when I'd rejected another invitation to a party with a bunch of rich snobs. She'd told me I wasn't the same person, that she understood what Kevin meant about me being frigid. That he was better off without me. "Our priorities shifted. She wanted to keep playing the party girl, and I was done. I needed more." Hence the reason I was here with Greg in the first place.

The waitress showed up again, this time with our food. I couldn't fault her timing. I held up my empty wine glass. "Another, please." Somehow, I'd drained it in that last painful confession.

I stared down at my plate, marveling at the beautiful presentation. But my appetite had disappeared.

What am I doing? I'd gone from playing at life and pretending everything was perfect, to facing the truth because of my brother and his new girlfriend. I'd caught a glimpse of real love, real purpose, and I wanted it for myself. The cupcake standard I called it, the bar I set for myself and what I wanted.

But here I sat across from my pretend boyfriend, playing make-believe all over again.

Chapter Eleven

Tears fought to surface, and I scooted back in my chair, excusing myself to rush to the bathroom. It was a battle, but I maintained my composure. I stuffed my feelings back into the trench where I kept them, burying them beneath happy thoughts of Derek and Avery.

The fake part with Greg wasn't permanent. It was a foot in the door, a sliver of a chance to grab hold of the man I'd wanted for a long time.

Once more in control, I practiced my smile in the mirror until it looked real again. Then I reapplied my lipstick for good measure. I straightened my shoulders, took a deep breath and returned to our table. Only to find Carrie had taken up residence, going so far as to pull up a chair.

I approached from the side. Greg's face was angled away from me, and I saw what she couldn't. His leg jiggled beneath the table while one fisted hand sat on top of his thigh. She tilted her head back in a tinkly laugh, showing off pearly white teeth and reached out to brush his arm. He froze, so I quickened my pace.

With a gentle hand on his shoulder, I let him know I was there. "Sorry about that. What did I miss? Nothing too exciting, I hope."

"Oh," she said smugly, "Greg and I were just reminiscing." But that smugness dimmed when my fingers wrapped firmly over his shoulder, my thumb tracing circles on his clavicle.

Greg brought his hand up to cover mine, distancing himself further from her. "You should eat. Your food's getting cold." Genuine concern laced his voice as he glanced up at me. "Everything all right?"

I'd forgotten just how much he always saw. I nodded. "Definitely. I can't wait to dig into this delicious looking pasta. Have you tried yours yet?"

He shook his head. "I was waiting for you."

Suddenly, we were the only two people in the place. Everyone else just melted away as I stared at him, joined by our hands on his shoulder. Those gray eyes mesmerized me, the stormy flecks of almost black contrasting against the lighter rings with a bluish tinge. They sucked me into their tempestuous gaze, holding me prisoner.

"Well, I guess I'll let you two eat." Carrie shoved away from the table, startling both of us and sloshing our wine to the brim of our glasses.

Greg cleared his throat. He hurried to let go of my hand, then awkwardly nodded at my chair. "Sit. Please."

So, I did, placing my napkin in my lap and gathering a bit of everything on my fork before sliding it into my mouth. It was perfection. "Wow. This is amazing." I moaned around another mouthful, startled to find Greg watching me instead of eating. "Oh, did you want to try some?" I stabbed a forkful, offering it to him.

He hesitated but took it, his smile growing as he swallowed. "That is good."

"It goes great with the wine. How's yours?"

"Good, though not as good as yours." Again, he hesitated, but then he said, "Would you like a bite?"

It felt like so much more than just a forkful of noodles, and I beamed when nodded. He'd been right when he said mine was better. But exchanging food felt like something a real couple would do. Judging by the glares Carrie shot our way, she bought our act—hook, line and sinker.

We were just finishing when our waitress returned with a piece of flourless chocolate cake and two spoons. "Dessert for the two love birds, compliments of Mr. Raymond."

I grinned at Greg, then at the waitress. "Please thank him for us. If it's as good as everything else has been, we won't be disappointed."

And it was. Of course, sharing it with Greg was a treat within itself. I automatically reached for the bill when she set it down, only to find Greg's hand on top of mine and a frown on his face.

"I can afford it, Rhonda. You don't have to pay for everything."

My frown matched his. *He always assumes the worst.* I snatched my hand from under his. "That's not it at all," I hissed.

Carrie watched us intently, not missing a thing.

Quickly, I plastered on a smile. "Your ex is still watching, and I need to thank my father's friend, but I'm more than happy to let you pay. We'll discuss this more in the car. For now, though, I'm going to lean over to kiss your cheek, and you need to act pleased about it."

He wasn't as good at pretending as I was, but he did an admirable job.

"I'll be back in a few, darling." It was an effort to keep my steps light as I approached Carrie. "We're getting ready to leave. I'd like to say goodbye to your dad."

Reluctantly, she went toward the kitchen, returning with her booming father in tow. "Rhonda, how was everything?"

More air kisses, ugh. "Delicious. And thank you for that amazing dessert. What a delightful surprise!"

We chatted for a few more minutes until Greg made his way over, sliding his wallet back into his pocket. After he'd said his thanks followed by a stilted goodbye to Carrie, he helped me on with my coat, and we made our way to the car. He huffed as he started it up then buckled the seatbelt.

I'd had enough. "I don't get you."

He settled against the seat, keeping the engine running as he turned his frosty gaze on me. "What? That I don't just let you be my sugar mama, paying for me like everyone else? You paid at the diner on the way up here, didn't even give me a chance. You don't need to pay for this too." He snorted, shaking his head. "No, thank you."

"That. Right there." I threw my hands in the air. "Sometimes you see more of me than anyone has a right to. Like, you knew I was upset when I went to the bathroom, didn't you?"

Confusion etched across his face as he nodded.

"Then you go back to seeing me like everyone else does. Just goodbye Jellybean, hello spoiled heiress." I slumped against my seat, rubbing two fingers over my left temple that had started throbbing. Silence sat between us as I stewed.

"What sort of explanation would you give me, if I asked for one?" His words were cautious, as if holding a pair of pliers over a ticking bomb and being told to choose which wire to cut. He wanted all the information first.

It was a chance, and I took it. "My parents always paid. I don't know if it was a status thing, a power thing, or a pride thing. But they made sure they always paid, so I had them as a precedent."

I sighed because it was so much more than that. "Even without their example, I was the richest kid at most of my functions. People just…assumed. Sometimes I'd wait to see if anyone would offer to pick up the check or at least split it. But it rarely happened." I shrugged.

A bitter memory popped into my mind, spilling out of my mouth. "I remember my first date, how I'd built up the romance in my mind. I imagined a candlelit dinner and snuggling at a movie afterward. I was so caught up in the daydream that I didn't notice at first when he slid the bill to me at our table. He even winked, like I was in on some joke with him."

I stared out of the window at the gravel-streaked piles of snow lining the edge of the parking lot. One was taller than the roof of our car. My quiet words had a despondent edge to them. "So, I stopped waiting. Now, I just pay." And, apparently, was condemned for it.

Warm fingers slid over my hand, engulfing it and spilling over onto my thigh. "Rhonda." Greg's voice was gruff. "Please look at me."

Slowly, I turned my head, glancing down at his hand covering mine then up at his handsome face.

"I'm so sorry. You're right that I judged you in there. I let my own insecurities get the better of me, and I was an ass." He squeezed my hand. "I'm sorry, Jellybean."

The apology wedged its way past my defenses, making a home in my heart. I flipped my hand over to clasp his. "Apology accepted." I managed a small grin. "And thanks for lunch."

He smiled then, a true stomach-flipping, dimple-making smile. "You're welcome. Now I need some coffee, and we should talk about what we're going to do about those favor bags."

We bounced some ideas around on the way to the coffee shop. I wanted the favor bags to be my present to Mandy since I hadn't gotten her a gift. But I wanted them done right, unique and classy. "Is there any sort of art district or shops nearby that sell local artists' works?"

Greg thought for a few as he merged into traffic. "There are a few up by Presque Isle—a pottery shop, a gallery, and I'm not sure what else. It'd be worth a shot."

It sounded like a good place to start. I hoped the fiasco at the decoration warehouse was a fluke and our good luck from earlier would continue. When we pulled into the coffee place, Greg offered to run in just as my phone dinged. I accepted, happy to sit tight. Pulling out my phone, I grinned when I saw Avery's name.

Hey girl! How's Greg treating you? What's new?

I quickly replied.

Fine, good. How are things your way?

Seriously, you run off with the chauffeur and that's all I get?

lol

I had to give her something or she'd pester me until I did. I typed out the first thing that darted into my head.

Um, did you know he has a dimple?

Really?!

Yep, only when he really smiles.

Do you want to lick it?

I stared at the phone for a long minute. Avery had a track record of blurting out weird thoughts, but this was unusual even for her.

Um...what?

This romance author I'm reading right now has a thing for dimples, and she's always going on about her main character wanting to lick them. Derek doesn't have any. So, I wondered if that's anything you ever thought about?

I wrinkled my nose.

No, not so much.

Damn, it's not Gina's thing either. I need to find someone to let me know what I'm missing.

You need help. And maybe a different book.

A gif came through. I stared in horror at a lizard licking a Cheerio, over and over and over. *What the hell?* Of course, Greg chose that moment to come back. I practically threw my phone into my purse as he opened the door and handed me my coffee.

"Sorry that took so long. Peppermint mocha for you." He handed me a tall cup with a brilliant smile which showed off his adorable dimple.

And all I could think about was a stupid lizard. *Dammit, Avery.* I had to bite my tongue to stop my laughter.

"You okay?"

It didn't work. I burst out laughing, ignoring him and grabbing my phone to yell at Avery once more. All the explanation he got was, "Avery needs serious help."

By the time we arrived at Presque Isle, I had calmed down. It was a scenic drive, the road hugging the shore of Lake Superior and taking us right by the ore docks.

"There's a park, too, if you keep going. Lots of trails to walk, a little lighthouse." He shrugged. "Not the best place in the winter, but in the summertime, it's something."

Why have I never been up here before? "I'd like to see that," I said quietly.

"I hope you get to."

I felt like a batter who'd just swung for a home run, but missed the ball completely, only connecting with air. I could almost hear the *whiff*. I covered my disappointment with a sip of my coffee. At least that was delicious.

Greg hurried around to escort me to the door, and when I walked in, I knew I'd struck gold. The shops all joined together on the inside, flowing seamlessly into one another. Shelves of pottery were interspersed with mini displays of jewelry, scarves and art. I even noticed a section with soap and lotion. Best of all, everything was handmade.

"Jackpot," I breathed.

I put my game face on and set about finding someone to do business with. Half an hour later, I had a more than satisfactory price for thirty-five local pieces each of mini art coasters, a handcrafted mug, earrings, the softest scarf I'd ever felt and a small bottle of lotion. Greg carried the boxes out to the car, along with enough business cards for each bag. Plus, we had a lead on the best truffles in town. He came back to help me to the car.

"Good recommendation, Just Greg." I grinned up at him, ridiculously pleased with our finds.

Once we were on the road to the chocolatier, he asked, "Is this the last stop?"

"Close. I need bags to put all these in. And I'd like a local bottle of wine or cocktail or something like that. Then I think that should be enough." I rested my elbow on the armrest between us, taking a sip of my still warm coffee before I set it down in the cup holder.

I stared out of the window as we wound along the shores of Lake Superior. Greg moved and his arm rested along the entire length of mine. My mouth twitched as I pretended to ignore him to see what else he would do. A minute later, he shifted again until his fingers dangled over mine. Our hands danced to the movement of the car for several long moments.

I held my breath when he shifted again, and his warm fingers settled over mine. A soft sigh escaped my lips as I gripped him back. My stomach did a quick little flip, and we sat like that for the rest of the quiet ride.

When he steered us into a parking spot in front of a row of shops, I reluctantly let go. He gave me a soft smile before he got out, hurrying around to help me out of the car. It was a relief to touch him again, and I gripped his arm as I stepped onto the sidewalk of downtown Marquette.

A heavenly smell permeated the air, so delicious I almost swooned just breathing it in. "Is that—?"

I turned around, and there was the chocolatier, the word Decadence scrawled across the window in looping white letters. If it smelled this good outside, I could just imagine the inside. Greg must have had the same thought because we hurried in, a jangling bell signaling our entry.

I'd never seen so much chocolate in one place. No matter which way I turned, I was met with a glass case full of it. Turtles, caramels, all sorts of things dipped in it.

"Hello, there." A friendly, middle-aged woman with curly auburn hair escaping her unruly bun greeted us. "Anything I can help you find?"

"Actually, yes. Are you Midge?" When she nodded, I explained how she'd been recommended to us and what we wanted.

She beamed—her smile as sweet as the desserts surrounding her. "Well, that Terry sure is a dear for thinking of me. You'll have to do a taste test, of course.

This way." She wove her way over to a counter on the opposite side of the room.

I took a different path than Greg, stopping to gawk at the various confections. This place was a dream come true. I was almost drooling when I finally made it to the counter where Midge set up a line of truffles.

"We have six different flavors—milk, dark, darker, coffee, white and cream." She leaned in to whisper, "Of course they all have fancy names, but that's what it boils down to." The bell jingled as another customer came in. "I'll leave you to it. Let me know if you have any questions."

One of each flavor sat on a tray before us, which meant we were once again sharing desserts. She'd thoughtfully poured two glasses of water as well. I picked up the white truffle, biting it in half and moaning almost instantly. "It melts in your mouth. This is phenomenal." I held the other half out to Greg.

He surprised me by leaning forward to eat it right out of my fingers. His soft lips brushed my skin, sending a delicious rush of heat through me. "Mmm," he said, smirking as I stared up at him in stunned delight. "Delicious." Then he picked up the cream one and carefully bit it in half, nodding his approval.

I swallowed in anticipation as he offered me the other half. It was only fair that I got the same treatment, right? I leaned forward, lips parted, stomach flipping. He slid the dessert into my waiting mouth, the pad of his thumb grazing my lower lip.

Dazed, I barely remembered to focus on the flavor of the truffle. The first tasted better.

Milk chocolate was next in line, and I sank my teeth into it. Heat flared between us as the chocolate melted in my mouth and desire pooled low within me. This was my new favorite. My tongue darted out to lick the chocolate off my lip.

I held the other half up for Greg, and my hand trembled, though I tried to hide it. He stepped forward, taking the truffle and my fingers into his mouth. His tongue flicked between my fingers even as his lips grazed my skin. I thought I might spontaneously combust on the spot. *No, I can't do that – it'll ruin all the chocolate.*

"That was really good, too." Greg's low voice pulled me back from my ridiculous thoughts. "Ready for the next one?"

No. But I nodded.

It was his turn to go first, neatly severing the coffee truffle and running his tongue over his lips. I had never been more jealous of a piece of food. When he placed the chocolate in my mouth, my tongue found a bit of it on his thumb. I greedily sucked it off. He drew in a sharp breath as his fingers grazed my cheek. I couldn't resist giving his thumb one last swipe with my tongue.

One truffle left. I didn't want it to end, but at the same time this torture was agonizing. What more could he do to me? I savored my half, this one by far my favorite. I moaned at the rich flavor. Dark chocolate had always been my kryptonite, and this was darker than sin.

"Good?" Greg's voice was as smooth and rich as the dark chocolate, his tone just as delicious.

I could barely nod. He gently took the truffle from me, without fanfare. Disappointment weighed on me. I started to move away when he reached out his hand once more.

"I think this is my favorite, but I think there's a way to make it better."

He swiped a bit across my lower lip, then leaned down to claim my mouth with his. Our bodies aligned as we feasted on each other. I tasted the truffle mixed with him and the barest hint of peppermint.

His teeth scraped my bottom lip just before he pulled away. "Yeah, that's my favorite."

Heat rushed to my cheeks as I stared up at him, speechless. I didn't have much time to recover when Midge sent the other customer on his way, coming to see what we'd decided on.

My negotiations were a little off, flustered as I was, but Midge remained patient. After discussing the amount needed and our timeline, along with our flavor preferences, she offered to have everything ready for us to pick up by ten a.m. tomorrow for a small upcharge because of the rush. I was more than happy to pay it.

Walking toward the counter, I noticed a rack of mini bottles of local wine and grinned. We ended up with everything we needed except the bags, and she recommended a gift shop one block away with a decent selection. It was a quick trip there. They had several options, so I picked out three styles in complementary colors.

I plopped back into the car, waiting for Greg to sit down before I said, "Home, Jeeves."

It was my oldest, most annoying joke, always met with a huff and a glare. Today was no exception, though this time amusement twitched his lips before he reached over to hold my hand.

Chapter Twelve

As we pulled into his parents' driveway, I studied the majestic house sitting regally on the hill. The snow-white mantle surrounding it glinted in the waning sun, which had already started its descent despite it not even being five p.m.

"Let's go inside first," Greg said as he put the car in park, "and make sure Mandy's not here before we bring in everything." He paused. "I mean, I'm assuming you want these to be a surprise."

"I think that'd be fun." I waited until he came around to open my door. "I guess I know what I'll be doing tonight." It was habit now to slide my arm through his, so I didn't fall on my ass.

"What's that?"

"Putting together gift bags." I waggled my eyebrows. "Big plans, Greg, I've got big plans for a scintillating night."

He chuckled, and we made our way inside. Mandy was off greeting guests at the hotel and helping them settle in. Greg spoke with his mother, who was also on her way to the hotel.

"We'll have dinner there if you want to join us. Rhonda, I can't thank you enough for getting all these details squared away." Julie frowned, wringing her hands together. "I do hope Erin arrives in time."

Me too, for Mandy's sake. I gave her a comforting smile. "I'm sure it'll all work out like it has so far. I don't think I'll be able to make dinner tonight. After being out all day, I'm ready for a quiet night in."

Her frown turned into a gentle look of concern, and she patted my arm. "Of course, dear." Turning to Greg, she said sternly, "You make sure she has everything she needs. You hear?"

He nodded with a solemn, "Yes ma'am."

With a quick goodbye, she bustled out of the door.

Greg arched an eyebrow. "So, I guess we're on our own. You hungry yet or want to wait a bit?"

"I'll wait. I just want to change into something comfy and get out of these shoes."

He offered his arm once more, a knowing grin sprawling across his face. This time I used him to balance against as I shed my heels and let out a sigh of relief.

"Better?"

"Much." I rubbed first one foot, then the other, before letting go of his arm.

We stood there for a moment before he glanced at the door. "How about I bring in all the stuff? I can take it right up to our suite since no one will bother us there. You go get changed."

He didn't have to ask me twice. I sat on the couch in my hip-hugging yoga pants and form-fitting T-shirt with my bare feet tucked under me when he hauled the first load into the sitting room.

He took one look at me and groaned. "Does it have to be those pants?"

"Who made you the wardrobe police?" I stuck my tongue out. "Are you going up to the hotel for dinner?"

The boxes slid to the floor with a gentle thump, surprise crossing his face. "No, not unless you don't want me here." Hurt underlined his words.

What? "No, I just wasn't sure what your plans were."

He surveyed the boxes then glanced back at me. "Same as yours and just as...what was the word you used? Scintillating?"

I gaped at him. "You're going to stay here and help me make favor bags?"

"Yeah. I mean, how else are you going to get them all done?" His eyebrows knit together, and his mouth crooked in puzzlement.

It was so unexpected, I couldn't contain my reaction. I leapt off the couch and threw myself at him, almost knocking both of us over with the force of my hug.

"Rhonda?" he murmured in my ear as he gingerly patted my back, "You okay?"

My voice was muffled from my face being buried in his shoulder. "Kevin never would have done this. Neither would Yolanda or Fawnda." I squeezed him tighter, and his arms wrapped around to hold me, too. "Thank you, Greg."

"You're welcome." His words came out rougher than I expected. He held me for another beat, then he tugged me off him. "I've got one more load, okay? I'll be right back." He waited for my nod before he left.

I was still stunned that he'd stay to help. Several times over the years I'd asked my so-called friends to work with me on one of my charity events, folding pamphlets, creating menus, stuffing goody boxes. Yeah, we'd had volunteers too, but if I was on the committee, I wanted to contribute, give it that personal touch. They'd promise to help, but when it came right down to it, it had always been me.

Greg just assuming we were doing it together threw me off-balance. My throat tightened, warmth blooming in my heart. This was the kind of relationship I so desperately wanted.

When he returned with the last two boxes, he disappeared into his room, coming back out in those ass accentuating, or maybe *ass-entuating*, sweatpants I'd drooled over this morning. He gave me a smug smirk, and I knew he'd done it on purpose as payback for my own outfit. At least he still wore a shirt, even if it was a soft, knitted one that hugged his torso.

"So, how do we want to do this?" He looked to me for guidance.

I surveyed the boxes, trying to formulate a plan. "Well, we're missing two key things." He started to protest, but I continued, "Booze and music."

A smile spread across his face. "I'll go raid the wine cellar."

"I'll get something going on my phone." While he was gone, I pulled up a playlist that reminded me of dancing with Papa. I cranked up the volume and pushed play, then got to work organizing our items for an ideal assembly line.

Most things were in order when he came back with two bottles of white wine, two glasses, and a corkscrew. He grinned at my progress. "Wow, that was quick," he said loudly, wanting to be heard over Journey blasting from my phone.

"I thought we could start from here with a gift bag and just go down the line. We'll have to add in the truffles tomorrow."

He frowned, assessing my setup. "What if we did half and half? You do these items, then pass the bag to me and I do these ones? Then we each have our own workspace and aren't interrupting the flow as much. I could be behind the couch, bring in the end tables from my room."

My smile came of its own accord. "I'll drink to that."

"Ah, I see where your priorities lie." His teasing smirk turned heated as his gaze drifted down my length. He swallowed then went to open the wine.

I returned the favor, watching him walk away. *This could be an interesting night.*

Handing me my glass, he held his up, waiting for me to touch mine to it. "Cheers, to you, Jellybean. For pulling all this off."

"I couldn't have done it without my getaway driver." I winked, and we both laughed, clinking our glasses together. The smooth perfection of the wine slid across my tongue, a note of apple lingering afterward. "Wow, that's delicious."

He grinned. "One of my favorites. It's local, and my parents stock it just for me."

I took another sip. "How much do they keep on hand? We might make a dent in their stash tonight."

It took a few rounds to find my rhythm. The scarf was my biggest hang up, and I decided to fold them all first so I could just shove them into the bag. Once Greg saw what I was doing, he plopped next to me and mimicked my movements. It was a small couch. Our thighs brushed whenever he leaned over to reach for a new scarf.

"Excuse me," he'd say, leaning more obtrusively each time.

I think after the fourth, or maybe fifth lean, he didn't shift back, just let our legs rest against each other. I had to refold the scarf I was doing at least three times. It was a particularly difficult one.

With the last scarf in hand, he leaned over to put it on the pile, but he shifted too far. He lost his balance, taking me down with him. Both of us ended up in a heap on the floor between the couch and the table, me beneath him.

"You were supposed to catch me." His elbows were braced on either side of my torso, one leg between mine. Those lips hovered above mine a hair's breadth away. "You okay?"

I shook my head.

At least he had the decency to frown. "Where does it hurt?"

I fought to keep my pout in place as I reached up to tap my lower lip. "Here."

"Oh." One corner of his mouth tipped up. "I suppose I need to kiss it and make it all better?"

I nodded. "I think it's only right, since you dragged me down here in the first place." I added a little challenge to my tone, excited to see heat flare in his eyes.

His lips brushed mine. "Better?"

But I wanted more, so much more. "Not quite."

He knew exactly what he was doing, the cad, and a smug smile crossed his face. Then he leaned down to press his lips against mine, slowly, gently, stoking the ever-growing fire within me. "How's that?"

"Greg, please." The words were out of my mouth before I could stop them, and I winced at the rawness in my voice.

He stilled, his heated gaze drilling into me. "Oh, Jellybean." His whisper was husky. "What am I going to do with you?" This time he kissed me with all the passion I craved. His body sank onto mine, his hunger for me evident.

I welcomed his weight, wrapping my leg around his, sliding my hands up his muscular back. One of his hands shifted under me, pulling me closer still. My breasts pressed into his firm chest as he ran his fingers through my hair. I moaned into his mouth, our tongues colliding. I never wanted this to end, but I also needed to breathe. We both broke off, gasping as we stared at each other.

"The bags," he bit out, finally. "We should finish the bags."

Unfortunately, he was right.

When he stood, I felt cold and too light, like I might float away without him there to ground me. Greg extended a hand to help me up while Bon Jovi sang about being halfway there. *Shit, if this is only halfway...I don't think I can handle the rest.*

I found my glass of wine, hoping it would douse the flames dancing inside me. I took a bracing sip then threw myself into stuffing bags. Soon I found a steady rhythm, the highlight being when I handed my bag to Greg and our fingers would brush. Liquid heat flared within me each time, then I'd have to make the circuit again to cool it off.

Just to repeat the cycle.

The first bottle of wine disappeared too fast. Greg poured the last of it into our glasses when I realized we only had five bags to go. Then what? My imagination raced. I rubbed my thighs together, taking an anxious sip of my wine. I hadn't had sex with anyone since Kevin several months ago.

As I made my circuit, old doubts crept in. Kevin's words about me being frigid, mixed with Yolanda's taunts about him being right. I'd never been one to orgasm easily. What if it was too much for Greg?

I couldn't handle that, not from him.

The last bag went to Greg, who took it with an easy smile that showed off his adorable dimple. Even in my wined-up state, I didn't want to lick it. *Sorry, Avery.*

The full favor bags rested neatly in the cardboard boxes, waiting for the finishing touch of the truffles we'd get in the morning. A heady feeling of accomplishment washed over me, pushing out some of the anxiousness that had crept in.

Greg walked over to slide an arm around my waist. "We did it, Jellybean. They're going to love them, especially Mandy. She's going to flip."

I leaned into him, allowing the heat to spread through me, the rumble of his voice relaxing me. "Now what?"

"Did you know we have a hot tub?" When I pulled back to look at him, he grinned. "That's right, in a closed-in gazebo out back."

My voice was low as I stared at the floor. "I don't have a suit."

He swallowed, shifting a little. "Neither do I. You can wear whatever you feel comfortable in." His voice dropped, a husky layer adding to it. "I thought I'd go in my boxers."

The image had my mouth going dry, and I pushed it away as I thought over the suggestion. It sounded amazing, a soak in the hot water with the jets. Especially for my feet which were killing me from being on them all day. "What about your family?"

"I'll just send them a quick text saying we're going to use the hot tub, but I doubt they'll be back for a few hours yet." He shifted, waiting for an answer. "We have robes here for the trek back and forth. And I have that other bottle of wine."

"Okay," I said, so quietly I wasn't sure he'd heard me.

But the smile on his face told me otherwise. "All right." He squeezed me to him for a beat. "I'll go find us some robes."

I bit my lip, feeling unsteady and unsure as he disappeared into his room. Pat Benatar's voice filled the silence. I turned off the music when Greg reappeared with a robe draped over his arm.

"I left yours on the bed, along with some slippers that I think will work better than any shoes you have. Meet you back out here?" He waited for my nod before he went into the bathroom, shutting the door.

I hurried to the bedroom, going through my options. As much as I wanted to, I didn't think I could get down there and throw my robe off to reveal my naked self. Not with the way Greg was always getting mad at me showing my skin. We'd get in a fight for sure.

Cute lingerie seemed the way to go, something dark but sexy. It could always come off if things went that direction. I settled on a lacy black bra and panty set. The bra clasped in front, had scalloped edges and made me look good, if I did say so myself. The panties were bikini cut, low in front, high on the hips but covered all the necessary parts.

I slipped on the fluffy robe, tying it tightly before sliding my phone into its deep pocket. The slippers were big, but I'd manage. Then I took a deep breath and walked out of the door.

Greg waited for me, the bottle of wine in his hand, plus two plastic glasses. "I couldn't remember if you'd said yes to more wine?"

"Please."

His relief matched mine. And I grinned, knowing I wasn't the only nervous one. I followed him through the cavernous house, a little on edge with how eerie the quiet was.

Relief hit me when we stepped outside, followed by awe as I drank in the scene. It was like walking into a whole different world. White blanketed everything while big, fat snowflakes drifted lazily from the sky. I stopped to stare up for a minute. The snow muffled all city noise, not that there was much to muffle since their property was surrounded by the cushion of the woods. An owl hooted, but otherwise it was still.

I stuck out my tongue to catch a massive snowflake as it sauntered down, giggling at Greg's amused expression. Then I shivered. "Okay, enough of that."

The path to the gazebo was lined with black lampposts, their yellow orbs haloed in sunny light. It looked like a scene from a postcard. Or Narnia. As he always did, Greg held the door for me.

He showed me around, flicking on lights as he went. Steam billowed as he flipped up one side of the cover, dragging the thick lid out of our way. It was a good-sized hot tub, able to hold at least eight people.

I deliberated whether I should be brave and go first. While I tried to work up the courage, Greg stepped over to the hooks and shed his robe. I forgot about bravery, losing myself in staring at him. His broad shoulders and intricate tattoo fascinated me, his sculpted back tapering down to a slim waist.

Then he turned around, and I drank him in — his muscular pecs, the ridges of his abdomen, the indents disappearing into his blue plaid boxers. My mouth went dry. All the moisture must have gone to my palms, now extremely damp.

I traced my way up again, and my fingers itched to follow. I gasped when I met his stormy gray eyes and saw the turbulent emotion swirling in them. He punched the button for the jets, then descended the stairs. His gaze never wavered from me, even as he lowered himself into the water, settling back against the tub.

Wait. That means it's my turn. My gulp was swallowed by the roar of the jets. I went over to the hooks then slid the robe off my shoulders, my back to Greg, and I wished I could hear if his breath hitched as mine had.

My fingers missed the hook twice before the robe found its mark. I toed off my slippers, steeling myself as I turned to face him. The cold winter air gave me goosebumps and pebbled my nipples instantly. Greg's lips parted, and I watched his chest move with a sharp inhale of breath as his gaze wandered over me. My confidence trickled back in, and the butterflies calmed. I took my time walking down the steps, adjusting to the steamy temperature of the water.

Then I didn't know where to sit.

The middle of the tub was deep enough to brush my belly button. Greg poured a glass of wine and held it out, not fully extending his arm. "There's a reclining seat over here." He nodded his head next to him. "It's Mandy's favorite."

Who am I to turn down an invitation like that?

I moved to the corner seat, surprised when I slid down the slope and ended up facing him, my legs positioned in front of me. Once I'd settled, I took the wine, thankful he'd had the foresight to switch to plastic glasses. The molded seat fit me comfortably with several jets that hit key spots across my body. I sighed as I relaxed.

When I slid my legs down the ramp, I bumped into Greg's thigh. "Oh. Sorry." I instinctively started to pull my feet back, but he caught my ankle.

He didn't say anything, just pulled one foot onto his lap, then the other. My breath stuck in my throat as a jolt of heat burst through me at his casual touch. Deft fingers massaged the arch of my right foot, and I melted. *Holy shit, that feels amazing.* I slid down a little more to get the jets right on my back, and my left foot brushed against something...hard.

Chapter Thirteen

My eyes flew to Greg's, tension coiling within me once more. I'd given Greg a hard-on. To my surprise, he didn't shy away, didn't act embarrassed, didn't stop rubbing my foot. He paused for a drink of wine, then languidly switched to the other foot.

I, on the other hand, couldn't breathe. *How can he be so calm?* I had undeniable proof of his attraction to me, and he just sat there. I wanted to climb into his lap and ride him right here, show Greg just how much I needed him. A thrill shot through me at the very thought. But this was Greg, and he had his own pace. The last thing I needed was to scare him off.

He finished massaging my left foot. "How was that?"

"So good, thank you." I wanted those hands on me in a million other places, even more now that I knew what they were capable of.

A gentle tug on my ankle had me biting my lip before I slid his way. Desire pulsed low in my stomach as I let him pull me sideways onto his lap, draping both legs to one side. I had to turn my torso to face him when I looped one arm over his defined shoulders.

"Hi," I breathed. *Is this really happening?*

"Hi." His gaze roamed my face then dropped to my lips.

His hardness pressed into my hip, teasing me. I needed so much more, but I forced myself to wait. One of his hands settled on my back, caressing my bare skin. I slid my palm up his chest, shifting so my breasts grazed his right side.

Desire pulsed between my legs as his other hand danced along my arm, sliding higher until he cupped my cheek. I leaned into the gentle touch, holding my breath as his thumb caressed me. He threaded his fingers through my hair and pulled me to him, his lips crashing into mine. Flames seared through me, and everywhere our skin met blazed with a scorching heat.

I tightened my arms around him, my breasts aching as I pressed them to his chest. I couldn't get enough of him. His hand would surely make an imprint in my back this time.

As our tongues danced together, I shifted enough to let my fingers slide down his smooth pecs, tracing the divots of his muscles. He followed suit, his calloused palms skimming up my sides and over my abdomen. Tentatively, he edged up higher and higher until at last he brushed my breast. I gasped into his mouth, but he just deepened the kiss as he cupped me.

His thumb grazed over my taut nipple, sending a jolt of pleasure straight to my core, and I writhed on his lap, bringing my hip tight to his erection. He bucked against me as I pressed my thighs together, wanting more. The jets shut off abruptly, and we broke apart at the sudden lack of noise.

Heavy silence hung between us as he stared at me, his chest rising and falling rapidly. "Room?" he bit out.

I nodded, unable to speak through my haze of desire. He stood up with me in his arms. Slowly, he let me slide down his hard, wet body. *How do I walk again?* When my brain finally started functioning, I followed him out of the tub, both of us dripping, but I didn't care. We pulled on our robes, then he flung the cover back on the tub, snatched up the wine bottle and away we went.

We barely made it inside the room before his lips claimed mine. The fire consumed me as I ran my hands over his shoulders, to his neck and into his hair. Our tongues tangled together in a furious dance while I shoved at the shoulders of his robe, needing to feel his bare skin.

He tore open my robe and pulled me flush against him, the heat of his skin burning after the frigid air. His cock jumped against my thigh, and I grinned against his mouth. I knew exactly what I wanted next.

My hands slid down his bare torso to the hem of his sodden underwear as I edged him backward toward the couch. I tugged eagerly on the fabric. The wet boxers clung to him, but I peeled them off as he tensed before me. They dropped to the floor, and he stepped out of them, deliciously naked.

His body was even more perfect than in my fantasies. I couldn't stop myself from running a hand over his chiseled abs, down to his hip. His muscles tensed beneath me as I neared his impatient erection. I ran my hand over his hard length, grinning at his impressive size. He sucked in a sharp breath at my touch. The smoothness of his skin taunted me, begging me to put my mouth on him.

This had to be a dream. Any second my alarm would ring, and I'd be yanked back to reality. I grazed my fingers over him, circling his damp tip.

He jerked in my hand. "Rhonda."

My name held a hint of warning, and I sighed as I let go. He leaned in to kiss me again, but I shook my head with a coy smile. I shoved his shoulders, directing him to sit, and I knelt before him, running a hand over his powerful thigh to his knee. Then I nudged his legs open, satisfaction coursing through me as his lips parted and his breathing increased.

This was a skill I'd honed to make up for not being able to come. If I took the offensive and made a guy go first, they let the matter drop.

But that's not why I was doing this for Greg.

I loved being in control, loved seeing his desire. I couldn't wait to see him uninhibited for once. He clenched his fingers into a fist as I kissed my way up his leg, closing the distance to his straining cock. I paused to shed my robe, grinning when he let out a tortured groan, and I hurried to pick up where I left off.

His cock bobbed when I ran a finger down it. I looked up at him through lowered lashes as I parted my lips over his glistening tip, and he seemed frozen. When I licked his shaft, he dropped his head back against the couch as he hummed. I took him fully in my mouth, pleased when his hand brushed my hair.

I wanted nothing more than to pleasure him, to hear him moan my name, feel him pulse in my mouth. I began slowly, my tongue swirling his head while I pumped him with my hand. His groans were music to my ears, the dampness between my legs growing with each guttural sound. His hand flexed on my head like he wanted to hold me there, but it was tentative. I took him deeper and deeper, suppressing the gag reflex until he was fucking my mouth.

Finally, he let go of his inhibitions, his fingers digging in as his rhythm built, and he thrust into me. Delight thrilled me as he let his instincts take over. I felt him harden even more. A hint of salty warning signaled he was close, then he came, shuddering into my mouth. My name burst from his lips as I drank him down, and it had never sounded so sweet. I pulled away, licking my lips.

His expression held a mix of awe and hunger as he tugged me up to meet his mouth. He reached for my bra. "My turn," he said, his voice husky with longing.

And I froze.

Greg's face was inches from my nipples, he sprawled naked before me, and I was minutes away from getting what I'd wanted for years. But icy fear gripped me. "Um, I just need to use the bathroom."

I ran. Deep gulping breaths did nothing for me. *What's wrong with me? This is Greg, the man of my dreams.*

But what if I can't get off? What if I do it wrong and I really am frigid like Kevin said? The thought of disappointment on Greg's face had bile rising in my throat.

I mentally shook myself, gripping the edges of the sink as I stared into the mirror. *Get a hold of yourself. You're better than this, and so is Greg.* I berated myself as I stalked back and forth, until at last I started to calm down. I used the bathroom, washed my hands, then I heard my phone ding where I'd left it on the couch.

Followed by Greg saying, "What the fuck?"

Oh no. I rushed out to see Greg with my phone in his hand.

"Is this the kind of thing you're into?" Frustration laced his voice.

I took my phone from him to see a picture of Kevin fucking another girl, her face in the throes of delighted orgasm. The caption read, *You know you want to be a dirty bitch, just like her. Someday, Rhonda.*

Shaking my head violently, I turned the screen off, trying to erase the awful image from my mind. My stomach sank as a dirty feeling crept over me. Would I ever escape the disgusting mind of my ex?

"Is that why you froze?" Greg said tightly. "Is that what the back seat of the limo was about? The night of the gala when you fucked Kevin and made me watch?" Greg clenched his jaw as he connected all the wrong dots.

My lips parted, and I sucked in a sharp breath. *That's where his mind went? Here he is jumping to conclusions without explanation. Again.* I kept my voice controlled and quiet. "No, Greg. Kevin is just a sick pervert who likes to torment me."

"Well, what happened just now?" He threw his hands up, exasperated and not even letting me respond before he continued, "You shut down again. And why didn't you tell me about him?" He rapped his knuckles against the phone, fury lacing his words.

Anger flared up in me. "For exactly this reason! Because you always assume the absolute worst of me." I raised my chin, ignoring the fact that I was only in my bra and panties. My fingers clenched into fists at my side, my nails digging into my palm. "I have to practically beg for a chance to explain myself. Why the fuck would I volunteer to spill my guts to someone who treats me like that?"

I stomped off, realizing at the last second I needed to go to his room for my clothes. After changing into my dry, comfy outfit from before, I dragged my two bags across the sitting room.

Greg perched on the arm of the sofa. "Rhonda —"

With a shake of my head, I kept walking, dropping my luggage in the other room.

"Don't go," he said quietly.

My glare hit him as I stalked back to grab my charger and my other bag. "I'll finish out this wedding sham with you. But when we get back, you'll need to find other employment. I can't be around someone who always thinks the worst of me." I had almost reached my bedroom when he spoke again, so quietly I almost missed it.

"What happened, Rhonda? That night in the limo?"

The words halted me in my tracks. I'd waited so long to explain but had never found the right time. I couldn't let the opportunity slip away.

I didn't look at him when I answered, staring at the floor instead. "The summer after I graduated, I realized just how much you meant to me. And you'd filled out, turned into exactly my type of guy. I tried all summer to get your attention, to show you I wanted more, but you ignored my advances. So I came up with a plan. The night of the gala…"

The lump in my throat grew as the memory weighed on me. "I spent hours finding the right dress. Just before it was time to leave, I downed a shot of tequila, so I wouldn't chicken out." I sucked in a shaky breath. "It took all the courage I had to kiss you, and you scolded me like I had no idea what I wanted. Like my feelings meant nothing."

Strained silence hung between us. I forced myself to keep going, and my words were harsh. "So I found a guy who made me feel validated. Kevin. He wasn't my first. But I needed it after the way you shredded my confidence that night."

Now the fun part. I didn't know if it was the wine or if I was just done caring, but I was going to tell him the truth. Every last bit of it. When I finally glanced at him, the pain on his face combined with the tightness in his jaw almost unraveled me.

It was a second before I could speak. "We got drunk, and he wanted to fuck so I took him to the limo. I thought it was empty, was actually pretty bored with the situation, until I looked up." I tightened my fists, digging my nails in further, welcoming the pain. "There you were, Greg, watching me. All I saw were those beautiful gray eyes staring at me, exactly the way I'd been dreaming about."

My voice cracked, but I pressed on, needing him to hear all of it. "Suddenly, it wasn't Kevin beneath me. It was you. Your thumb on my clit, your dick I was riding." I raised my chin. "When I came that night, it wasn't Kevin's name on my lips."

Greg's face was pale and his expression strained. His mouth formed my name, but no sound came out. I kept a tight hold on my anger as I pivoted and strode into my room, slamming the door behind me.

* * * *

Unsurprisingly, I slept poorly that night. But when someone tapped on my door the next morning, I was shocked to see it was after ten. "Come in," I said, clipping the words because I expected Greg.

Mandy appeared instead, carrying a mug. "Greg thought you might like some coffee. Sorry you had a headache this morning." She shot me a sympathetic look. "He also said you need to get dressed. Our family friend just arrived, and Greg wants you to meet him. They'll be up in fifteen minutes. Yoga pants are fine." She paused, oozing concern. "I just want you to know that Wayne's a good guy, okay?" With a pat on my arm, she set the mug down and left the room.

What's that all about?

It didn't take long to get dressed, and I sipped my coffee in the sitting room while I waited. I caught up on my group chat with Gina and Avery, then scrolled through some of my feeds until Greg opened the door, peering in.

"Oh, good, you're up." He stepped inside. An officer in blue walked in behind him, and Greg raked a hand through his hair. "This is Officer Wayne Merriman of the State Police. He's a friend."

I gaped at them, having the sense of mind to put my coffee down before I dumped it in my lap.

The tan-skinned officer pulled up a chair in front of me, and said gently, "Ms. Elgin, Greg here filled me in on your situation."

My glare could have withered flowers, but Greg just gave me a sad smile.

"I assure you I will keep this quiet and am only here to help."

Greg sighed. He perched on the sofa with a safe distance between us. "Please, Rhonda, let him help. No one should be exposed to something like that. It's harassment."

The knowledge that he was right weighed on me. I was beyond tired of Kevin's involvement in my life. Tired of the pictures, dirty words and borderline threats. Most of all, I was tired of dealing with this alone. If Greg and Mandy vouched for this officer, that was good enough for me.

I opened up my phone, swiping to the folder of screenshots and saved photos. "His name is Kevin Ferguson, my ex-fiancé." I told him the whole story.

Officer Wayne frowned. "All these photos seem to be similar. Do you know why?"

I shifted in my seat. The truth was uncomfortable, but it needed to be said. I steeled myself, raising my chin and making sure all my shields were in place. "I'm not known for my ability to orgasm during intimacy. In fact, it's only happened once."

When I said the last part, I stared straight at Greg, who blanched then hung his head. *Good.* "Kevin seemed to take that personally, as an affront to his sexual prowess. He keeps sending me these to prove how good a lover he is, and what I missed out on." I shivered at his twisted mindset.

The officer's frown deepened. "I see. Well, you can either stop down to the office to make a copy or —"

I shook my head. "There's no need. I have them backed up on my laptop and can make you an encrypted USB drive right now if you don't mind waiting." I returned a few minutes later with a tiny black stick. "If you give me your business card, I'll email you the password. Thank you for your time and your discretion."

Greg opened the door for him. "Thanks, Wayne. I appreciate it." Once the officer was gone, he turned back to me. "Jel —"

"Don't you dare!" I stood up, my finger in his face. "You don't get to call me that anymore. I meant what I said, Greg. This" —I pointed between us—"whatever fucked up thing this was, is over."

I took a calming breath, forcing myself to put on a pleasant expression. *How many times have I pretended over the years? I can do it again. I can do it now.* I donned my charitable smile. "Thank you for bringing Officer Wayne here. It was long past time I handled this situation with Kevin. Now, if you'll excuse me, I have your sister's shower to get ready for." I glided by him to my room.

Thankfully, I had a lot to do for the shower, including going early with Julie to decorate. Unfortunately, Greg came along because we needed someone tall. I just kept busy directing people.

When Mandy asked if Greg and I had fought, I stuck as close to the truth as possible. "My ex-fiancé sent me some upsetting pictures, and I'm a little overwhelmed. Sorry if I'm not as talkative as usual."

Her brow furrowed. "But everything's okay with you and Greg, right?"

"Oh, he was kind enough to introduce me to Officer Wayne and help me with the situation. I'm just a little off with the whole thing, so he's giving me my space."

She seemed to buy that. "Well, if you need to talk…"

"Actually, what I need is to keep busy," I said lightly, "so this is perfect. Any word from Erin?"

Her face fell, and she sighed. "It's not looking good. The storm seems to have settled over Minneapolis, and she's not sure she'll be able to make it."

Oh, how awful. I patted her arm. "Don't give up hope yet."

The shower progressed beautifully, and it gave me two hours of reasons to ignore Greg. Everyone loved the favor bags. Mandy wouldn't stop gushing over them. It was a good thing I'd gotten a few extra since several aunts showed up at the last minute. And not much food was left afterward.

That night I helped Mandy write out thank you cards, because it was better to just get it over with. We watched *The Holiday* on TV while we worked. When *Home Alone* came on, we didn't bother changing the channel. We were so busy chatting, the TV was relegated to background noise. When she excused herself to the bathroom, I found myself focusing on the movie.

It was the part where John Candy offered Kevin's mom a ride with his polka band. And it lit a light bulb in my head. *Maybe we can get Erin here after all.* I kept the idea to myself, not wanting to get her hopes up. We finished the thank yous, our hands cramped from writing, as well as stuffing and sealing envelopes, but they were done.

"Tomorrow the fun begins. Rehearsal dinner, bachelorette party. Almost the big day — da-dum-dum-dum." I grinned at her, and she beamed.

"I'm so glad Greg brought you." She sagged against the couch, her smile turning soft. "I've never seen him so in love. He watches you constantly, like he's trying to anticipate what you'll need next. If he makes you feel anything like Peter makes me feel..." She shook her head. "I hear wedding bells in the not-too-distant future."

A bark of laughter nearly erupted from me, but I clamped my mouth shut just in time. The idea that Greg loved me was absurd. *And marriage? Yeah, right.* I dodged admitting to anything by saying, "I've seen the way Peter looks at you. He's head over heels, and you are a lucky woman." It was the right thing to say because she gave me a big hug before leaving, the broad smile still on her face.

Mine matched, but only because I was still laughing at the idea of Greg being in love with me. When pigs flew maybe. When Marquette was snowless and sunny in mid-January. When Jamaica froze over.

Speaking of Greg, I had to break radio silence and actually talk to the guy. *Fuck me.*

Chapter Fourteen

I trotted up to our suite. Of course Greg was just getting out of the shower, only wearing a towel slung low on his waist. Droplets of water clung to his bare chest. *Why couldn't I have stayed with Mandy for five more minutes?*

I stammered, "Um, I need to talk to you about my idea, when you have a second."

He smirked, running his fingers through his damp, sandy hair. Leaning against the door jamb, he shrugged. "I've got time."

Double fuck. "Since Erin can't fly here, do you have any chauffeur friends near Minneapolis we could hire to drive her over? I know it'd be asking a lot with the holidays and the storm, but maybe it wouldn't be too bad once they got out of that area."

His towel slipped lower, revealing the sharp ridge of his hip bone. Memories of just what lay under that towel flooded back to me. My knees wobbled, so I went to lean back against the sofa and nearly missed, thinking I was closer than I was.

"Let me make some calls." His smile was genuine, and when the dimple appeared, it pierced my heart like an arrow. "Good thinking, Jel—" He caught himself just in time. "Rhonda."

"Thanks," I muttered, then raced to the sanctuary of my room.

The next day was harder. I didn't have anything to do until that evening besides avoid Greg. I ate breakfast with Mandy, talking about the plan for her bachelorette party that evening. Greg kept trying to get my attention, but I avoided looking at him.

Finally, he cleared his throat. "Rhonda, can I have a word?" He stood near the stairs, sounding so forlorn that I couldn't say no. Not in front of Mandy.

So, I kept my mouth shut, reluctantly walking over to him. He led me upstairs. Evidently it was private, whatever he had to say. *It better not be any sort of apology or explanation, because I'm not ready to hear it.*

"Two things," he said when we made it to our suite. "One, Erin should be here tonight. I pulled some strings, found a guy and paid through the nose, but they hope to arrive in time for rehearsal dinner." He crossed his fingers.

Where even yesterday I might have flung myself at him or squealed and danced around, now I gave him a reserved smile. "That's great. Mandy will be thrilled." She deserved to have her friend at her wedding, and I was happy for her.

Greg cleared his throat. "The other thing is I'm sorry—"

I held up my hand, shaking my head and backing away.

But he stepped closer. "I know I hurt you."

My wounds were too raw for this. I turned around, my hand on the door handle, but he held it shut.

"I know it's too soon for an explanation, but I'm not giving up, and I want you to know that." He stood close enough that I felt his warmth, and my body betrayed me, a thrill shooting through me even though I told it no. "You're worth fighting for."

The anger drained out of me at his quiet words, replaced with resignation. My fingers slipped off the doorknob. "Please, Greg. Just let me go."

He stayed still for a beat, hovering behind me. "Only for now, Rhonda." He stepped back, though he didn't remove his hand. "I booked you and Mandy spa appointments this morning. I thought it might be a nice way to relax. Especially after yesterday's excitement. You should get ready."

This time he moved his hand, opened the door and let me go through, but I was too stunned to move. Any guy I knew would keep me close after a fight, to weasel his way back in my good graces. I wasn't a stranger to apology gifts, but booking me a spa appointment? Only if it was a couples' spa with a hidden agenda.

I stared at my bare feet, feeling off-kilter and unsure. "Thank you."

He leaned over so his face appeared in my peripheral vision. "You deserve to be pampered. Now go tell my sister, or you'll be late."

Mandy was thrilled to say the least, her delighted squeals and exuberant hug making even my grumpy ass smile. The place Greg had picked was just the right amount of bougie—lavender permeating the air, dim golden lighting in every room. My masseuse talked enough that I felt comfortable, but she wasn't a chatterbox. Her hot stones had my tension melting away until I was an oozing puddle of relaxation on her table. Ninety minutes wasn't nearly enough.

My legs were practically noodles when I was given a bottle of water and donned my fluffy, oversized robe. Mandy appeared with a glazed-over look on her face that probably matched mine, and we giggled at each other. Next, we enjoyed mani/pedis in adjacent chairs, complete with delicious mimosas to sip on. I couldn't remember a more relaxing morning.

Greg picked us up in the Town Car, and I forgot to be mad at him for a second. I grinned before I caught myself, my heart leaping at the sight of him. I pushed the joy away, telling Mandy to take the front since she hadn't had much time with Greg. She chattered the entire way home while I stared out of the window.

I caught Greg's eyes in the rearview mirror just once, a sight I was all too familiar with. A pang shot through my chest that this would be ending soon. I didn't feel like glaring at him anymore, but I was a far cry from the lovesick woman I'd been at the beginning of this trip.

When we got back to their house, I said I was so relaxed from the massage I wanted a nap. I holed up in my room for the rest of the afternoon taking the easy way out. I caught up with Derek and Avery, then actually laid down for a bit until it was time to get ready for the rehearsal dinner.

My phone dinged as I started doing my makeup. Greg and I were supposed to meet the rest of the family for the dinner but didn't need to attend the rehearsal since we weren't in the wedding party. Mandy's text was to me and Greg, saying Erin had arrived, along with, 'Thank you' and a thousand exclamation marks.

I smiled while I finished getting ready, enjoying being the hero. Though, Greg really deserved the credit.

A light tap sounded on the bathroom door, Greg's deep voice echoing through the wooden barrier. "Almost ready?"

I'd wanted to leave a little early to be positive everything was all set. One last glance in the mirror assured me I'd put on all my finishing touches, so I pulled open the door, only to suck in a breath at how amazing Greg looked.

The bright blue button-down shirt clung to his sculpted torso, his black slacks emphasized his long legs, and a black belt accentuated his trim waist. His sandy brown hair was artfully tousled. I smelled the peppermint on his breath from here. How was I supposed to be okay sitting next to him all night?

His lips parted as he stared at me. "Wow, Rhonda, you are gorgeous."

I preened at his words, happy to have the same effect on him. My off-the-shoulder black dress tapered in at the waist then flared out again. The hem hit just above my knee. It was elegant, classy in its simplicity, and the shape flattered me. My dark hair was down, in loose curls that cascaded to my shoulders. "Thanks."

"You have—" He frowned, reaching out to touch a piece of my hair. I felt a gentle tug, then he carefully let go. "One of your curls was being unruly, but it's better now. Shall we?"

Sure, as soon as the butterflies in my stomach get the memo that we aren't doing this anymore. Traitors.

We headed down the stairs, and he took a deep breath. Then he started talking. "So, Carrie and I dated through most of high school. I thought she was it for me."

I gaped at him as he continued, giving me more details without me even asking.

"She moved here when I was in the tenth grade, but it took a while before I found the courage to ask her out." He told me about dating her, the different things they'd done together, how close he'd felt to her.

I soaked up every word, stunned he was simply telling me all this. I'd never heard this much about his past. Ever. Once we were in the car, he glanced at me anxiously, as if making sure I really wanted to hear this.

I gave him my softest smile, nodding. "Please, don't stop."

So, he kept going. "I started college up here, at Northern University, just to be close to her. When she graduated and broke up with me, I was devastated." He paused, and his voice got quieter. "I guess when she caught a glimpse of her future tied to me, she thought I was holding her down."

"That's awful." My heart went out to him.

He drove in silence for a few minutes. "It's one of my biggest fears, that I'll be the one to hold someone back, be the thing that keeps them from reaching their potential, the brick that makes them drown."

Past comments floated through my head. That he could afford to pay for lunch, that maybe I'd choose him if we were on the same level. He wasn't only judging me in those moments, he was judging himself, and he'd always come up lacking.

I knew firsthand what those inner voices could do. How they could snuff out even the brightest hope and stir up every insecurity. Guilt hit me, knowing my judgment of his motives hadn't helped. I wasn't always the easiest to get along with, hadn't given him the benefit of the doubt.

The need to reassure him welled up in me, and I said, "Greg, you were always the bright spot in my day. Whenever I was down, I could count on you being there with a smile or a joke. Whenever my parents ignored me, you listened. When Papa died and no one bought me jellybeans, you did." I rested my hand on his forearm. "You don't drag people down, you lift them up. I've always admired that about you." I gave his arm a quick squeeze, then returned to my side of the car.

We were stopped at a red light, and he stared at me so long that the light turned green. People behind him began honking.

He blinked as if startled, then whispered, "Thank you." And we started down the road once more.

Silence sat between us as a third passenger for the rest of the drive, but it wasn't exactly uncomfortable. I filled in some gaps of who Greg was, shifted my view of him. I wasn't excusing his accusations or the way he jumped to conclusions, but it helped to know he wasn't just judging me.

When we pulled into Raymond's, there was a difference between us. Where I'd thought the door to anything involving us was firmly shut and barred, now I wasn't so sure. Daylight filtered in along the edges as if it had cracked open.

He came around to offer me his arm, and I took it, grateful for the support in my high heels again.

Carrie greeted us as soon as we stepped in, not even waiting for us to take off our coats. "Oh, thank God, you're here. Dad is on his way, but he had car issues and he won't answer the phone now that he's driving. One of our cooks didn't show up tonight, and the other is still new." Panick underlined every word. "We have a full house, plus your party will arrive any minute."

"Let's go see what our options are." I glanced at Greg, handing him my coat. "Don't say anything to Mandy until I come back." *No need to worry her if we don't have to.*

He nodded.

Carrie led me into the kitchen where the cook banged pots and pans around, muttering to himself. I called him over, and the three of us studied the menu, figuring out which dishes they could pull off. As we were talking, I mentally sifted through my years of charity events and the various issues I'd worked through. I'd dealt with similar situations before, with success.

"Okay, guys, here's the plan." I clasped my hands in front of me as they listened eagerly.

"Give our party a limited menu, say three options of easy to make meals. Be sure you have enough ingredients first, so you don't run out. If you can make it in big batches, even better. You could even do the same for the entire evening. Set up a chalkboard or whiteboard, call it 'the specials' and don't even hand out menus. Say you're only serving those today."

Carrie let out a relieved breath. "You're a genius. If we can do three dishes for your party, we can handle the rest of the guests. Dad's still coming in, and we have enough waitresses to cover my hostess position." Her shoulders dropped, and she said in disbelief, "We may get through this yet." She shot me a genuine smile which I returned.

"If you know what the dishes are, I'll start spreading the word and getting orders, so you can begin prepping."

Carrie pursed her lips to one side as she assessed the cook. "How about chicken fettuccine Alfredo plus white fish, or eight-ounce ribeye served with mashed potatoes and either green beans or a side salad?"

I nodded. "Perfect. I'll let you know what I find out." I hurried out of the steamy kitchen, pleased with the solution.

Greg waited for me in the entryway. "Any luck?" My smile must have given me away because he chuckled. "I knew you wouldn't let us down." He wrapped an arm around my shoulders and pressed a kiss against my temple before I even had time to protest.

I resisted the urge to lean into him, realizing how much I'd missed his affection. Instead, I half-heartedly pushed him off me. "Are they here yet?"

A flash of disappointment crossed his face as I stepped back, but he recovered quickly. "No, but any time now."

"Okay, I need to start putting orders in. We have three options for dinner tonight."

Greg began texting everyone as I tallied up orders. His family came pouring in not long after I gave Carrie the final count. I even double checked to make sure the number of people matched. It did. We sat near an alcove next to the bar which made it super easy for us to get refills on our drinks, further eliminating the need for more staff. Mandy never even knew there was an issue.

Before our food arrived, Mandy grabbed my hand, beaming as she tugged me over to meet Erin. Her friend was on the petite side, with dark hair cut in a sassy pixie cut. She was all angles, sharp cheekbones, pointy chin,. Her wide, dark eyes stood out against her ivory skin.

"Rhonda, this is Erin," Mandy said, almost bouncing on her toes from her excitement. "Erin, Rhonda."

Even Erin's grin had a sharp edge to it, but her words were laced with gratitude. "Nice to meet you. I hear I have you to thank for getting me here and taking on my maid of honor duties. Thank you so much."

Her focus shifted to over my shoulder, her grin growing wider. "And your boyfriend. Get over here, Greg!" She gave him a quick hug. "Long time no see, huh? Last I heard you were a chauffeur. Now you're saving damsels in distress and dating Michigan royalty."

Greg chuckled, his dimple making an appearance as he slid an arm around my waist. "That's me."

I shifted so I wasn't plastered against him, wishing I could pull away but not wanting to make a scene. His hand was warm on my hip. I wanted to forget everything between us, wave a magic wand and make it disappear.

But I couldn't.

Next Mandy dragged me over to meet her other bridesmaid, Lauren. I didn't blame Lauren when she didn't stand up. Her rounded belly rested between her and the table, but her smile never dimmed. Her husband, Remy, seemed quite nice too. He was standing up with Peter as well but wasn't planning on joining us for the bachelor party tonight. For obvious reasons.

We made it through the rest of dinner without mishap. When Raymond arrived, he came out to greet us all personally, then pulled me aside to thank me with exuberant cheek kisses and a bone crushing hug. As the evening wound down, the older, married adults went their separate ways leaving me, Greg, Mandy, Peter, Erin and Peter's best man, Dale, for our night out.

Dale grinned. "All right, let's get this show on the road."

Mandy frowned at Peter. "You behave, mister. Or else. Remember our deal."

"Oh, I remember all right." Peter smirked wickedly at Mandy.

A pretty blush spread over her cheeks. Each group had a separate chauffeur for the night, since we wanted to be able to drink without worrying about driving. We headed to the parking lot where Peter kissed Mandy — a sappy, romantic kiss. They were so over the top, it was funny.

"Wait, Greg, you forgot to give Rhonda a goodbye kiss," Mandy admonished, affronted on my behalf.

A mischievous smile spread over Greg's face. "You're right. How could I?" He strode right up to me, purpose in every step.

I had nowhere to run, no excuse to give. Mandy's hands were clasped under her chin, and I could practically hear her sigh. *Damn her romantic notions.*

Greg reached for me, pulling me flush against him. He brushed one knuckle under my chin, guiding my lips to his, then I forgot to think. The rest of the world faded away until it was me and him and the way I fit so perfectly against him. When he stepped back, one hand stayed on my waist as if he knew just how unsteady I was.

"Why are you doing this?" I whispered. The butterflies were back, doing a tango in my midsection, and I could barely hear my voice over my pulse pounding in my ears.

"Because my life is better with you in it," he whispered back. He kissed my forehead and strode off to the other limo, leaving me to question everything.

Our first stop was a cute bar on this side of town called The Funky Parrot. It had a tropical theme, overlooked Lake Superior, and was one of Mandy's favorite places. She linked arms with me and Erin as we sashayed in. Music blared. I didn't recognize the song but loved the heavy beat. The inside was done up with lots of clean lines and stainless steel, so the flashing, colored lights reflected off the shiny surfaces.

"Shots!" Erin called, dragging us to the bar. She bought us each a shot of tequila to get things started, complete with lime and a saltshaker. We downed them on the count of three.

I made a face, hurrying to bite the lime, which didn't make it much better. My next drink was a Jack and Coke which I was happy to sip.

Cardi B came on, and Mandy squealed. "I love this song! Let's dance!"

The alcohol hadn't kicked in enough for that yet. I held up my drink. "Maybe in a few."

She frowned, but Erin looped her arm through Mandy's, and they danced their way to the middle of the floor.

"Can I get a glass of water too?" I shouted to the bartender. After he slid it to me, I took a long drink, turning sideways to watch the girls dance.

A low, familiar voice spoke behind me. "Are you a parking ticket?" Greg waited for me to turn around before continuing, "Because you've got fine written all over you." His dopey smile brought out his adorable dimple, and I couldn't help but laugh.

Chapter Fifteen

"What was that?" I asked.

Greg plopped onto the bar stool next to me. "A pick-up line. I'm hitting on you."

My stomach flipped at the idea, though I wasn't sure I was ready for it. For him. "What are you doing here?" I sipped on my drink, unable to stop smiling.

"Besides hitting on the prettiest girl in the room?" The intensity of his gaze made me duck my head, until he added, "Just going where Peter wanted to."

I bumped him with my shoulder. "Stalker."

He spun around to order a rum and Coke, glancing back at me. "I know I said it before, but you really do look beautiful in that dress."

"Thank you," I said slowly, getting the feeling he wasn't quite finished.

His smirk told me I was right. "Know what else you'd look beautiful in? My arms." He winked and took a drink.

Laughter spilled out of me, and I couldn't turn away from him. This new side of him held an irresistible charm that pulled me in like a magnet.

"Do you like my shirt?" He leaned over so I could feel it, waiting for my nod. "It's boyfriend material."

I snorted, clamping a hand over my mouth.

Even he couldn't keep a straight face at my reaction. Then he changed the subject. "Why aren't you dancing?"

"I hadn't been hit on enough yet. My confidence was lacking." He laughed at my deadpan delivery, but then I told him the truth. "The alcohol hadn't kicked in, and dancing was never my strong suit."

His eyebrows shot up. "I seem to remember lots of dance classes in someone's younger days. Leotards and tap shoes, tutus and tights."

I blinked at him. "Tchaikovsky didn't prepare me to dance to this."

Shaking his head, he signaled the bartender. "Six pineapple upside-down cakes, please." Then he disappeared, coming back with the rest of our crew.

We all lined up, tossing back the overly sweet shot. I grimaced afterward since pineapple wasn't my favorite, but Greg's fingers laced through mine, and he tugged me toward the floor.

"Greg—" I started to protest.

"Dance with me if I'm wrong, but dinosaurs still roam the earth, right?" His eyebrows bounced up and down as we moved closer to the floor.

I groaned.

"I've got more. I'll keep going until you say yes."

It was my own fault—I hesitated.

"Did you hear the latest health report? You need to increase your daily intake of vitamin ME, and just one dance will do that." He tugged again, then we were out in the middle of everyone.

A song I knew started up, Dua Lipa, one of my favorites. Mandy and Erin wiggled and writhed with Peter and Dale. Greg kept his hand latched onto mine as if he were afraid I might bolt at the first chance I got. He frowned, then spun me around so my back was to his front.

Placing both hands on my hips, he said in my ear, "I know you've got moves, Jellybean."

It was the first time I'd let him use the name since our fight, and it felt right. His body found the rhythm of the song, moving behind me. One of his hands slid over my abdomen, the other down my thigh as I began swaying with him to the beat. My stomach flipped, and I pressed against him.

The song changed and the tempo slowed way down. I thought he'd turn me around to face him, but he just held me there. His thumb slid up and down my hip bone while his other hand sprawled across my stomach. I leaned languidly into him, tilting my head to rest my cheek against his chin. The alcohol combined with how I always reacted to his presence had me melting in his arms. *Could I trust this? Trust him not to hurt me again?*

When the song ended, his lips pressed a featherlight kiss to the bare skin where my neck and collarbone met, sending delicious shivers throughout me. "Thank you for the dance."

As one, our group headed back up to the bar for more drinks. It didn't take me long to finish my Jack and Coke, then I sucked down my water. Mandy and Erin were ready to move on.

"Guess we're heading to the next place." I didn't know what else to say to Greg. *Goodbye? Thanks? Kiss me?*

Wait, scratch that last one.

He raised his glass as I awkwardly stood there waiting for I didn't know what. Mandy giggled as Peter nibbled on her ear while Erin rolled her eyes, pulling on Mandy's hand. I told myself I wouldn't look back, but just before I walked out of the door, I turned. And Greg smiled big enough for that damned dimple to appear.

The next place was halfway across town, called The Wagon Wheel. Mandy warned us that we'd be overdressed but would be forced to participate in line dancing, at least once. I'd need more shots before that happened.

We bee-lined to the bar but before we could order, Greg's deep voice said, "My friends bet me I couldn't talk to the prettiest girl in the room. How about we use their money to buy us a drink?"

I gasped. "How'd you get here already?"

"We paid extra for the NASCAR limo, complete with nitro." He winked. "What are you ladies drinking?"

A terrible idea popped into my head and out of my mouth. "I think a Blow Job sounds great."

He froze, and Mandy's head whipped toward me. I stared at him, the challenge clearly written in my jutting chin.

Greg's jaw worked a few times, but he turned to the bartender. "I'll take six Blow Jobs please." His face turned red as the words came out, and the three of us girls erupted in a fit of giggles. Greg glared at me, but amusement lay beneath it.

We lined up to do the no hands shot. Mandy, Peter and Dale tossed theirs back, laughing at each other before darting right out to the dance floor, hopping in on the song like pros. Erin took her shot, but didn't join the others on the floor. She hovered to one side, chatting with a guy in tight jeans and a belt buckle the size of a dinner plate.

Greg still stood next to me, with his hands behind his back. A muscle ticked in his cheek as his gaze lingered on me. "I remember the last time I watched you do one of these."

The words were for my ears only, and he wasn't referencing a shot. The image of his dick disappearing into my mouth popped into my head, my lips parting as I stared at him.

He just smirked. "Good. Now it's not just me."

Unnerved he'd gotten even more under my skin, I decided to exact my revenge. I tossed my hair over the shoulder away from him, so it fell in a cascading backdrop behind me then I glanced up, licking my lips and letting my desire show. I lowered my mouth to the glass ever so slowly.

His jaw worked back and forth, letting me know I had him. I wrapped my lips around the glass, tossing it back, nice and smooth with no hands. It dropped to the counter with a mere *tang*. It was my turn to smirk. "Your turn."

He swallowed hard then gamely bent, lifting the glass with his mouth, and tossing it back. When he leaned down, the glass slipped, skittering across the bar. He hurried to grab it, a sheepish look appearing on his face.

But I wasn't about to let him off the hook. "So, all out of pick-up lines?" I quirked an eyebrow at Greg. "Or did I throw you off your game with that shot?"

He stared at me long enough that I began to wonder what was going on. Then he blinked and said, "There must be something wrong with my eyes. I can't seem to take them off you."

"Boo." I gave him a thumbs down as I leaned against the bar.

"You want another shot? Or a sipping drink?" His lips were so close, they nearly brushed my ear.

It took me a moment to form an answer. "Shot."

"I was hoping you'd say that. Two Slippery Nipples, please." Just hearing him say that word had mine tightening under my dress. He handed me my shot, brushing against my chest as he did. "Your Slippery Nipple, madam."

Heat pooled low in my abdomen. Greg talking dirty was not a fantasy I'd engaged in up to this point. Shame on me. I took the shot. *Wait, no, we're over. No more pining after him, dreaming about him, dancing with him.*

"Are you good at math?"

I shook my head, half paying attention.

"Me neither. But that's okay, cause the only number I'm concerned with is yours." His arm brushed against me.

The punchline sank in through the alcohol haze, and I smiled. "I like that one."

But he stayed serious. "I always thought that happiness started with an h."

I frowned, waiting.

He touched my cheek. "Turns out mine started with u."

My inhibitions melted away, and all I wanted was Greg's mouth on mine. So, I closed the gap, threading one of my hands into his hair before tugging him to me. He groaned my name against my lips. I didn't want to stop when he pulled away, but I sensed the storm raging within him.

"I'll be back, Jellybean. Order me another shot, then we're dancing." He kissed my hand and disappeared.

I ordered two straight up whiskeys this time, and a big glass of water which I gulped. I wasn't one to fall for the cheesy lines or over the top sappy bullshit, but I knew Greg. I knew when he was teasing, and he'd meant every word of that last one. I felt off-balance, as if the ground had shifted beneath me, and I was still waiting to see what landmarks remained in place.

"All right. What'd ya get us?" His hand was on my waist, and his words rumbled through his chest now pressed against my back.

My stomach flipped, and I leaned into him. "Whiskey. Bottoms up."

We drank, then his hand slid to my ass, and he gave it a little pinch.

I smacked him. "What was that for?" Shock and a teensy bit of delight darted through me.

He chuckled. "You said bottom, and I couldn't resist. You, Jellybean, have a fine ass."

"A fine-ass what?" I couldn't help but tease.

"A fine-ass ass!"

We both laughed, then we weaved our way to the dance floor where we made complete and utter fools of ourselves. Half the time we were facing one another when we were supposed to be facing the same way. Sometimes I dosied when he doed. And whenever I kicked, it usually ended up connecting with someone else.

When the song ended, we stumbled off the floor, deciding it was safer to take up residence at the bar. Thankfully, the rest of the crew wasn't too far behind. Erin was begging to go to The Black Jacket, but Mandy didn't seem to want to let go of Peter. I knew exactly how she felt. Somehow, Erin talked her into one more place.

This time I knew what to say to Greg. "One more for the road?"

The side of his mouth tipped up in a half smile. "I have the perfect one. Want to go outside and get some fresh air with me? Because you just took my breath away." He offered me his arm.

"That is perfect." I kissed his cheek before getting into the limo. The tinted glass made it impossible for him to see me, but I watched him until he was out of sight. And he never looked away from my window.

When I saw him at the next bar, his back was to me, and I nearly gave myself away by squealing. I'd hoped Peter would meet us there since that seemed to be his game plan, but I hadn't been sure. I took a deep breath before I walked right by Greg, then paused, turned, and said, "Do you believe in love at first sight? Or do I need to walk by again?"

He threw his head back and laughed, his arms shooting out to pull me toward him for a sound kiss. "That's my gimmick," he growled.

"I can Google, too." His smirk made my knees weak, and I was grateful his arms were around me.

"Speaking of. Is your name Google? 'Cause you have everything I'm searching for." He waggled his eyebrows, so over the top.

I cracked up. "Do you have a Band-Aid? Cause I scraped my knee when I fell for you."

"Ooh." He grimaced. "I have a question. If you're here, who's running heaven?"

I stuck my finger in my mouth, pretending to gag. I glanced around, trying to find our group. "Where is everyone?"

"Probably at the bar." We started walking that way, and he leaned down to say, "So do you have a name, or should I just call you 'mine'?"

My jaw dropped as I gaped up at him. That was a little audacious, even for him, but I loved it. *Mine.* The word echoed through me. His smile was smug after he'd rendered me speechless, and I just shook my head.

Until I remembered another one and reached out my hand. "I'm going for a walk. Mind holding this for me?"

He frowned, staring at my hand. Then the joke clicked, and I got to watch his whole face light up. A chuckle rumbled through him before he slid his hand into mine, and we walked side by side to the bar.

"There you are!" screeched Erin. Her voice had gone up an octave since the night began. "Now we can do our Leg Spreaders."

I froze, staring up at Greg. "Did she just say...?"

He nodded. "Sounds like a good idea to me. I'll get yours." The heated look he gave me told me he wasn't talking about alcohol.

The shot went down easily, but I was so done with fast drinking and loud bars. I desperately wanted to chill. I could tell Mandy was over the scene, too. Erin was plenty wound up, but the way she downed shots between every song, I knew she'd regret it if she didn't stop soon.

I leaned into Greg. "I think Mandy's ready to call it a night. She's got a big day tomorrow."

He trailed a finger along my bare shoulder. "What about you?"

"I'd like to get out of the noise. Go somewhere quieter." Honestly, snuggling with Greg was at the top of my want list.

"I'll talk to her." He headed in Mandy's direction while I snagged another glass of water.

Dale was ready to go, too, and Mandy tasked him with convincing Erin we were done. I didn't know what he whispered in her ear, but after he straightened up, she threaded her fingers through his and dragged him toward the door.

Peter came up to us, scratching the back of his head. "So, um, Mandy and I were kind of hoping to have the limo to ourselves for a few. Do you guys mind riding with Erin and Dale?"

"TMI, for sure." Greg grimaced.

I laughed, nudging Greg before telling Peter, "We're fine with that. You guys have fun."

Greg stuck his fingers in his ears. "Not listening."

Mandy walked up, giggling at her brother before she sidled up to Peter. "I take it you told him."

At his nod, she moved over to wrap her arms around her brother's waist. He reluctantly dropped his hands to hug her back. She came over to me next, whispering her thanks. I squeezed her tight and told her to have a good time.

We waved as they went to their limo, and I clung to Greg as we crossed to ours. He opened the back door, letting me go in first. I was unsurprised to see Erin and Dale making out in a fervid embrace. *At least they're still upright.*

I was more than happy to sit with Just Greg. He draped his arm across the back of the seat, and I snuggled into him, using his warmth to fight the cold. Hauling my bare legs onto his lap, he adjusted my skirt, so it covered as much of me as possible. His right hand rested on my bare knee as the driver pulled us out onto the road.

Darkness filled the spacious back seat. Even the streetlights were filtered through the tinted windows. It was enough to keep my panic at bay, though, especially since I was in Greg's arms.

He began tracing circles on my knee as I leaned against his shoulder. His fingers edged higher, beneath my flared skirt. Anticipation coiled within me as desire pooled between my legs. I ached for his touch, but this was Greg. And there were other people in the back seat, even if they were oblivious to anything but each other.

But he kept going. He slid right up, nudging my thighs apart. I bit back a gasp as I stared up at him in astonishment.

He whispered against my ear. "Just tell me to stop, and I will."

I clung to him as his deft fingers found my damp panty line. "But—?"

"If you're worried about them," he said, nodding in the direction of Dale and Erin, "they're occupied." He nuzzled my neck, his lips grazing just below my ear as he added, "And if you're worried about the end result, don't."

Doubt swirled in me, but I didn't stop him. He pulled aside the edge of my panties, and one knuckle brushed against my clit. Sparks danced through me, my thighs tightening around his hand.

His breath hitched. "Do you like this?"

I nodded, not trusting myself to speak as he glided between my slick folds.

"I like it too, Jellybean. I've been dying to touch you since...well, for a while now." His eyelids lowered, voice husky as my grip on his arm tightened. "As long as you enjoy it, then the rest doesn't matter."

He stroked me just right, and I bit back a moan before I whispered haltingly, "But what if I don't...?"

His lips brushed my cheek. "Then we do it again until you do. I'm a patient man. And I'm willing to figure out what makes my Jellybean tick."

Those words echoed in my head. *His Jellybean*. The claim followed by one of his fingers slipping into my pussy had me gripping the edge of his jacket with a tight fist. It was a wonder I didn't shatter on the spot.

I kept my lips clamped together and my face buried in Greg's shoulder to muffle the sounds of my pleasure as he established a perfect rhythm. His finger eased in and out of me while his palm brushed my swollen clit in a tantalizing dance of friction. The rest of the drive was like that, a mixture of torturous words and movements that stoked a fire inside me. I could hardly sit still by the time we pulled into the driveway, and I was thankful we were dropped off first.

He removed his fingers. "I can't wait to taste you, Jellybean. I want to fuck you with my mouth. I bet you taste so sweet."

"Greg," I whimpered.

"We just have to make it upstairs."

It was torture not to run. I made it into our suite, turning around to wait for Greg. Desperate for him.

He kicked the door shut. "Just tell me what you want, Jellybean."

The words tumbled out of my mouth, the heat between us burning away any remnants of hesitation. "Kiss me."

His lips met mine hungrily as he dipped, gripping the backs of my thighs to haul me against him. I wrapped my legs around him. Desire coiled low in my abdomen, and every step he took pressed his eager length against my needy clit. He kept one hand on my ass, but his other roamed freely, up my thigh, skating my ribs, brushing my breast.

When we reached the couch, he lay me down and lowered himself on top of me.

"Take my dress off." I lifted my arms, and he pulled the fabric over my head, flinging it across the room. I hadn't worn a bra, and the cool air tightened my nipples instantly.

He sucked in a breath at the sight. Of me. "Damn, you are exquisite." He didn't move, though, waiting for my next command.

Power is a heady feeling. "Taste me." With one finger, I circled my already aching nipple.

Greg didn't need to be asked twice. His mouth covered my sensitive peak, sucking gently at first. When I moaned, he sucked harder, and a thrill burst through me. His fingers cupped my other breast, brushing my other nipple. I arched into him. Then he switched sides, lavishing his attention on the other. He came back up to cover my mouth with his, pressing his hard cock against my desperate clit.

Needing more, I decided to play a little dirty. "Ow."

He froze, then moved off me. "Are you okay?"

Shaking my head, I pouted, "I'm hurt. You should kiss it and make it better."

His forehead crinkled. "Where are you hurt?"

I trailed one finger down between my breasts over my damp panties to rest between my legs. "Here." I bit my lip, wondering how he'd react. I remembered what he said about tasting me, but saying and acting were two different things.

He hesitated. "Are you sure, Rhonda?"

My heartbeat quickened at his concern for me, and I knew what he was confirming. That he didn't want to go too fast and overwhelm me again. I nodded. "I'm sure."

A smirk appeared as he ran his hands down my hips to my panties. "Then these have got to go."

Chapter Sixteen

He dragged my panties off, and I was naked before him, except for my heels. There was no ice this time, only delicious, intense heat, and I couldn't get enough of it.

Greg knelt before me clearly in awe as he spread my thighs apart. He ran his warm fingers up and down my legs, over my hips. "I love touching you."

I stared at him, anticipation intensifying with his every movement. His fingers danced along my folds, then slipped inside, and I let out a moan.

He grinned. "Ah, that's what I wanted to hear."

His breath warmed my inner thighs as he leaned closer and flicked his tongue up my seam. I groaned. His fingers began pumping in me as his tongue circled my clit. I wove my fingers through his hair, trying to hold out against the rising wave of pleasure pulsing with me.

A hint of doubt crept in, but I remembered Greg's words. That the end result didn't matter as long as I was enjoying myself. *We can check that off the list.*

The tension kept building, a bomb on a timer, counting down. I stopped worrying, stopped thinking, as I lost myself in Greg's delicious attention. He kept up a steady rhythm, and before I knew it, I was gasping for breath as the first wave hit me.

But he didn't stop there. He sucked on my clit again, keeping pace with his fingers until the earth shattered around me. I cried out his name as I closed my eyes and stars filled my vision.

I opened my eyes to find him staring at me with a satisfied smile as he slid his fingers out of me.

"You tasted just as sweet as I thought you would," he said, with a smirk. "I think I know what your problem was."

I was mush, almost too tired to answer. The bliss of the orgasm combined with the alcohol and my lack of sleep the night before. "What's that?"

"You were fucking the wrong guys." His gentle, whispered words bit through my sleepy haze.

I managed to glare at him. "Whose fault was that?"

His palm slid under mine, and he brought my hand to his lips. "Mine, Jellybean. All mine." Then he picked me up like a rag doll and carried me to my bed, my eyelids heavier by the second. He slipped off my shoes, dropping them to the floor with a gentle *thunk*.

My protests were almost incoherent. "I might be able to stay awake for sex." I really wanted to return the favor.

But when I tried to reach for him, he just chuckled. "Oh, Jellybean, this was all about you tonight, okay?"

I frowned. "But—"

"Listen, you haven't slept well for a couple nights. You've had plenty to drink. And you're in post-orgasm bliss. Take advantage of it." He tucked me in and kissed my forehead.

I sighed, then grabbed his hand, my words a little mumbled. "Couldn't you stay? Just to snuggle?"

A tormented groan escaped him. "If I stay, you wouldn't be sleeping, and that's what you need." His lips brushed mine once more.

That's Greg, always looking out for me...even when I don't necessarily want it. His fingers slid out of mine, and a flicker of disappointment skittered through me, but I knew he was right.

"I'll be here in the morning, okay?" He padded into the other room, making sure not to shut my door all the way so the light could filter in. "Sweet dreams, Jellybean."

The wedding day dawned bright and early without me. I slept in until nine. The sun was up, though its shine was buried deep behind a layer of clouds and snow. The storm had arrived. My head felt heavy, but I was relieved to not have a hangover.

I stretched, the sheets brushing against my naked body. *Naked?* The memories came rushing back in a flood. Every detail, every intimate moment. I lay there stunned, replaying all the things Greg had said, had done. He had claimed me. Tasted me.

And admitted it was his fault I'd been with the wrong guys.

Part of me didn't want to get out of bed. What if it had all been a delicious dream? And if it had been real, where was I on the whole 'mad at Greg' scale? I covered my face with a pillow just as a gentle tap sounded on the door.

I peeked out as the door edged open, mortified to see the object of my thoughts peering in. I flung the pillow away and yanked up the covers.

Greg just chuckled. "Morning, Jellybean. Any reason you're not out of bed yet?"

Oh shit. I recognized that teasing grin, and I was too embarrassed to answer.

"Thought I'd check on you, make sure you have everything you need." His gaze trailed over the covers as if they were see-through. "Want to come out and play?"

I shook my head, clutching the covers to my chin.

"Why not? I saw everything last night." He stalked to the foot of the bed, toying with the edge of the blanket. His fingers crept under the edge, stroking my calf and I squealed, rolling away. He pounced on top of me, pinning me down with his weight plus the covers. "I just wanted to say good morning."

Our faces were inches from each other. I tried not to breathe on him since I hadn't brushed my teeth, but he leaned down and kissed my cheek.

He hovered there. "No good-morning kiss?"

I bit my lip, not saying no.

Greg trailed kisses closer to my mouth until his lips pressed to mine. He sighed happily. "That's better." The smile made his dimple appear. "Get dressed, and I'll take you out for breakfast."

Once the door was shut, I stayed in bed for a few long moments, almost expecting him to come popping back in, yelling, "Gotcha!" This playful, flirtatious side of Greg was unexpected, but I loved it. It seemed he finally felt comfortable enough to be himself.

Maybe those invisible barriers between us had truly crumbled.

Convinced I had the room to myself, I hurried to get dressed. I pulled on my one pair of jeans and a worn sweatshirt along with thick socks, planning on wearing the boots Greg had bought me. When I opened my door, I almost tripped over a beautiful mixed bouquet of flowers in a vase. The card simply read *'Thanks for letting it be me'*.

If I took longer to get ready than he expected, I wasn't going to tell him that his note had blindsided me, and I'd needed a minute to compose myself. I trotted downstairs where he waited for me, lighting up as he took in my casual outfit. He was dressed similarly. His smile widened when I reached for my boots.

Since we were already going out, the frozen shoreline appealed to me, and I suggested. "I thought maybe we could go out to Presque Isle again if we have time. Take a walk."

A frown crossed his face. "We'll have to see how bad the weather gets. A blizzard up here really means something." When my face fell, he touched my chin. "But we'll see, okay? Right now, it's just a little bit of snow for us yoopers."

The wedding wasn't until four p.m., so we didn't have to be back till one. We were caught in that happy bubble of pre-wedding anticipation, feeling like we had all the time in the world together. A day of endless possibility stretched before us. And I was happy to take advantage of every delicious moment.

Breakfast was a comfortable affair. Greg took me to a nearby cafe with hearty breakfast sandwiches. They had great service, a homey atmosphere and the conversation never lagged between us.

When our stomachs were full and we had coffee to go, Greg declared it safe enough to venture to Presque Isle. The drive was snowy, and he took it slow, but it must not have been too dangerous because he held my hand the whole time. After we'd parked, he produced a red hat with a pompom on top for me as well as a pair of thick gloves.

The sharp wind blew off the coastline when I stepped out, for once not waiting for Greg to open my door. I met him in front of the car with a grin, blinking away the snowflakes that flew into my face. It was an entirely different world. The trees were coated in white, snow clinging to their branches. There was a quiet beauty in the monochrome scene of white, no hint of green or blue that came with spring. It was peaceful, almost reverent. I felt odd even speaking.

Then he went to his trunk and got out two pairs of what appeared to be tennis rackets with leather straps on them.

I frowned. "What are those?"

"Only way to access the shore this time of year. Snowshoes." He grinned.

They weren't hard to put on, but walking in them took some getting used to. The surface area was much different, so it felt like I was waddling.

But we did it. The snowshoes allowed us to stay on top of the snow, instead of sinking into it. As we trekked, I admired the drifts and the frozen waves. A cardinal zipped past, a bright flash of red against the pristine wall of white. When I needed to catch my breath, I tugged Greg to a stop, and we stood for a few minutes just staring into the frozen expanse of Lake Superior.

My family's livelihood came from that and the other Great Lakes surrounding our state. I'd grown up knowing them, hearing about them. But they still took my breath away. The wind picked up even more, slicing through me with cold as sharp as a razor.

"Ready?"

I nodded, my breath coming out in foggy puffs before me as we trekked back to the car. I was grateful to take off the snowshoes, happy to walk normally once again. When Greg started the engine, I reached over, cranking the heat up to full blast. "Do you miss it?" I asked. "Living up here?"

"Sometimes." Greg turned on the wipers to push away the snow that had built up while we'd been walking. "It has a certain beauty, an untamed quality that begs to be conquered."

Once we were on the road, I waited anxiously for the heat to kick out. It was nice to be away from the wind, but my hands were still freezing. Greg started talking again, surprising me when Carrie's name left his lips.

"After Carrie dumped me, I was in a bad place." His gloved hands tightened on the steering wheel. "I flunked out of Northern. My dad and I fought constantly. He wanted me to take over the family business, said I was wasting my potential." His lips twisted into a wry smile. "That's why it's been so long since I've been back."

I forgot about the cold. I just wanted to wrap Greg in my arms and hold him until the obvious pain of his father's words disappeared. It amazed me, the power of words, the hurt they could cause.

"It was my mom who thought of her brother. Uncle Harry took me in, found me a job, and I got to meet you." His dimple appeared, although the grin was tinged with a hint of sadness. "There's a lot of things I miss about this place, but if I had to do it over again, I wouldn't change a thing."

His hand left the steering wheel to rest palm up between us. I didn't hesitate to grab it.

Maybe the heat had kicked on. Or maybe the sweetness of his words warmed me. Either way, when I thought about it, I couldn't bring myself to want anything to change either.

When we got back, Mandy begged me to go with her to the hotel while she got ready. "You've been my good luck charm so far, and it wouldn't feel right without you there."

I couldn't say no, so I grabbed my dress, my shoes, my makeup and kissed Greg goodbye. When we arrived at the hotel, Simone escorted us to the room where we could get ready. Erin and Lauren joined us a few minutes later.

Mandy hated her first hairstyle but couldn't say why. At last, I dragged it out of her that it was too poufy in front, and the stylist toned it down. The end result was intricate and beautiful, a sweeping updo with looping braids, twists and curls befitting a princess. When Mandy put on her dress and tiara, her veil flowing down behind her, that was exactly what she looked like.

Erin and Lauren had their hair done in simpler updos that were also elegant. Their dresses were black, not a traditional bridesmaid color, but, being New Year's Eve, Mandy had thought black, silver and gold would be perfect. Erin, as the maid of honor, had gold accents. Lauren had silver, and their groomsmen would match.

About half an hour before the wedding was supposed to start, Greg texted me that he had arrived. I glanced over once more at the full-length mirror, making sure I was ready to go. I'd gone with part of my hair pulled back, keeping it out of my face to show off my dangling, swirly earrings. The rest of my hair cascaded over my shoulders in large curls.

My dress was a dark teal. Its simple fitted bodice had one shoulder strap on the left side and the flowing skirt reached to the floor. A slit opened to my right thigh, and I wore a silver tennis bracelet on my right wrist.

"You look great, Rhonda. As always." Mandy swallowed. "I don't know what I would've done without you this week. Thanks so much for being here." Her voice cracked on the last word.

I scowled as I admonished her. "Don't you even think about crying! You'll ruin your makeup." We both laughed, and I pulled her in for a hug, squeezing tightly. "Thanks for letting me be a part of all this." We shared a shaky laugh before I left.

In the hallway, I took a moment to compose myself before going to find Greg. The elevator opened at the lobby of the main floor to a bustling crowd of people. I had to push my way through them, fighting the flow of traffic to reach the hallway outside of the ballroom where Mandy's wedding would be held. Greg's voice found my ears before I saw him. Then I found him, and he stole my breath.

The dark gray pinstriped suit was tailor-made for him. He could have walked straight out of a magazine, and I had to tell my heart to slow down for surely I would die if it kept up this pace. As I made my way toward him, I saw he was talking to three guys and some of his words reached me.

"Oh, she's a handful all right." He chuckled as all the guys exchanged grins. "A real diva."

I paused for a split second as doubt spiraled through me. *Does he mean me?* I nibbled at my lip, waiting to see if he said more, but I caught his attention and he turned.

His eyes widened as he took me in. "Rhonda, wow, you look absolutely amazing," he said with a full smile as he scanned my length. "Guys, this is my girlfriend, Rhonda Elgin."

He introduced me, but I tuned out their names, even as I robotically grinned and shook their hands. Had his eyes widened because he *had* been talking about me? Or because of my appearance?

No, Greg wouldn't talk about me like that. Right? I waited for my resounding, confident self to answer back, but only silence greeted me. The seedling of doubt sprouted in my upper abdomen, just below my rib cage, and I didn't have the ability to squash it.

The ushers led us to our seats, in the second row from the front on the bride's side. A black swath of fabric ran up the aisle between the myriad of white chairs, leading to a flower crested archway at the front of the ballroom. The white and peach roses would complement the silver and gold accents of the bridesmaids' outfits. Dull afternoon light filtered in through the many large windows spaced around, the whited-out view another reminder the blizzard was now in full swing.

"How'd the afternoon go?" Greg asked.

"Fine," I said, trying not to sound too stilted. I needed to just let it go, and I tried to shove his words aside, but they hovered in my mind as I described the issue with Mandy's hair and how profusely she thanked me.

Greg started to respond, but the music changed. We all turned to watch Peter lead his grandmothers then his mom in. Mandy's mom was next. Julie gave me a happy smile and a little finger wave. Then Peter took his place at the front of the room, puffing his cheeks as he blew out a nervous breath.

An instrumental song started, and Lauren walked by with her husband, taking their places at the front of the room. Next came Erin and Dale, walking along in perfect time with the beat, though Erin held Dale's arm a bit stiffly. There was an awkward tension between them, making me wonder just what had happened after we'd left last night.

Pachelbel's *Canon in D* started up as the minister signaled us to stand. We turned as one toward the back of the room where Mandy appeared on her father's arm. She was gorgeous in her floor-length strapless gown, beaming behind her gauzy veil. Her sweeping train trailed behind her — every step placed in complete and utter confidence, as if certain she were doing the right thing.

What would that feel like?

I couldn't help glancing at Greg. He had his hands clasped in front of him while he intently watched his sister walk down the aisle. I scanned the room. So many other couples were holding hands, with fond smiles on their faces as they leaned into one another. *Yeah, we're new, but couldn't Greg give me something?*

The seedling of doubt sprouted roots that threaded through my stomach.

When Mr. Peterson gave away his daughter, a pang hit me, right in my gut, as I realized I'd been so close to doing this with Kevin. When Mr. Peterson lifted his daughter's veil and kissed her cheek, I imagined my father doing it for me.

Not that I'd wanted to marry Kevin.

No, that ship had long since sailed, but the idea of my father giving me away to a man I loved was so poignant and beautiful that I sniffed. Then I dug into my clutch for the emergency pack of tissues I'd thrown in there. Just in case.

The ceremony was short and sweet, a few readings, a few songs, "I do"s and a kiss. Then we were cheering for the first-time-ever-Mr.-and-Mrs. Peter Harris. Being in the second row, we didn't have to wait long for the reception line. But we did have to hang around before going to the reception itself because Mandy wanted Greg in some of her pictures. She insisted I be included, too, which felt weird. It made her happy, though.

Finally, we were dismissed along with the rest of the family to make our way to the reception. Greg reached to hold my hand for the first time that night. I must have made an odd face because he asked, "What?"

I didn't want to explain, to start anything at his sister's wedding so I shook my head. Seats at the reception were assigned, and we sat with Greg's parents. His uncle Harry was at our table too, along with his wife Pamela and their three children, all about my age. Their youngest boy, Trevor, had just graduated high school earlier this year and just about drooled over me, until Greg put his arm around my shoulders.

The back-off look he shot Trevor had the younger man almost falling out of his chair in an excuse to find somewhere else to be. It was hard to hide my chuckle and it felt good to be claimed. Some of my doubt receded.

My stomach growled as the DJ announced that everyone needed to take their seats so he could introduce the newlyweds. They danced through the door, Lauren and her husband first, as well as she could with her protruding stomach. Next came Erin and Dale, both of them loosened up a bit, flushed cheeks a telltale sign they'd already begun drinking.

Then it was time for Mandy and Peter, who shimmied their way to the head table. Everyone started clinking their silverware against their glasses before they'd even sat down, calling for Peter to kiss his bride. I beamed as he dipped Mandy backward, kissing her soundly.

The wedding party went through the food line first, but our table was next. I gaped as I surveyed the many dishes. Pot roast, chicken, mashed potatoes, white cheddar macaroni and cheese, green beans almondine, the softest rolls ever and a beautiful spring mix salad. My eyes were way bigger than my stomach, and I sat down with my plate piled high. No way could I eat all this.

Greg sat beside me, and he chuckled. "Get a little carried away there?"

"I'm hungry!" I protested. "And everything just smelled so good."

"I'll plan on not going up for seconds, then. Until I see what you don't eat." His tender smile had my stomach flipping, making me feel warm and cozy like I'd been wrapped in a blanket straight from the dryer.

"Sounds perfect." *He's perfect.* I stared at him a minute longer before I started eating. The phrase 'too good to be true' flitted through my mind as doubt wriggled in my gut. *It can't just leave me alone for five seconds?* I sighed. *Maybe I can bury it in food.* I tried my best, but in the end, I was just too full.

Chapter Seventeen

My food coma made the toasts drag on forever, then it was time for the opening dances. Peter and Mandy danced for their first time to *All of Me* by John Legend. It was so perfect, watching the two of them gaze at each other as if the rest of us didn't exist.

Maybe we didn't. Not for those few moments, anyway.

Then Mandy danced with her father. Once again, I thought about dancing with my dad. I hadn't gotten as far as picking out a song, but the idea of it made me a little sad. My dad and I weren't particularly close.

Greg's voice pulled me out of my thoughts. "Rhonda?"

"I'm sorry, what?" I asked, startled.

His smile dimmed a little, a hint of uncertainty making his dimple disappear. "I asked if you wanted to dance to the next song. It's for couples, but we don't have to."

"No." I sighed, wanting to kick myself. "I mean, I'd love to dance with you. I owe you after all."

His face fell at my last sentence. Maybe I should have kept my mouth shut and pled the need to use the bathroom or something. The doubt spread further, fed by my own bumbling idiocy.

"All couples to the dance floor," the DJ boomed. He started a slower Ed Sheeran song. "Okay, so we're going to find out who here has been together the longest. Anyone married for less than a day, off the floor." Everyone chuckled as Mandy and Peter hung their heads and shuffled off the dance floor.

"Anyone together less than a year, off the floor." Greg and I glanced at each other before heading back to our seats.

Disappointment wriggled in me that our time on the floor had been so short, though I was relieved not to face the awkwardness building between me and Greg. He sat with me as they went through everyone left on the floor. Peter's grandparents won, together for over sixty-five years.

I snagged a glass of champagne as a waiter made the rounds, more than ready to have a little help for the next round of dancing. Maybe it would drown the doubt too.

Greg glanced around the crowded room. "I feel like I should mingle. There's a lot of family I haven't seen in a while. Want to come?" he asked hopefully.

I shook my head, holding up my glass of champagne. "Nah, I think I'll just sit and sip for a while. It was a long afternoon."

Disappointment scuttled across his face, but he blinked, and it was gone. Then I blinked, and so was he. What had happened to the open, easy conversation of this morning? Where were the dimpled smiles, the hand-holding and casual touches? This weird tension between us had my overly large dinner sitting in my gut like a brick.

I took another sip, hoping I could ease the tension, one way or another.

Harry sat next to me, asking how things were with me and my brother. I caught him up on Derek's success, how he'd graduated with his Master's and the way his app reshaped the shipping industry. But then I ran out of Derek anecdotes and the conversation circle back to me.

So, I excused myself to the bathroom. I definitely didn't want to answer questions about Greg at the moment, and as for what else was going on in my life, I had nothing.

What am I doing? I washed my hands, reapplied my makeup and repositioned a bobby pin to tuck in an escaped curl. I thought about Derek who'd already accomplished so much. Then I stared at my reflection, once again playing dress up with a fake date.

Same old, tired song.

It was New Year's Eve, for crying out loud. This was the time for resolutions and new leaves and promises. I straightened up, looking myself dead in the eye. *This will be my year. I'll find myself, no matter what it takes.* I didn't need a guy to do that, though it would be nice.

Gina's advice echoed in my head. I needed to know what I wanted to do with my life, be it charity work or a job or what, then go after it. *I'm Rhonda fucking Elgin, after all.* I was known for my drive, my go get 'em attitude.

I just needed to figure out what I wanted to go get. *That* was the dilemma. My shoulders sagged a bit, and

I sighed, then dried my hands on a paper towel before walking out of the bathroom door.

For now, do I go back to the table and face the Harry inquisition? Or find Greg? I scanned the crowd, finding my date not too far away, talking with a small crowd of people our age. He seemed the logical choice, and I could avoid more questions from Harry that I didn't have the answers to.

I snagged another glass of champagne from a passing waiter, then wove my way to Greg's group. They were all laughing as I came up behind him.

He was obviously in the middle of a story, and he continued, "And after we get done singing happy birthday to Derek, they come in. She always has to make an entrance." He shook his head.

His words had me frozen, mid-step. This time I had no doubt he was talking about me. My tardiness to my own brother's surprise party was due to a tagalong visit from our mutual friend Piper. She was a musical legend, a country pop star I'd managed to score for the night. Though she'd been a huge hit for the party, it had been a chore getting her there.

Of course, my late arrival hadn't been my fault but here I was, still taking the blame. His earlier words about being a diva entered my mind, and my stomach sank.

One of the guys nodded to Greg, directing his attention to me.

Greg smiled. "Hey, Jellybean."

But I couldn't play that game, not now. I pivoted, rushing off to the safety of our table and the mind-numbing questions from Harry. Anything was better than having that knife shoved into my gut, yet again.

The figures on the dance floor writhed in tune to the heavy beat. Ties were no longer on, collars unbuttoned, and high heels sat abandoned in heaps next to many a chair. The party was officially in full swing. As soon as I sat down, someone yelled they were going to cut the cake, but I couldn't bring myself to get up again.

I didn't know how much time passed before I felt a light brush of fingers on my bare shoulder. It could have been minutes. It could have been an hour. When I glanced up, I saw Greg's face etched with concern as he sat next to me, a glass of water in his hand.

"Everything okay?"

The beat pulsed within me, shoving brutally around inside my head. I felt one misstep away from a panic attack, as if the combination of the crowd and the noise were closing in on me. But I played it cool, keeping my charitable smile in place. I noticed the glass of water he was sipping on. "No champagne?"

He grimaced, rubbing his stomach. "Too much food. It just didn't settle well with the champagne, so I thought I'd hold off. Maybe later." His lips pressed together, and I knew he wasn't going to let my deflection go. Sure enough, he said, "You want to talk? Maybe go outside and get some fresh air?"

That sounded heavenly. But I found myself shaking my head before I could stop the action.

His eyes narrowed, seeing too much. His voice lowered, though it couldn't go too quiet with all the noise. "I can feel you pushing me away, Jellybean, and I don't know why. Talk to me."

The pleading note in his voice almost undid me, and all my doubts nearly came tumbling out.

But Harry chose that moment to reappear. "Rhonda, would you care to dance?"

Eric Clapton started singing about a lady in red, and I latched onto Harry's hand as if he were a lifeline. We danced. The next song came on, another slow one, and Greg appeared over Harry's shoulder, tapping him.

"I believe I'll cut in."

Fuck. I owed him, though, from that stupid bet, so I plastered on my fake smile and tucked one hand in his, the other resting lightly on his shoulder.

Greg didn't waste any time. "This is bullshit, Rhonda. I thought we were past all this." His grip on my waist tightened, pulling me flush against him as I sucked in a startled breath. There was no space between us. He leaned down to nuzzle my neck, his hips swaying in beat with mine.

I stiffened, fighting the lump in my throat even as a thrill went through me at his touch. "So did I." And I shoved away from him, leaving him alone in the middle of a song on the dance floor.

He didn't follow me. I grabbed my clutch off the table then fled to the bathroom, knowing if he tried to, he wouldn't be allowed in. Thankfully, the bathroom was spacious enough that I could lean against the far wall with my hip against the sink, and not be in anyone's way. I pulled out my phone.

Maybe I'd text Avery. She'd know what to do. But when I swiped open my screen, a new sort of horror waited for me, one that had me biting my knuckle to keep from screaming in frustration.

Kevin had texted me again, from a new number. Another disturbing picture, this one with a caption that read,

Tell Avery her mom says hi. And thanks for the book. We wouldn't have found each other without it.

My phone dropped to the tiled floor with a loud clatter. I hurried to pick it up, afraid someone would see the awful photo. *Oh no. Avery has to be told.* Her mom was with Kevin, one of the most vindictive and manipulative people I knew.

Avery's dad had Alzheimer's, and Avery was doing everything she could to get him the proper care. Her mom, a well-known author and YouTuber, had embraced a much more vivacious lifestyle since her father's diagnosis. So far, she had managed to keep a lid on it, not wanting it to ruin her career. Kevin could very well be the final straw that broke that camel.

Avery had to know right away. This wasn't the sort of info one should get in a text. I wouldn't even know what to say, and I definitely couldn't send the picture. I tried to imagine explaining Kevin's message to Avery via text, and my stomach sank. I needed to tell her in person.

After stuffing my phone into my purse, I hurried to find Greg, who was not happy to see me.

"I know, Greg. I'm sorry, but all this," I said, gesturing between us, "doesn't matter right now. There's something more urgent that I have to take care of immediately." I sucked in a deep breath, then blurted out, "I have to go home."

He gaped at me, disbelief written all over his face. "Rhonda, not only is it New Year's Eve, and my sister's wedding, but there's a blizzard outside."

All his diva comments ran through my head at his disdainful tone, but I pushed the mute button on my inner commentary. Whatever he thought of me, I didn't care at this point. My friend needed to know the truth, and I was sitting on a ticking time bomb.

I glared at him. "You promised you'd stop jumping to conclusions about me. I swear this is important. I know what I'm asking of you, and if I could drive myself, I would." *Damn that champagne.* "Greg, please."

He sighed. "It's not that I don't believe you, but I think I deserve an explanation."

"You do," I said, and he raised his chin, waiting. "But I can't give it to you here. It's sensitive. I promise I will explain, though." I held my breath, hoping it would be enough.

His gaze softened. "All right, Rhonda. Just let me say goodbye."

Relief crashed over me like a tsunami, my knees almost buckling from the force of it. We hurried through our goodbyes. Mandy and Peter exclaimed in concern but wished us luck. When we got outside, I had to cling to Greg's arm out of necessity.

We were halfway to the car when he asked, "Okay, now can you tell me what's going on?"

I wished we could wait till we were in the car, but I stopped, making sure my feet were firmly planted before I dug out my phone. "Kevin is with Avery's mom, that's what. If anyone gets wind that my ex-fiancé is hooking up with Mabel Milbourne, how's that going to look? The press will have a field day, not to mention what will happen with Mabel's career. And who would suffer in all that? Avery's dad."

The frown on his face deepened as he swiped through the pictures. "We can't just send her a text or call her?"

I gaped at him. "Is that the kind of news you'd want to hear over the phone? Plus, neither Avery nor Derek know about any of the situation with Kevin. I can't explain that in a text message." His mouth tightened as

I hurried on, "And no, it can't wait. I know Kevin. The sooner he can leverage this situation to his advantage he will, either for money or fame or something. Avery needs to know ASAP."

Greg still didn't move.

"Look," I said, annoyed and freezing. "Avery is my first real girl friend. Ever. And this could easily blow up into a crisis of major proportions for her. Because of me." I stared down at the snow swirling around my frigid feet. "I want to be there for her. I don't want her to find out because her mom sends her a shitty postcard, or the tabloids run some grainy picture. *I* want to tell her. And if you don't want to drive me, I'll start calling until I find someone who can."

With a sigh, he handed me back my phone. "No, I'll drive you. At least send that to Officer Wayne."

I did as he asked with no argument, emailing the photo and a short explanation. Greg walked me the rest of the way to the car. Just before he opened the door, movement made me freeze, a glint of light and a shifting of shadows. Had someone been watching us? Had they overheard our conversation?

"What now?"

"I thought I saw something." I peered into the darkness, squinting through the flurrying snow when I heard the door open behind me.

"There's nothing there. Just get in." He sounded more than exasperated.

I sighed and turned to find him holding open the back door of the car. If he had taken a knife and stabbed it into my heart, it would have hurt less. Our façade was truly over then, this game was very much done. I choked on a sob, diving into the car and locking the door behind me.

Greg's muffled voice sounded, separated once more by a barrier, just like it should be. His fist met the window as he called my name.

But I buried my face in my hands. I heard his car door open, heard him climb in the front.

"Rhonda, I didn't mean to. It was a mistake, I swear."

"Just go." I kept my face hidden as the tears poured out, watering the tree of doubt that choked out the flowers of hope.

His voice was strained when we stopped at his parents' place. "I have to get extra supplies since it's New Year's Eve. We should have plenty of gas, food, and water, since not much will be open, especially up here. Plus, we need to pack. Wear your warmest clothes and your boots."

His tone held no room for argument. I stumbled out of the car, not bothering to wait for assistance. And promptly fell on my ass.

His jaw clenched as he helped me up, and his touch scalded me even through my coat. As soon as we were inside, I wrenched away from him, tearing off my heels before I ran up the stairs. I packed in record time. My bags bumped as I dragged them down the staircase where I waited on the bottom step.

"Rhonda—" He tried again.

With my composure firmly in place, I cut him off. "Stop, Greg. I get it. Whatever this experiment was, it failed. It's over. I'm too much of a diva, I'm great fodder for stories at parties and I'm perfect for sitting in the back seat. Thanks for driving me home." I took my own bags out of the door to the trunk where I waited for him to open it.

Then I climbed into the back seat, wishing very much for that barrier to slide up between us so I had some protection between me and the guy responsible for shredding my heart into the raw, throbbing mass that it was.

* * * *

The drive was slower than usual, and Greg kept both hands on the wheel. The snow flew at our windshield like a million white arrows racing by. High beams were useless, only illuminating more flakes. *At least it's coming straight down.* If the wind started blowing, there would be surprise drifts to avoid on top of everything else.

The hypnotic stream of snow in the headlights combined with the champagne to lull me to sleep. I woke up when I slammed against the car door, my seat belt jerking tightly across my lap and chest. My breath left me in a whoosh. Startled, I automatically looked to Greg.

"Hold on, Rhonda," he called between gritted teeth as he tried to straighten out the car.

I'd seen him do it before, had faith he'd do it this time, kept waiting for us to settle back onto the road and go on our merry way. But it never happened.

Instead, we went careening toward the ditch, and time slowed as we flew to the opposite side of the road. I bit back a scream as we toppled over the embankment. The world went upside down as the car flipped onto its roof. Metal scraped against the rocks and roots above my head until we stopped with a dull thump.

Greg was in the back seat, beside me before I could even take a full breath. "Rhonda! Rhonda, are you okay?"

I hung suspended from the ceiling. *How'd he get out of his seat belt so fast?*

"Are you hurt?"

Carefully, I assessed myself. "I don't think so." I'd be sore from all the jerking around, and would probably have some bruises, but nothing was sprained. My ribs all seemed intact.

I felt lucky to be in one piece.

"Here, let me help you down." He put his hands on my waist, holding up my weight so it wasn't on the seat belt anymore. "Go ahead and unlatch the belt. I've got you."

Regardless of everything between us, I trusted him in this moment, and I pushed the button. I didn't even fall. He smoothly lowered me onto the floor...roof of the car. Then he smothered me in his embrace, his face pressed to mine, his arms wrapped around me.

"I'm so glad you're okay." His words came out in a choked whisper.

I began to shake as the fear hit me then, his and mine. Adrenaline ripped in on its heels. "What about you, Greg? Are you okay?" *He has to be okay, right? To be able to do everything he just did?* I pushed away from him. My hands flew over his torso frantically, trying to feel any bumps or breaks.

"I'm all right, Jellybean. Probably a few bruises in the morning, but I'm in one piece." He kept rubbing my arms, trying to soothe me.

I realized as I stared at him that the lights were on in the car. He'd somehow done that as well, so I wouldn't be suffocating in darkness.

His hands gripped my shoulders. "I have something to tell you, and I need you to stay calm, okay? Lots of deep breaths."

My chest tightened at his words, and I dug my fingers into his forearms as panic began fluttering inside me.

Chapter Eighteen

"We landed upside down, in a ditch." Greg's words came out slow and measured. "I'm not sure how deep the snow is, or what the situation will be once I get outside."

How deep the snow is... I read between the lines. "Wait, we could be trapped here?" The walls felt closer, the air thinner. My breaths came in stuttering gulps. Did the lights just flicker?

"No, Rhonda, I won't let that happen. I'll get us out. It just might take some time, and we have to stay calm. Can you do that?" He watched me, full of compassion and empathy — along with an undercurrent that scared me but warmed me at the same time.

It gave me the strength to say, "I'll try."

His hand came up to cup my cheek, his thumb sliding back and forth. "You're so brave, Jellybean. Always ready to conquer anything. I have something else to tell you, and I hope you won't be too mad at me."

Greg paused, glancing over my shoulder. "I took a different route, knowing how late it was when we got started. I own a place up here, a cabin I rent out most of the year to hunters or tourists for the summertime. It's empty right now, and I thought maybe we'd need a place to crash. I didn't mean to do it quite so literally, but I think we're nearly at my front porch, or at least my driveway."

The odds of crashing close to shelter were slim at best through many parts of the Upper Peninsula. A lot of Michigan's northern section was state forest or national parks with no buildings of any sort. To land so close to a place that he owned had to be a miracle. Or some sort of fairy-tale plot in one of Avery's cheesy romance novels.

I frowned. "Why would I be mad about that?"

"I don't even know at this point." He sounded so defeated.

It made me want to pull him back to my chest and hold him until we were both whole again. But there were more pressing matters.

Like not freezing to death in this icebox.

"What's the plan?"

"Well, I have an emergency kit in the trunk with a flashlight and all sorts of other stuff. Plus, our bags are back there. The seat folds down if I can get this lever to work." He pulled on a latch buried in the crevice of the seat, and the seat tilted, revealing a dark trunk.

Everything was backward since the car was upside down. He had to push the seat up, and of course it wouldn't stay. I offered to hold it, because no way was I crawling into that small, pitch-black space.

Greg leaned in, tossing bags out. After more than one landed on my toes, I stretched to one side and only used my fingers to keep the seat propped up. With a triumphant noise, he emerged, the emergency bag in hand. Thankfully, the flashlight was a crank one and not battery operated. Once he'd wound it up, he pulled his gloves on and stuffed a bottle of water into his pocket.

Then he turned again to me. "I'll be as quick as I can, okay, Jellybean?"

I pressed my lips together, trying to keep a lid on my emotions, but I couldn't help throwing my arms around him once more. I squeezed him tightly, and he held me, one gloved hand smoothing my tangled hair.

He touched a kiss to my forehead. "Goodb—"

I clamped a hand over his mouth. "Don't you dare say that to me," I said furiously. I blinked several times before I could speak again. "See you soon." I watched him fight a smile behind my fingers, one that spread across his face as soon as I removed my hand.

"See you soon."

We'd agreed that I'd stay in the back seat since the snow would have to go somewhere, and some of it would end up in the car. He'd get out, find the cabin, and come back for me. I watched him shove the passenger door, his muscles hidden under his winter layers, but I knew he was straining. The door slowly opened wider and wider, some snow spilling in like we knew it would.

Time was of the essence now. The cold had seeped into the car, sucking out the heat. Greg would be completely exposed to the elements, and the snow was still coming down. He offered me a reassuring wave before he disappeared completely, shutting the door behind him.

The car already seemed smaller. I sat down hard, pulling my knees to my chest and wrapping my arms around them. I kept glancing at the windows, but they were in solid white. *Nothing but walls in every direction, no light, no sky, no moon, no —*

I cut off my train of thought, knowing it would get me nowhere fast. *Greg's cabin.* I'd think about that. *Would it be big and spacious?* I laughed because knowing Greg, it would be a one room hut, built out of Lincoln logs with a fireplace you had to cook over, minimalist all the way. And neat as a pin.

How long would we be stranded there? If we even made it to the cabin. *No. When* we made it to the cabin, I'd have to talk to him, tell him I'd overheard his stories about me. My chest ached once more, hoping this wasn't how we were going to end things.

I glanced around the car. Was the light growing dimmer? I wondered how long he'd been gone. Why hadn't I checked my phone when Greg left? I pulled it out now, surprised to see it was one-thirty-five a.m., officially over an hour into the New Year. *What a way to begin.*

My breathing started coming in shorter, quick breaths, and my eyes darted from window to window. I couldn't focus on anything but the walls and the solid white behind the panes of glass.

Still hugging my knees, I started rocking back and forth. *What else can I do? Count.* That's right, one technique my therapist had suggested was counting. *One Mississippi. Two Mississippi.*

Two hundred of those miserable moments later, and I hated the state. *Why Mississippi anyway? And where is Greg?* I was going to die here, a Rhonda-sicle, frozen and alone in an upside-down Town Car with dirty pictures from Kevin on my phone. I wouldn't even live to exact my revenge on that sleazy scumbag.

Just then the door on my right opened, and more snow tumbled in. A bright light shone in my face, making me hold up my hand as I squinted.

"Sorry that took so long," Greg said, his cheery voice making me tremble as I wrapped my mind around his presence. "Hand me a bag, will you, Jellybean?"

He came back. He found the cabin. My relief at his appearance overwhelmed me, and I dissolved into a tearful puddle, burying my head in my knees.

"Oh, shit, Rhonda." His voice drew closer as he continued murmuring, "Rhonda, hon, I'm sorry. I'm here, it's okay." His arms came around me, encompassing me, knees and all.

Together we rocked. My tears froze on my cheeks, and I started shaking.

"Jellybean, you need to get warm." He picked me up, maneuvering me out of the car. His big boots crunched in the knee-high snow as he marched through the dark, the flashlight's narrow beam lighting our way. Wood reverberated beneath his feet when he connected with the cabin's porch, and he set me down in front of the door. "Go on in, you just gotta punch in the code. It's your birthday, month and day. I'll grab our bags."

Wait, what? Why would his code be my birthday? I stood stunned for a second before common sense sunk in, and I punched in ten-eighteen. The keypad beeped, the deadbolt opened, and I walked in. An LED lantern sat on the dining room table, lighting the spacious room with high ceilings. A stairway sat beyond, leading to a second floor. But I found my way to the plush couch, plopped myself on it and promptly passed out from sheer exhaustion.

* * * *

I knew I was dreaming. It was one of the recurring nightmares I'd had since being locked in that closet. The dream always took place with me trapped in the trunk of a car, banging on the lid as water rose steadily. Like someone had pushed the car into a lake with me in it.

But this time was different. I heard Greg's voice calling my name, and I answered him. It was enough to pull me out of my nightmare but panic still held me tight in its grip. I rolled to one side, my covers tangling around my legs and my shirt catching under me. The collar pulled taut against my neck, and I couldn't bear it. Couldn't handle one more thing restraining me. I flung the covers off and ripped my shirt over my head.

The dim light showed an unfamiliar room, and I was in an unfamiliar bed.

When the bed dipped beside me, I shrank away until the sweet scent of peppermint cut through my panic. "Greg," I gasped.

"I'm here, Jellybean. What do you need?"

I dove for him, and he caught me, cradling me to his bare chest as he rocked us back and forth in the safety of his embrace. It didn't matter that I was nearly naked, this was bigger than that. I gulped in ragged breaths as I clung to him. I needed to ground myself in the present and one of the therapist's techniques jumped to my mind.

Five things I could see. Though the light was dim, it was enough. I saw Greg's bare shoulder, pine plank walls, a trunk under a window, a quilt draped over the trunk, and a sturdy end table with my phone resting on it.

Four things I could hear. The wind howled outside. Snow battered against the pane of glass. Greg's heart beat beneath my ear, steady and calm compared to my racing one. His chest rose as he inhaled between murmurs, and I focused on his husky voice.

Three things I could touch. All of them were Greg. His chest beneath my cheek. His strong arms cradling me. His thighs beneath me, supporting me.

Two things I could smell. *Peppermint and cedar, of course.* I drew in a heady breath, then another, and another.

One thing I could taste.

I leaned back, my gaze locking on his lips. I reached up to thread my hand through his hair, tugging his mouth toward mine. "Please?" I asked when he hesitated.

His throat bobbed as he swallowed, but he didn't protest. His soft lips met mine in a tentative kiss that I lost myself in. Sparks jolted through me, burning the remnants of panic in their wake.

Greg finally pulled away, sucking in a ragged breath. "You okay?"

I nodded, wishing things were okay between us. I wanted more, wanted to push him to the bed where—

I shut down my thoughts and climbed off him. "Thank you," I said softly.

His jaw clenched as he stood up and raked a hand through his hair. "You're welcome."

He turned to the door, and my nightmare sprang once more to the front of my mind. The walls already felt like they were closing in, more with every step he took away.

"Wait, Greg!" I called frantically. When he turned back toward me, I held out my hand, reaching for him. "Please. Please stay with me." He frowned, but I didn't give up. "It's the only way I'll sleep. I can already feel the panic coming for me." I sounded broken to my own ears, but I couldn't bring myself to care. "Don't leave me."

A whoosh of breath left him, and he hurried back to my side, scooping me once more into his arms. "I'm here, Jellybean, for as long as you need me."

I huddled there for several long seconds, relief coursing through me as I soaked in his offered comfort. I knew things couldn't go back to the easy way they'd been before the wedding. But we'd both been through an ordeal tonight, and I was grateful he was here.

I moved out of his embrace, laying down with my back to him. I scooted until my ass touched his hip, silently begging for him to hold me again. He read me loud and clear, his arm sliding under my head. His warm body curled around me, and I pressed against him. I felt safe in his embrace, folded neatly in his arms as if they would ward off any hint of bad dreams. Soon the rhythm of his chest brushing my back steadied, and I knew he'd fallen asleep.

I stayed awake, trying to still my jumbled mind. The door was propped open, illuminating a hallway beyond, and an LED lantern gleamed through. Warmth flooded me at the image of Greg making sure my door was open enough for me to have light. My throat grew tight as I slid my hand up to cover his, where it rested against my abdomen. I really could sleep safe tonight, thanks to Greg.

In more ways than one.

Stiffness, and not the fun kind, greeted me when I woke up. I groaned before I remembered I wasn't alone. Or was I? There were no arms curled around me, no warm body pressed against my back. Greg's side of the bed was empty and cold. He'd been up for a while then.

The muted light coming through the window gave no hint to what time it was. I tried to stretch, but it was too painful, so I gave up. I would have just been content to lie here forever, without exploring how excruciating standing would be. But I had to pee. *Stupid bladder.*

With a heavy sigh, I braced myself then just went for it. *Bad idea.* My neck and right shoulder screamed at me. Okay, I needed to baby them a little. So I shifted more onto my left side and managed to shimmy off the bed. Straightening fully also hurt but at least it was bearable.

I was still shirtless, only in my panties but I couldn't even think about getting dressed. The less movement, the better. Each step was carefully measured and executed, bringing me that much closer to the door.

At last, I reached it, hoping there was a bathroom nearby. I peered down the hallway. To my left was the landing before the staircase, with another door between me and the stairs. Two doors beckoned across the way, and I took my chances on the farther one. A full-length mirror startled me, hanging on the wall at the end of the hall.

I lurched into view, biting back a gasp at the multi-colored stripe slashing across my torso. *Holy shit.* I stared at the band, dark red and deep purple that hovered on being blue mottled together from the top of my right shoulder to my opposite hip. Another gasp sounded behind me, and I saw Greg in the mirror.

"Jellybean." My name came out as an apology, dripping with guilt and remorse. "Does it feel as bad as it looks?"

I forced myself not to hold in my tears. "I'm pretty stiff."

His jaw clenched as he held in his emotions. "I've got some salve that'll help." He turned on his heel, his footsteps slamming on the stairs. "Get back to bed."

It was an order, and I bristled at it. I ignored his command as I headed for the door I thought was the bathroom. My hand touched the cold metal knob, and I pushed it open to find I was right. I let out a sigh of relief just as those footsteps pounded back up the stairs.

"Rhonda—"

"Dammit, Greg," I bit out, mortified at having to explain it to him. "I have to pee, okay? So let me do my business, then I'll happily go collapse back into bed. I'm not up because I want to be." I would have shot him a glare along with my scalding words, but my neck wouldn't cooperate. Instead, I shuffled into the bathroom.

When I opened the door a few minutes later, a chagrined Greg stood across the hall. "I'm sorry," he said softly. "Please let me carry you back to bed."

The thought of trying to walk back made me want to scream. My nod was small. "My right shoulder is the worst, and my neck."

He picked me up, so my left side was cradled against him, his hand strong across my back, finding a non-tender place before he scooped me up. When he lay me down on the bed, my shoulder barely jostled at all.

Chapter Nineteen

I'd just started to relax when I remembered our mission. "Avery!" I pushed up with my left elbow, wincing at my sudden movement and the searing pain.

Greg flinched just watching me. "Rhonda, you're in no condition to go anywhere. I know you want to help your friend, but the blizzard is worse now. And you can't even walk to the bathroom, let alone sit for hours in a cramped car." When I started to protest, his forehead crinkled in admonishment. "What would Avery tell you to do?"

My lower lip jutted out. "She'd probably yell at me for trying to drive to her in a blizzard in the first place."

"That sounds about right." We both chuckled. "And I'm sorry to say, there's no phone service here. We're lucky we landed near shelter, and that neither of us were hurt worse than this." He gestured to me. "So, let's just be thankful for that. We should focus on getting you better, then we can concentrate on leaving, okay?"

I sighed. "Okay." I glanced up at him. "What about you? Are you okay?"

"In better shape than you, that's for sure." One side of his mouth tipped up. "I've got a few bruises, but nothing like these. And I'm a little stiff, but I knew it was coming. You got tossed around like a rag doll back there, going every which way while I could lean into it. I propped myself against the ceiling when we flipped." He winked. "One of the advantages of being tall."

The humor didn't quite hide the guilt, and I opened my mouth to set him straight.

But he held up a white tube. "I fell down my steps one winter, bruised my entire side and hurt my back. I've still got a bunch of supplies from it, but this was the best stuff." He unscrewed the cap, then hesitated. "May I?"

There was no way I could reach my problem areas myself with my limited mobility. "Please." I shifted onto my left side, baring my neck and shoulder for him to start with.

"It might be cold."

I winced at the temperature difference, but then a pleasant tingling sensation spread wherever he rubbed in the salve, accompanied by a menthol smell. I hummed at the instant measure of relief that followed his touch. He rubbed gently as he went, working my sore muscles enough to get the blood flowing.

A throat clearing was all the warning I had before he asked, "When we were dancing, I said I thought we were past all this, and you said you thought so too. What did you mean by that?"

His question caught me off guard. I tried to turn my head before I thought about it, ending up in a wince mixed with a groan. But his hands just moved to my shoulder, and I could picture him patiently waiting for my answer. I didn't give it right away, holding on to it until he finished with my back because I needed to see him. His hands moved to the front of my shoulder, working toward my collarbone.

"I heard you telling your friends diva stories about me." His eyebrows furrowed, like he was confused, so I said, "Like how I had to make an entrance at Derek's birthday party."

Those magic fingers stilled as he stared at me. "Jellybean, I was talking about Piper. Somehow a bunch of the guys found out I'd chauffeured her around, before she became a big star. They followed me all night, begging for stories. So that's what I was doing, telling them about Piper the diva."

I blinked, taking my turn at being confused. Guilt washed over me at how I'd thought the worst of Greg. I'd blamed him and jumped to conclusions, the same way he always did with me. His hands started working again, but he didn't meet my stare.

With my left hand, I reached to touch his wrist. "I'm so sorry Greg. I did the same thing I accused you of doing when you first saw the picture Kevin sent."

His mouth tilted up a fraction of an inch. "Now I know why you got so pissed."

Shit. "Yeah, it sucks, doesn't it? Which is why we should both promise to never, ever do it again. As long as we're together." It was a peace offering and a leap of faith all rolled into one.

"Is that what we are?" Hope buoyed his words.

For once, he hadn't shut me down and answering hope blossomed in me. I grinned, then rubbed my thumb over the back of his hand. "I don't let just anyone cover me in ointment. No matter what they say it does." This time the smile tipped his lips up far enough that his dimple appeared, so I knew I was forgiven.

"I should hope not." His gaze followed the red and purple stripe, his throat bobbing. "This might hurt the most because of the bruising, but I swear it'll help."

With a bracing breath, I removed my hand from his. "It's okay, Greg. I know you'd never hurt me on purpose." And I grit my teeth as his fingers began covering my bruise with the salve.

Finally, the torture was over, and he put the cap on the ointment, wiping his hands on a towel he'd brought. "I have soup or oatmeal plus the food we packed. You should eat so you can take an anti-inflammatory."

It made sense. "Soup, please."

"Okay." He brushed a kiss against my forehead and covered me up. "Back in a few." He flinched as he straightened, so fast, I barely caught it.

"Wait."

He paused.

"If you sit here" — I patted my left side with my good hand — "I can get your back, the parts you can't reach. With the ointment."

A crease furrowed his brow.

"I'm sure you're hurting too, Greg. Let me do this. Let me help." I knew it wasn't much, but I wanted to do something for him. He always looked after me.

He nodded, stripping off his shirt as he walked around to the other side of the bed. His torso had a diagonal line of bruises from his neck to his ribs, but they were much spottier than mine. And not nearly as dark. He slid back on the bed until he was within reach.

"Where does it hurt?" There weren't any bruises on his back, but I'd bet his shoulders were stiff from trying to steer the car.

"Both shoulder blades."

Thankfully I had full mobility of my left arm, and I could reach his broad back. He hissed as the cool cream touched his skin. I took my time rubbing it in, making sure I covered the full area. "Anywhere else?"

"My neck."

I frowned. "You're too tall!"

He chuckled, moving to lie on his side, still facing away from me. "Better?"

I spread the cream over his tense neck, grinning when he groaned under my touch. "I should be asking you that."

Rolling over, he stared at me with an intense gaze. "I am. Thank you." A wave of emotion passed between us, heady and strong. He blinked then scooted off the bed, his movements more fluid than before. "I'll be back with that soup."

I stared at the ceiling until he returned, wondering what would happen next between us. I couldn't handle much more of this roller coaster, and I hoped things calmed down. He helped me sit up enough to get half a can of soup in me, then I swallowed some Motrin.

"You should take some too."

"I will. After I finish off your soup." He pulled a pill bottle out of his pocket after a moment's hesitation. "My back acts up once in a while after that fall I took. Muscle relaxers got me through, and I always make sure I have some on hand, especially when visiting up here." He glanced at me. "You ever had Flexeril?"

"Once."

He nodded. "Good. No bad reaction?"

"No," I said, wanting to shake my head, but refraining at the last second. "Other than sleeping a lot."

His lips tipped into a soft, gentle smile. "That's the best thing for you right now. Want one?"

I couldn't argue. "Just half." Normally I wouldn't share someone's meds, but this was a unique situation, and we weren't anywhere near a doctor to get some of my own. I could only guess the status of the car. And from what I knew of cabins in the Upper Peninsula, I doubted there were any neighbors to call on for help.

Before I could analyze the situation much more, I drifted into a deep sleep.

Time passed in a foggy dream. I knew Greg woke me up for medication, I knew I got up to use the bathroom, and I knew I ate. But I had no idea how much time passed between each incident or what day it was. Everything just blurred together.

Finally, I woke up on my own, mostly clear-headed. I lay there, marveling that I could turn my head without wanting to scream when I heard footsteps in the hall.

Greg appeared in the doorway, smiling when he saw me awake. "Hey!"

I grinned back. "Look." I showed him that I could turn my head, and he seemed appropriately impressed. "You cannot imagine how good this feels."

"I'm so glad you're starting to feel better." He set down the bowl of soup and glass of water on the end table.

"You're moving better, too."

He grinned. "I am. You rubbing that ointment on me made all the difference."

Warmth bloomed in my chest. "What day is it?" His frown made me want to laugh. I wasn't the only one caught in a time warp.

"Monday, I think. You've been out for a couple days."

Wow. "Morning? Afternoon?"

"Two in the afternoon." He grimaced. "Sorry about the late lunch. That just happens to be when your meds line up."

What a sweetie, watching out for me like that. "How's the blizzard?"

He grimaced. "Don't let the quiet fool you. I have a feeling this might be the eye of the storm. We'll have to wait and see." He sighed, looking at the dull sky through the window. "It'll take a bit to shovel us out. Besides, I want to make sure you're fully recovered before we even attempt an escape."

I sighed too, knowing he was right. "Does anyone else know where we are? What if we're stuck here forever?" I almost kicked myself after I asked it, not wanting to know the answer. *Stuck in a remote cabin with Greg forever? Sign me up.*

His chuckle rumbled between us. "My family knows about the cabin, and they know I'm smart enough to head this way if things were bad. So, they'd probably check here first. But it'll be a while before they can even get to us, with the road conditions."

The word family struck a chord with me. Derek and Avery would be missing me sooner than later since we'd been texting often. I didn't want them to worry. "There's really no phone around here?"

He shook his head. "Not unless we go into town."

Resigned, I reached up to brush a piece of hair off my forehead and instead encountered a greasy clump.

Ew. As I touched more of my hair and further assessed myself, I realized I was in desperate need of a bath. "Greg? As good as that soup smells, there's something that smells more." I waited a beat. "Me. I've never needed a shower more in my life. Or a bath. Or something." A bath sounded heavenly, provided I could get clean first.

He chuckled at my melodramatics. "Lucky for you, we have one of those. And the water heater is hooked up to the wood burning stove, so you have unlimited hot water at your disposal."

I pretended to swoon. "You sure know how to sweet talk a girl." I worked my way to a sitting position. To his credit, he let me feel out how much help I needed, not babying me, but he stayed within reach in case I wanted him. I managed to walk to the bathroom on my own.

He showed me where everything was, made sure I got into the tub okay, then left me to it. I thought sitting was safest. Luckily there was a shower wand, so I brought that down with me. I washed my hair twice then thoroughly scrubbed everything else, rinsed and ran a fresh tub of water. The effort wore me out, but it felt good to have actually done something.

I lay there, relaxing and enjoying the change of scenery, as well as the hot water that eased some of the lingering stiffness in my body.

Greg poked his head in. "Just checking on you. Need anything?"

"Some water to drink would be nice." I added a please as he disappeared.

When he came back, he had a water bottle in his hand. "Here you go."

I smiled up, not the least bit bothered that I was naked before him. "Thank you." I took a sip, staring at his handsome face, thinking of how sweet it was that he'd taken such good care of me. "And thanks for everything, Greg. I'm feeling a lot better. That's all because of you."

He couldn't seem to figure out where to look. His gaze would drift lower down my body and shoot back up to my face. Then he'd shift his weight. "You're welcome."

The words had an edge to them, and I watched the anger build in him. I set the water bottle down and asked quietly, "Why do you do that?"

"What?" The edge was harder, sharper.

I tried not to flinch. "You're mad at me. Why do you always get mad when I don't have clothes on?"

My words seemed to knock the wind out of him as they hung in the air between us. He sank to his knees next to the tub. "Jellybean, look at me." The sharpness was gone, replaced with an earnest pleading I couldn't resist.

I kept my chin tilted down, but I glanced up at him through my eyelashes.

"It's not you I'm mad at. It's never been you." He laced his fingers through mine, bringing my hand to his lips. "You are beyond gorgeous, and I can't always control myself around you." There was an awkward pause.

When he spoke again, his voice was lower and huskier. "Like now for example, I feel like a horny teenager with no self-control." He brought my hand down to brush against the front of his jeans, against the erection straining behind the denim. He inhaled sharply when my fingers grazed the bulge. "The only person I'm mad at is myself."

I sat in shocked silence for a long moment, too stunned to even move my hand. "It's not me?"

Pain laced his face, and he reached up to cup my cheek. "It's only you, but not like that. You are exquisite. So beautiful it hurts." He thrust against my hand and leaned over to brush his lips against mine once more. "But never because you did anything wrong. You're perfect."

The words sent a wave of desire through me so strong I almost gasped. He wanted me. All those times he'd been mad, it was because he'd been out of control over me. I bit my lip. "Greg."

He shook his head. "No, you're in no condition to—"

I shut him down with a lusty smirk. "Well, if you won't, then I will." I removed my hand from him, sliding it down my peaked breast, around the splotchy bruises of my stomach and between my legs.

He sucked in a sharp breath. "Rhonda."

"I'd rather have you, Greg, but I'll take what I can get." I moaned as I thought of his hand replacing mine.

He swallowed hard as he watched my fingers nestle between my legs, worry creasing his brow.

"I promise I won't get carried away, but I need this." I reached for his hand. "Touch me. Please."

He hesitated as I tugged, but then he gave in and let me guide his hand between my legs. I shuddered at the delicious feeling of his skilled fingers circling my clit, relieved that the only tension between us was sexual. I relaxed against the tub, groaning when his fingers slipped inside me and his palm hit my swollen clit.

The growing bulge at the front of his jeans had me licking my lips. I assessed my movements, deciding I was up for giving him the same pleasure. He had to pause to help me undo his jeans with his wet fingers, the denim dark where the water had soaked in. Then he shoved his pants down along with his boxers, his eager cock springing up to greet me.

I wrapped my hand around his hot length, grinning when he sighed and thrust against me. My grin fell when his fingers eased down my leg once more to slip back inside me. I arched into him instinctively before he shot me a reprimanding glare. *Right, I promised not to get too rowdy.* His expression softened as he stared at me, then he leaned over the edge of the porcelain tub to claim my mouth with his own.

A wave of giddiness shot through me as I relished being with him. This ease between us, the mutual pleasuring, the incessant need. I wanted it all, and I poured my feelings into that kiss as I stroked his rigid cock.

He deepened the kiss, changed the angle, both of his mouth and his hand. The increased friction against my clit sent pleasure waves through me. He slid a second finger in me, and I fought the urge to arch into him once more. I settled for moaning into his mouth.

I felt him harden in my grasp, and I wondered which of us would cave first. A flutter went through me, signaling I was close. But I fought it until his tongue began thrusting in time with his fingers. I broke our kiss, crying out as I clenched, my orgasm taking over in a flash.

So much for him losing control. My hand was still wrapped around his shaft, and I turned my concentration to him. I expected him to remove his hand, but he kept touching me, teasing me. Did he think I'd come again that easily?

I pumped his cock slowly, loving the groan he let out. I wished I could take him in my mouth, or better yet, feel him fully inside me. But I knew I was already pushing my limits by doing this much.

Increasing my pace, I added a swipe of my thumb over his sensitive ridge on my way up. He hummed, the velvety skin hardening even more, a sure sign he was close. My thumb grew slick with precum, making it easier to slide along his thick shaft. His lips crashed on to mine as he pressed into my hand. I pumped harder as he groaned into my mouth.

Then he went rigid above me, hot liquid spilling over my hand. A Cheshire Cat grin spread across my face as I lay back. A ripple of pleasure went through me as I realized he hadn't stopped either. His lips tipped up in a cocky smirk as he swirled his slick fingers over my needy clit. I clenched at the motion, surprised to find myself so quickly on the brink once more.

I really had been with the wrong guys.

I leaned my head back against the tub, shifting as he slid two fingers inside me once more. His palm hit just right again, and I moaned. I wanted to writhe at the building pleasure within me, but I had to stay still. I settled for panting breaths and gripping the edge of the tub with my slick fingers, coated in Greg's cum.

"That's it, Jellybean. Come for me," Greg said, his voice full of gravel.

The command was enough to send me tumbling over that edge. Bliss crashed over me in wave after wave as I cried out Greg's name. He finally removed his hand, giving me a much-needed break.

Holy shit.

I felt like I had no bones left in me. When I saw the grin on his face, it was so smug, I had to chuckle. "Well don't you look like the cat who ate the cream?"

"I wish."

I shook my head slowly when I realized the double entendre. "Yeah, yeah. I think I'm ready to get out."

He glanced down at his state of undress. "Give me a second, to um, clean up, then I'll help you."

I was thankful for that. Getting into the tub was one thing, but getting out? I wasn't sure if I could manage on my own. Between the journey to the bathtub and the orgasms, I had no energy left. Not to mention trying to pull myself up with my still tender shoulder. It took some doing, and he ended up wet too, but finally I was out of the tub, on my own two feet.

"Ready for soup yet? And a nap? Muscle relaxer?"

I pondered my options while I dried off. "How about clothes and a change of scenery? Got any movies in this place?" I frowned. "Do we even have electricity? Like, are we on the power grid?"

He laughed. "No, it's a generator. Definitely out in the sticks here. But yes, we have a TV, Blu-ray and movies. So, you get dressed, I'll take your soup downstairs, and you holler when you want to come down. Your suitcase is in your room." Greg turned to leave, then said over his shoulder, "Don't you even think about coming downstairs without me."

My lips tipped up, happiness spilling over at the thought of someone caring enough to scold me for being too independent.

Chapter Twenty

I let Greg carry me downstairs. I wasn't ready for sleep, but I was ready to be a slug again. He set me down in front of his movie collection.

After perusing the two shelves, I wrinkled my nose. There wasn't a rom-com in sight. He appeared just then with soup, along with a bowl of popcorn that smelled amazing. I hated to admit how tired I was getting of soup.

"Thought you might like a change of pace."

I grinned. "You read my mind."

Once the food was on the coffee table, he came back to the shelf of movies. "Find anything?"

"Nothing good."

He clasped a hand to his chest like I'd wounded him. "How can you say that? *Lord of the Rings* is on this shelf."

Crossing my arms, I sniffed. "Never seen it."

His jaw dropped. "What? Never?" When I shook my head, he threw up his hands. "Well, I know what we're watching. Good thing we're snowed in with nowhere to go, Jellybean, 'cause you've got some making up to do."

He helped me settle into the couch. It took a minute to find a comfortable position, and he found some extra pillows I could prop myself up with. After he'd put the movie in, he picked my legs up, sliding under them so my calves rested comfortably on his thighs. Then he handed me the bowl of popcorn which I put on my lap between us, and we started the epic tale of *The Lord of the Rings*.

Three hours later, the end credits rolled. Partway through, we had shifted positions, ending with Greg's head on my lap and my feet on the coffee table in front of me. His steady breathing told me he'd fallen asleep at some point.

I sat there, content to think about the movie and marvel over Greg sleeping on me. Never in my wildest dreams had I imagined being holed up in a rural cabin with him, so completely comfortable with each other that this was our evening. I studied the shape of his face, the long eyelashes that curved against his high cheekbones. His lips parted slightly, and he seemed so peaceful.

He'd taken such good care of me these past couple of days, but he'd been in the wreck, too. And I knew there was a lot to do here to keep the heat going, the generator filled, on top of taking care of me. A pang of guilt hit me, that I'd needed so much on my end for recovery. I wished I could've helped more.

The least I could do was let him sleep. Easing over, I managed to reach the remote where it lay in front of his stomach, then I shut off the TV. In the absence of the noise, I heard the wind howling again along with snow battering against the windows. He'd been right about the blizzard, too. I sighed, but there was nothing I could do, so I leaned my head back to rest, just for a few minutes.

The next thing I knew, Greg was tucking me in upstairs. My eyes flew open, meeting his in a flash of panic.

"Easy, Jellybean, I just thought you'd be more comfortable in your bed." His voice was low and soothing as his hand stroked my hair. I relaxed again with his touch. "Want any medicine?"

I tried to assess my soreness through my groggy haze. "Yes, please."

He had some ready, along with a granola bar. Then I drifted back to sleep. Sunshine, actual honest-to-goodness sunshine, streamed in my window the next morning. I hadn't realized how rare that was until now. This was probably the second day since we'd been on this trip that I'd seen her golden rays on full display, not muffled behind a thick layer of clouds and snow. It felt glorious.

The sunniness carried over to my mood, because I felt amazing, too. The stiffness and pain were almost gone. I only had a few twinges when I stretched, dressed and made my way downstairs, smiling as I went. I'd been so out of it, I hadn't really noticed the details of the cabin, its white pine log walls, the wood trimmed panes of glass, the sleek hardwood floor beneath my feet. Cozy, but sleek, and perfect for Greg.

The stairs were wide slabs of wood, each swirled with age rings and knots but sanded to a smooth finish. They were beautiful. At the bottom was a landing, then three more stairs perpendicular to the others. The artwork hanging on the wall of the landing caught my attention.

It was mine. I stopped in my tracks, startled to find it here. I must not have seen it yesterday, either too busy looking at Greg, or I'd missed it because of the angle he'd carried me. It was a large, ugly thing I'd done not long after graduating high school. Yolanda had been crushing on a local artist who taught a four-week class.

I'd worked really hard on it, though. Just staring at it brought back the smell of the thick oil paint, the rubber cement I'd used to glue on the strips of news headlines and the bottle caps. I'd made a limo out of various bits of mixed media, a limo because Greg was my constant, the one I'd always been able to count on.

My painting had been featured in a local art show, with an honorable mention for its use of mixed media. I had been so proud, sitting on my stool and waiting for my family to arrive. Every time a person had walked in, my hopes bubbled up, then obliterated when I didn't know them. I watched jealously at Yolanda's steady stream of people coming in to support her.

While I had no one.

Ten minutes before the show was over, I was ready to give up. To ask Greg to take me home where I could throw away the stupid painting and never see it again.

Then he'd ambled in. My heart leapt into my throat as warmth spread through me. Of course, Greg was here. Of course, he'd come in early, just to see my painting. He was my constant, my friend. And it took all my willpower not to barrel over to him for a huge hug.

That was the day my feelings shifted. As I watched him meander his way through the exhibits toward me,

I realized the warmth spreading through me was more than friendship, more than excitement at seeing a familiar face. My breath caught as I looked at him, truly seeing how handsome he actually was.

I thought back to all the guys I'd dated, and they all fell short when I compared them to Greg. His gorgeous eyes, filled out body, and warm smile didn't hurt either. When he reached my painting, I was speechless for the first time.

"Hey, Jellybean," he said.

I gave an awkward wave as my heart pounded in my chest. A crinkle had appeared in his brow as he studied the limo, and he'd stared at me for several seconds before looking back at the painting. A flash of longing zipped through me, and I'd finally found my voice.

"What do you think?"

One corner of his mouth tipped up. "I've never seen anything like it."

"Thank you, Greg," I said softly. He'd turned to me with a frown, so I added, "You've always been there for me, and I really appreciate it. Especially today."

He gave me a sharp nod. "Of course." And he'd stepped away as the distance between us grew.

The walls he put up only made me want him more. I'd given him the painting when he dropped me off that night, but I'd never seen it again and he'd never brought it up.

To find it here, now, had me reeling.

"Greg?" I called. My voice echoed back to me off the cavernous ceiling. Disappointment rolled over me when I didn't get an answer.

Maybe he was outside.

I wandered through the dining room to peer out at the front porch, but I couldn't see much besides snow. I glanced at the painting again. He'd kept it. I'd pursued him that entire summer with no hint of reciprocation, but he'd kept my painting. Hope sprouted within me.

The smooth hardwood floor was cool under my bare feet as I padded into the kitchen. A small corridor branched off behind the pantry, and I saw a back door, so I investigated. It led to another porch, and I could barely make out Greg near a lean to several yards away. He was filling the wood burning stove.

My stomach rumbled and I decided to find something to eat, but when I turned, I noticed a key rack on the wall. Dangling from one key was a familiar blue lanyard.

The one I'd given him for Christmas when Papa had died.

The back door opened up, and Greg appeared in a snowy flash. He quickly shut the door. Stomping his feet to rid them of snow, he grinned at me before he began stripping off his many layers.

I picked up the lanyard and waited. When he was down to his jeans and long-sleeved shirt, I held it out to him. "You saved this. And my painting." It wasn't really a question, but I hoped that just maybe he'd explain. I searched him, his face so familiar I'd memorized it. Would I see anything different this time?

One corner of his mouth tipped up as he took the lanyard from me. "No one had ever made me anything before."

I followed him into the living room where he sank onto the couch and patted the cushion beside him. I plopped down, waiting.

He ran his fingers over the woven plastic. "Do you know what my favorite candy is?"

I shook my head, wondering what that had to do with anything.

"It's jellybeans," he said quietly. "My favorite flavor of gum?"

"Peppermint." My forehead crinkled as I stared at him.

"Yeah, but do you know why?" He waited a beat for me to answer, and again I shook my head. "The summer after you graduated that's all you chewed. I used to like spearmint. But then you started asking me for gum before you got out of the car, and if I didn't have your flavor, you'd crinkle up your nose." His gaze drifted over my face. "I switched to peppermint."

"Your lock code is my birthday." I stared at him, needing him to put the pieces together for me. The tentative hope growing within me had already been scorched to ash once. This had to come from Greg.

"And my favorite holiday is Christmas because I get to give my favorite person her favorite present..." He paused so I could finish the sentence.

"Jellybeans." I felt like this was all a fantastical dream, that maybe I was still in my half-drugged state, and I'd never actually woken up. I desperately needed him to connect the dots. "Greg, what are you trying to say?"

His shoulders slumped, and he sighed. "I'm not good with big speeches." The smile he gave me was tight. "According to Carrie, it was my biggest fault."

He'd been, what, nineteen when they broke up? But I needed a concrete admission from those lips. Maybe we could work up to it. "Did you date anyone else after her?"

"Not seriously." He turned the lanyard end over end. "I was a mess when I met you, but you helped me even then, Rhonda. Having someone to look out for took the focus off myself and my problems."

He paused, glancing at the painting. "It killed me when no one showed up for your art show." The words were strained, his voice low and taut.

I felt like we were closing in on what I needed to hear. "I can't believe you still have that awful thing. And hung it on your wall, no less." My eighteen-year-old self would have died to know that twenty-four-year-old Greg had kept the painting. Cherished it even.

"It's not awful. It's a piece of you, and no part of you is awful." He touched my cheek, a featherlight brush of his knuckle that sent a thrill coursing through me. "Watching you at the art show...Rhonda, that was when my eyes were finally opened to the beautiful woman you'd become. It was all I could do not to pull you in my arms, to comfort you, to hold you..." His voice dropped. "To kiss you."

His throat bobbed as he swallowed. "I set some hard boundaries for myself right then, especially since you were my employer's daughter."

Shock rippled through me. He'd seen me, even then.

"The night of the gala, when you asked me how you looked...then you kissed me —" The words came out rushed, sounding desperate and wistful. "I was so surprised, so entrenched in the little fence I'd set up for myself that I couldn't see past it. And later, you made me see. In the back seat of the limo."

His voice grew husky, deeper. "I didn't even know you were with anyone else at first. All I could see was you. By the time I realized it, it was too late." He swallowed, ducking his head. "I didn't even know what to feel that night. Hurt, anger, embarrassment."

He paused for a moment, then the words poured out of him, not even giving me time to process. "So, I left. I tried to forget you. Tried to date other girls and find someone else. But you ruined me, Rhonda." Raw emotion filled his voice as he said, "You're like the sun, bright and beautiful, but also blinding. Every other woman seems washed out and pale in comparison."

"It's taken me forever to get here, to figure out how to say anything to you. My Jellybean dilemma," he whispered in one husky breath. "I love you, Rhonda Elgin."

My head spun, hearing those words. There wasn't enough oxygen in the room to help my brain comprehend them. I felt dizzy and completely unmoored, as if I was back in that car, spinning end over end.

"Rhonda?"

I allowed every ounce of my overwhelming happiness to spill out into my smile. "And you don't think you're any good at making speeches." I flung my arms around him. His words flowed through me, like a shaft of sunlight thawing the last bit of ice in my soul. We clung to each other for what felt like forever before I pulled back. I kept hold of his hand, though, that contact a vital part of me right now.

It was my turn. I already knew he loved me, but I wanted to tell him my side. He deserved that much, at least.

I smiled up at him. "You've always been important to me. I could depend on you like no one else. You showed up." I squeezed his hand, basking in the warmth radiating through me. "You always made me feel seen. Whether it was jellybeans or dance recitals or art shows, I'm so grateful you were there, Greg. I'm so glad I had you as a friend."

I glanced once more at the painting. "The art show was when my feelings shifted."

He grinned, moving closer so our thighs touched.

"The moment you showed up, I wanted to barrel over and throw myself into your arms. I couldn't even speak when you came over." I squeezed his hand. "I tried that whole summer to get you to notice me, but you never did. I thought kissing you would show you my true feelings."

Chagrin washed through me. "I'm sorry, Greg. I know I took you by surprise, and I know I went about it the wrong way." I sighed. "Not to mention the whole thing in the limo."

I stared at the floor as I thought about the days after the gala. "Then you left." It hurt just to say the words, but I went on, forcing them out. "If I couldn't have you, my choice didn't matter. Kevin was predictable, easily manipulated, and he didn't care what I did as long as it didn't take away from his fun. We would have gotten married then led two separate lives, a power couple in name only."

Greg let go of my hand, putting his arm around me and pulling me to him.

I nuzzled his chest, grateful for the comfort. "But when I saw what Avery and Derek had, it reminded me what I was missing out on. Then you started showing up everywhere. At Liam's, when we played darts and pool. At my house when you brought Avery's clothes and stood up to Kevin. Then you drove me home from the gala."

His deep chuckle rumbled through me. "Another gala." He tugged me even closer, and I happily pressed into him.

"Thank you for seeing me," I said, quietly as I rested in his embrace. "And for being there when no one else was. I love you, too, Greg Peterson." The words felt right, hanging between us. All our time apart, all our rough patches and misunderstandings, had led us here to this moment. I did love him, more than I ever thought possible.

"Rhonda." My name was part growl, part plea as Greg bent toward me.

I instinctively moved to meet him, twisting so our torsos melded together. Our mouths collided, hungry, passionate, desperate to solidify the claims of love we'd just staked.

He pulled back, abruptly. "Wait, you're in no shape to—"

"Greg," I cut him off, "what did we say about making assumptions?"

He chuckled, but the laughter turned to a moan as my lips covered his once more. I threw my leg over his lap to straddle him. His hands slid down my hips to cup my ass and pull me tight against his growing length. Need coursed through me as I ground against him, gripping his shoulders.

Too many clothes separated us. I tore my mouth from his to yank off my shirt, and he frantically followed my lead. I wasn't wearing a bra, and the heat of our skin meeting almost made me burst into flames. His hands skimmed up my ribs, avoiding my bruises, as we devoured each other. I couldn't stop touching him, his shoulders, his pecs, his abs.

Every time we'd explored before paled in comparison, because now he was mine.

Greg pulled back, muttering, "Hang on. As much as I want this, I think we should move to the bedroom. You're not a hundred percent yet, and I don't want you getting hurt."

I pouted, brushing my chest against his once more. "Fine. But this *is* happening."

Fire flared in his stormy eyes, and a slow, predatory smile spread over his lips. "Damn right, it is." He kissed me gently, then nuzzled my cheek. "And you're going to come all over my cock." His gruff whisper made me freeze on his lap.

Why would he bring that up now? What if — ?

His hot breath cascaded down my neck. "Because we'll keep going until you do."

Excitement pulsed within me at the promise, pushing away my doubts. I rocked my hips, grinding against him again. "Well, what are we waiting for?" I leapt off him, tugging on his hand, desperate to continue.

I paused at the landing, looking up at him with all the wanton desire coursing through me. He groaned and yanked me to him, making my stomach flip. His mouth claimed mine as his hand cupped my aching breast. I arched into his touch, moaning.

He pinned me gently to the wall, so I was caught between the hard planes of pine and those of his firm torso. One hand cupped my ass, and I looped my leg around his, craving that friction.

"Someday, I'll fuck you, just like this," he growled. "Would you like that, Jellybean?"

My impatience got the better of me as his dick rubbed over my apex. "Just get me upstairs, Greg."

Chapter Twenty-One

He carried me to the bedroom as I covered him with kisses. He sat heavily on the bed, me still on his lap, my apex pressing against the straining front of his jeans. His lips sought mine as he scooted backward, our desperate need for each other not ebbing for one second. I moved with him, my legs framing his.

When his back hit the wall, he gripped my ass, grinding his hard length over my aching pussy. My hips started moving on their own as I rocked against him, needing the friction. He tore his mouth from mine, blazing a trail of scorching kisses down my neck. When his lips clamped over my aching peak, I threw my head back at the pure jolt of pleasure that shot straight to my core.

"Damn, I love these." He swirled his tongue once more around my nipple before moving to the other side. "You on top makes this perfect." He paused. "What's your favorite position, Jellybean?"

Embarrassment crept in, until I remembered this was Greg. "I don't have one yet, but I bet you can change that."

An unspoken promise smoldered between us, and my breath caught in my throat, knowing he'd rise to the challenge.

Then horror crossed his face. "Shit! I don't have any condoms."

We stared at each other for a long moment as I went over our options. Desire roared within me, my desperation for him a painful ache that needed to be fulfilled. But I'd never had sex without one before.

I knew that Greg would understand. If I said no, we'd find another way to sate ourselves. But I wanted him, all of him. I wanted to feel his cock pounding into me, wanted to reach that peak with him inside of me.

So I said, in a voice not much louder than a whisper, "I have an IUD. And I got tested after Kevin. He's the last one I..."

Greg searched me, as if looking for any hint of hesitation. "I get tested at my yearly physical. I'm clean, and I haven't been with anyone since my test." His lips pressed together briefly before adding, "If you're sure."

I didn't even pause. "I've never been more sure of anything." I ground against his hard length, feeling more desperate by the second. "Greg, I need you inside me."

He groaned my name, threading his fingers through my hair and pulling my mouth to his once more. "I want to taste you," he murmured against my lips.

"You already are." I couldn't help but tease.

His smirk was devilish as he shook his head. One finger traced my mouth. "Not here." His finger trailed down to my yoga pants, gliding between us until he rested over my heated core. "Here."

I nodded breathlessly, remembering the last time he'd feasted on me. How delicious that orgasm had been.

Gently rolling us over, he knelt between my legs. A wicked smile played on his lips as he tugged the fabric down my hips, my panties joining the pants on the floor. Anticipation surged within me as he knelt between my legs, his hot breath caressing my inner thigh. His lips parted as he ran a finger down my folds. "So wet already." His tempestuous gaze met mine, holding a hint of awe. "All this for me, Jellybean?"

"Only you," I grit out as he slid a finger into my depths.

His tongue lapped at me, and he hummed in pleasure. "Good, because you're the only one I want, Rhonda. The only one."

It was torture of the most exquisite kind, the agonizingly slow pace he started with. I writhed beneath him as my release built within me. Soon, I begged, pleading for more. But he would not yield, increasing little by little until my chest was heaving and my fingers hurt from how tight they clenched the sheets.

The orgasm blindsided me, stealing my breath as wave after wave after wave rocked me. Greg lapped up each one until I finally stopped quaking. I lay in a heap of bliss, feeling boneless from the tsunami of pleasure he'd given me.

"I changed my mind," he said, grinning as he took off his jeans.

Furrowing my brow, I didn't have the energy to actually ask the question. But I was more curious than concerned, his smile telling me I had nothing to worry about.

"*You're* my new favorite flavor."

His dimple appeared, and I grinned back, reaching for him. He carefully lay on top of me in just his boxers, pressing against me enough so I knew he was there. His lips brushed mine. The kiss was soft and gentle, starting slow just like he had between my legs.

"I know what you're doing." I frowned.

"Yeah? Already learning my tricks?" He leaned down to nuzzle my neck with his chin, making me squirm.

Which created more friction, just where I needed it, and heat spread through me. Greg raised up, his arms caging me in as his body hovered over me. A hint of panic trickled in, my claustrophobia raising its head at the most inopportune time. I froze, and he sensed it.

"Jellybean?" he asked, full of concern.

I swallowed, my mind racing for what I needed. I blurted out, "I want to be on top." Me being in charge, unhindered and not pinned down was of the utmost importance in that moment.

"Of course." He didn't ask for questions or explanations, didn't jump to conclusions. He simply moved off me to stand beside the bed. "You still good?"

Already feeling freer, I nodded. "I just felt a little…caged in, I guess," I explained before I reached for his boxers, sliding my fingers in the hem. "But I want this, Greg. I want you."

Relief shone on his face, and the tension melted from his shoulders. I tugged his boxers off, letting them slip to the floor as his magnificent cock jutted before me. I couldn't help running my fingers over its heated length, and I grinned when Greg groaned. He hurried across the bed, settling his back once more against the wall.

Then I crawled to him, slowly, pressing kisses along his thigh. I couldn't resist licking his hardened shaft from the base to the tip of his dewy head. His fingers clenched into fists at his side, but he didn't rush me. I pressed my breasts against him as I trailed kisses up his chiseled abdomen, over his sculpted pecs. When I finally tilted up for a kiss, he pulled me to him.

His lips were brutal in their exploration. Our tongues danced together as I settled my apex against his scorching length. I glided over him once, twice, using the wetness from my arousal to my advantage. He gripped my ass, his hips bucking as he held me in place.

"I can't believe you're finally mine, Rhonda," he gritted out as I ground against him. "Say it again."

I cupped his cheek as I positioned myself above his waiting cock. The love I had for this man was nothing short of overwhelming, and when I searched his face, the feeling echoed in the depths of his intense gaze. The blunt tip of his dick nudged my entrance, and I smiled softly as I whispered, "I love you, Greg," then I lowered myself onto him.

His eyes closed, head tilting back as he let out a soft, short breath. But they flew open again when I sat down all the way, our groans mingling together. He filled me perfectly, hitting all the right spots as I moved on top of him.

I gripped his shoulders as the memory hit me, that moment in the back seat of the limo. An image of Kevin swam before me. But as I kept moving on top of Greg, Kevin melted away and only Greg remained.

Just Greg.

I surged up to press a heated kiss to his lips, then wrapped my arms around his neck. With every movement, another of my broken pieces mended, and I basked in the warmth spreading over my entire body.

"Rhonda, you feel amazing." His lips closed over my nipple.

I could only moan and ride him harder. Then he slipped one hand between us, pressing his thumb against my clit. The friction added a whole new layer to all the incredible sensations. Each pleasure point sent jolts cascading through me, flooding me with bliss. The big ball of ecstasy exploded within me, and I cried out his name.

He watched intently as I shuddered over him, his gaze never leaving me as he waited for my orgasm to subside.

Feeling a little self-conscious, I asked, "What?"

"You're beautiful when you come." One hand came up to cup my cheek, and I smiled, running my fingers over his chest. A pleased grin spread over his face as he pulled me in for a kiss. Just before our lips met, he paused. "I told you you'd come all over my cock." He captured my mouth, thrusting his tongue inside me.

I felt myself clench at his words, desire stirring all over again.

"Ready to keep going?" He moved his hips, and I moaned in response. "Do you mind if I'm on top now?"

I shook my head, not caring what happened next, just needing more. *How is that possible?* He chuckled, the vibrations rumbling through me, hitting my core. In one swift move, he turned us over, never removing himself from me. *Holy shit, that's hot.* I stared as he hovered above me, drinking in his strong shoulders and sculpted chest.

"Are you going to come again for me, Jellybean?" he whispered huskily as he thrust into me, slow and deep.

I arched up to meet him, unable to answer. The tension gathering low in my stomach built higher with each plunge. I clung to him, our breaths mingling as we rocked together. His pace increased, stoking the fire burning inside me, matching the one blazing in his stormy gaze. His thumb stroked my cheekbone. I knew he saw me, everything inside me, and he loved every bit.

I ran my thumb along his jawline, pouring all my love into him as I stared back. I couldn't look away. We were joined in every way, our breaths coming faster and faster as we neared that peak. Together, we tumbled over, shudders wracking our bodies before he collapsed on top of me, careful to not give me all of his weight.

"Rhonda, Jellybean, I love you." We lay there, in post-orgasm haze, still connected, until our heartbeats fused together. Even our breathing matched.

When we did pull apart, I felt more whole than I'd ever been. And whenever I even glanced his way, I thought I'd burst from the wave of happiness that flooded me.

"What's next?" Greg asked, the same happiness shining out of him.

"Shower, food. Next *Lord of the Rings*?"

He smiled. "Perfect. I'll go find us some food then."

I watched him walk away, then headed for the shower. Clean, satisfied for the moment and dressed once more, we scrounged for snacks then settled on the couch for the second *Lord of the Rings*. It was a long movie. And it was a long time to just sit still with our hands to ourselves.

How had I ever thought I didn't enjoy sex?

The rest of the day was like that, we played board games, ate, eventually watched the last of the *Lord of the Rings* trilogy. Each time we interrupted our activity to make love, I thought, this was it, this time would be enough. But it never was. Greg was mine, and sometimes all it took was a sideways glance for me to pounce on him. Or I grazed my knee against his, then found myself lying flat on my back.

We went to bed that night, together, wrapped tightly around each other. I was sore, tired and spent, but more content than I'd ever been.

"Good night, Jellybean. Love you." Greg kissed my hair.

I snuggled tighter against his chest. "Night. Love you too, Just Greg."

* * * *

It was mid-morning the next day when Greg sighed. We'd already had breakfast and made love twice. I handed him the last of the dishes I'd just finished drying, then hoisted myself onto the counter.

"What?"

He bent down to put away the pan, giving me a wonderful view of his ass. When he stood up, he let out a sigh. "Not that I wouldn't love to stay here with you forever, because I would." He leaned into me, pushing my legs apart and clasping his hands at the small of my back.

I kissed his forehead. "Me too. But the real world awaits, and I'm better now." I searched him, concerned at the worry I saw lingering. "Although I was under the impression we were stranded here with no vehicle, no phone, no way of contacting help…?"

His lips tilted up ever so slightly. "That's all true. But I do have a snowmobile, and you are in much better shape now than when we arrived."

A snowmobile? It sounded so absurd, I couldn't help a small giggle.

It was his turn to ask, "What?"

"Remember how I pitched a fit about driving your SUV up here?" A wave of guilt slammed into me. *If I hadn't been such a diva—*

"Yes, I do, and stop that train of thought right there." Greg's hand came up to stroke my cheek. "You didn't control the weather. You didn't make Kevin send that awful photo. And you didn't lose control of the car."

I recognized the same guilt in his voice. "You're not allowed to blame yourself either. Because of you, we're here in one piece. I know what a good driver you are, Greg, and I know if there was any way to keep us on that road, you'd have done it." With that out of the way, I frowned trying to remember what I'd been saying. "Anyway, my point was, considering the fit I threw about the SUV, imagine telling me a week ago that I'd be grateful to have a snowmobile at my disposal."

Our laughter wasn't much, just a few chuckles, but they lightened the mood.

"So, what's the plan?" I listened intently as he started outlining his ideas.

It'd be a quick trip, and I had two options—stay here while he went alone which I immediately vetoed. Too many things could go wrong. *What if he got stranded out there, and we were separated, with no one ever knowing where either of us was?* Option two—I'd ride along to the nearest town, where he'd call around until he found a friend who could help us out. Then we'd hightail it home to Avery and complete our mission.

"When do we leave?" I ran my fingers along the short hair at the nape of his neck.

"I'll have to find snow gear for you, fuel for the snowmobile, and make sure it starts. But there's something I need first." He shifted closer to me, scooting me to the edge of the counter and aligning my center with his rock-hard erection.

"Oh?" I looked up, as innocently as possible. "Whatever could that be?"

He just grinned, his dimple appearing seconds before his mouth devoured mine.

It was a couple of hours before we had everything ready to go. I knew it was time, and I really needed to tell Avery about Kevin, but a huge part of me didn't want to leave my little bubble with Greg. I forced my thoughts aside as I concentrated on prepping for the weather.

I had my own boots of course but finding other snow gear that fit me wasn't easy. And going without wasn't an option. After I'd put on all my layers, I tugged on my helmet then we tromped outside.

"How am I supposed to get on this thing?" I muttered more to myself than Greg.

"What?" he hollered, his voice muffled from the helmet.

I shook my head, but he gestured for me to wait. Removing one of his mittens, he fiddled with the side of my helmet. I heard a click, and his voice echoed in my ears.

"Can you hear me now?"

"We can talk to each other!" I beamed, loving the idea of helmets with built-in radios. They were state of the art, complete with tinted face shields to block out the sun. No squinting required.

He sat down on the snowmobile, pulling his mitten back on. "So, what did you say?"

"I just forgot how hard it is to move with all this crap on." I grinned when his chuckle bounced back to me.

"Do your best." He started the engine then scooted forward, waiting for me to climb on.

I awkwardly plopped down behind him, then wrapped my arms around him as best I could. My helmet hit his with a sharp thwack. "Sorry."

Another chuckle. "Just hold on tight. There are handles on the side if that's easier, not that I don't like snuggling."

Oh. I found the side handles and heaved a relieved sigh. "So much better." I still scooted forward, so my chest was pressed against his back. I wanted him to miss me if I fell off.

"Remember what I told you? Lean with me. It'll help keep your center of gravity if you don't fight the turns. Use me as a shield. I'll block most of the wind and snow for you. Ready?"

I swallowed hard, letting out a deep breath that fogged up my helmet. *Dammit.* "Yep, let's go."

The snowmobile lurched forward on top of the several feet of hardened snow as Greg steered us to the road. Good thing he was driving because I couldn't even tell where the road was supposed to be. Scanning the yard, I realized I had no idea where our car was. Between the fresh accumulation and the wind, it was now just another lump under the snow.

Even when he said we were on the road, I didn't see it. It didn't seem to be plowed. He hadn't been kidding about the cabin being in the middle of nowhere. The nearest town was a good thirty-minute ride, and we still wouldn't be able to use our cell phones. We were in that remote of an area.

"How you doing?"

His voice startled me back to the present. "Good. I'm actually enjoying myself." It was fun zooming along the wintry landscape, trees and bushes and snow flying by. "Maybe —" I hesitated.

"What?" He steered us around a big drift, and I leaned with him.

"Maybe we could do this again, for real. Have a vacation up here and do the tourist thing." I held my breath, remembering how he'd brushed me off when I'd suggested this very thing over lunch at Raymond's.

He turned slightly, as much as the helmet would allow. "You'd want to come back?"

I nodded, then rolled my eyes at myself as I realized he couldn't see me. "Yeah, and again in the summer. I want to eat on Raymond's deck while watching the sunset." I almost didn't catch his next words, they were so low.

"You were serious, at lunch." His tone was oddly tight, and I wasn't sure if I felt relieved or embarrassed that he'd remembered.

"Yeah. I was."

Silence passed between us, the only sound the whine of the engine as Greg took us up a hill. "I'd love that, Jellybean. We'll make it happen."

I wasn't brave enough to release my death grip on the handles, so I settled for leaning harder against him, a sort of no hands hug. The rest of the ride passed in radio silence. I was ready for a break from the engine noise and a change in position when we pulled into what passed for a town in these parts. It had a blinking yellow light with a gas station on a corner. *A blazing metropolis.*

Greg pulled into a parking spot near the door, then waited for me to dismount. He pulled off his helmet and smiled. "We made it."

I smiled back, thrilled to stand upright and stretch my cramped muscles. *Hopefully this place has a bathroom.* Greg held the door open, plastered with a big sign saying, "Snowmobilers welcome!" *I guess we came to the right place.*

Chapter Twenty-Two

Helmet tucked under my arm, I stepped into the warm air and immediately started sweating. I removed my coat, then unzipped the top of my snow pants.

"Hey Zeke," Greg greeted the man behind the counter.

"Greg! I didn't know you were up. How are you, man?" The red-haired guy clasped forearms with my boyfriend, grinning a wide, toothy grin.

With a shake of his head, Greg chuckled. "Long story. But we're just lucky we were able to make it to the cabin. Can we borrow the phone? And the bathroom? We'll want a couple subs, too, if you've got the stuff."

A sandwich had never sounded so good, and I lit up when Zeke nodded. Greg directed me to the bathroom, after taking my helmet and coat. It was tiny, even worse with my extra clothes, but I managed to do my business without freaking out too badly.

When I opened the door, Greg leaned against the wall right outside, a sheepish smile on his face. At my crinkling forehead, he shrugged. "I know it's a small bathroom. Just wanted to be here if you needed anything."

His thoughtfulness caught me off guard. How long had it been since I knew someone was watching out for me? "Thank you." I kissed his cheek, noticing he'd also shed his jacket and helmet.

"I put our stuff on a table over there." He pointed to the back corner where three rickety tables sat surrounded by mismatched wooden chairs. "Zeke is making my sandwich. Why don't you let him know what you want? I'll finish up here, make a few calls, then we can have lunch."

I wandered to the counter to see about sub options. I settled on a club and chatted with Zeke while he put it together. Then I made sure to pay. It was the least I could do. Greg's voice caught my ear, and I couldn't help smiling when he kept talking since it meant he'd gotten a hold of someone. *Good.*

I took our sandwiches to the table Greg had claimed, picking the sturdiest looking chair to sit on. The store seemed to have a little of everything, which made sense as it was the only option for miles. From alcohol to plates to butter, there was even a small section of toys and several packs of birthday candles next to boxed cake mix. Despite the warped floors and the peeling paint, the shelves were organized and dust free. I was happy to support Zeke.

Greg made his way over, with a grin on his face. "My friend, Joe, will drop a car off tomorrow, mid-morning." He took a quick bite of his sandwich, then winked before heading back to the phone.

I watched him curiously, wondering who else he needed to call.

He grinned at me as he waited for someone to pick up. "Yes, I'd like to make a reservation for two."

What?

"The third Friday in June." He winked at me. "Special request? The table with the best view of the sunset. And make sure it's a good one, will ya?"

Completely overwhelmed, I put down my sandwich. *He's really done it. He's even remembered the random date I threw out.* I couldn't believe it, and I gaped as he strode back over to the table, sitting in the chair next to me.

His smile was on the tentative side. "You're still free, right?"

A huge grin split my face as I stared at him, joy flooding me. How could I have gotten so lucky? "But it's so far away. Are you sure—?"

He tsked, shaking his head at me. "You told me it was only me. Too late for take-backs now."

I laughed, then threw my arms around his neck. With a loud kiss on his cheek, I squeezed him tightly. "I love you."

"I love you, too. Now eat up. I'm anxious to get back to the cabin. We've got lots to do before Joe comes." The heat underlining his words stoked the ever-present fire within me.

Suddenly, I couldn't wait either.

* * * *

A loud, rumbling engine broke the normal stillness the next morning, promptly at ten. "That must be Joe." Greg hurried over to peer out of the window.

I quickly joined him, surprised to see an SUV as well as a tow truck in front of the cabin. I glanced at Greg for answers.

"Joe runs a towing business. Figured he could get the Town Car out, plus drop off a vehicle for us to drive home in. Two birds and all that." He shrugged.

A curly haired guy in a greasy ball cap with a red-flannel shirt and a Carhartt vest stepped out of the tow truck. He paused to tap on the SUV window, where a similarly dressed man got out. They tromped up the steps onto the porch.

"That's his boyfriend, Caleb." Greg opened the door, leaving Joe's hand suspended mid-knock. "Hey, man! Good to see you." He pulled him in for a one-armed hug, complete with back slapping. Caleb got a firm handshake and a smile. Then Greg turned to introduce me. "This is my girlfriend, Rhonda."

My grin grew wider as the word echoed through. *Girlfriend*. It was the first time he'd said it and meant it for real. I could have walked on water if he'd asked me to.

Joe stepped forward, gripping my hand firmly in his calloused one. His smile was genuine, and I liked him immediately. "Nice to meet ya. Heard ya had quite the scare the other day, glad yer both all right. This here is Caleb, my partner."

I shook Caleb's hand as well. He gave me a shy smile, which I returned, trying to make him feel at ease. I got the sense Joe was the talker of the pair. "You guys want some coffee or water or anything? Sit and chat for a few before we head on out?"

They looked at each other, a whole conversation passing between them, though, not a word was spoken. Joe shook his head. "Nah. You two got plenty of miles ahead of ya, and we've got work to do ourselves. We'll just get on with it. But next time yer in the area, Greg, you owe us a fish dinner."

Greg grinned at him. "Best deal I've made this year." They shook on it, and we all went out of the door.

I wasn't allowed to carry one bag, open my door or do anything for myself. They were so sweet. After Greg pointed out the heap of snow that was supposed to be our car, we hit the road. I watched the cabin disappear, sighing as I turned to face reality once more.

It had been nice to hide out in a little bubble away from the pressure of the world. It had been a welcome relief from wondering what I wanted to do with my life, who I wanted to be. Not to mention I'd loved having Greg all to myself.

Now we were headed home, and the questions pressed in once more. With each passing mile, I felt heavier. I still had to tell Avery about Kevin. Which meant I had to tell her and Derek about him harassing me. I wrinkled my nose, wishing I'd never kept it a secret in the first place. *Ugh.*

Greg's hand brushed mine, startling me from my bleak thoughts. "You okay over there?"

I traced the outline of his profile with my gaze, then I turned my palm over to lace my fingers through his. "Just wishing we didn't have to leave the cabin."

He gave my hand a squeeze. "I know what you mean."

It was a couple of hours before we came back into the range of cell service. As we drove merrily along US 2, my phone started dinging. Then Greg's followed suit, and he grinned. "Must be nearing civilization again."

Never would I have expected those words to not fill me with joy. Instead, the sinking feeling continued as I pulled out my phone to read through my messages. Most were from Derek, and they grew more concerned with each text. "I need to call my brother."

Greg nodded. "Yeah, you do." He showed me the screen of his phone where Derek's name was plastered on it, with the number seventeen indicating the amount of messages from him.

Swiping to Derek's contact info, I held the phone up to my ear and listened to the shrill ring.

"Rhonda?" He sounded out of breath.

"Hey, Derek."

"Holy shit, you're okay! Damn, you scared me. What the hell happened?" His tone went from terrified to furious in about three seconds flat.

I bit back a laugh, knowing it would only infuriate him more. But it was nice to be cared about. "Greg and I had a little accident. We got stranded at his cabin in a place with no cell service, and no way to contact anyone. But we're on our way home. Actually, we're almost to the bridge." I saw its green towers in the distance, and longing pulsed in me. We were really leaving the U.P.

I cleared my throat, focusing once more on my conversation. "Can we come over tonight? I'll fill you in on everything.

"Of course," he said, then paused. "You sure you're up for it? As much as I'd love to see you, it could wait till tomorrow."

"No." My chest tightened, and I hope my words weren't strained as I forced myself to say, "No, it needs to be tonight. I'll let you know when we get closer, okay?"

"Sure thing. Talk to you soon."

After he'd hung up, I sighed, feeling as if a black cloud hovered over my head.

Greg's deep voice sounded far away. "Hey, Jellybean, talk to me. What's going on?"

I didn't want to shut him out. I wasn't trying to, but I didn't know how to explain what I was feeling. "I don't really know. It's just the thought of telling Avery about Kevin and her mom, I guess. What if she somehow blames me, and I lose another friend?" *My only real friend.*

He frowned. "Avery's not like Yolanda and Fawnda. She wouldn't do that to you."

I hoped not. "And telling her means I have to fill Derek in on this whole harassment thing with Kevin. He's going to be upset that he didn't know, that I kept it from him."

With a reassuring smile, Greg reached over to rest his warm hand on my thigh. "Yeah, but you're telling him now, and he's a good guy. You know he'll forgive you."

Eventually. But we had a history. Things were just getting good between us again, and it had been mostly my fault. Avery had helped bring us back together, had made me see how awful I'd been to him. And I didn't want to lose him again. I liked having him in my life.

The miles ticked by. Greg allowed me my mood, settling for shooting me concerned looks and making sure he had some sort of physical contact with me. I appreciated it.

We decided to head right to Derek's, and I texted him when we were close. We pulled up in front of their apartment, and I felt frozen to the seat.

Greg opened my door, offering his hand to me despite the rugged boots I wore. "Come on, Jellybean. Derek and Avery love you. They want to know you're all right, and they've been worried about you. It'll be good to have this out in the open, you'll see." He tugged on my hand, then pulled to his side where I clung to him, the sweet scent of peppermint grounding me. "Besides, I'm right here. And I'm not going anywhere." He kissed the top of my head.

I could do this, with him by my side. *Together.* Stepping back, I gave him a little smile. "Thank you."

Derek opened the door of his apartment. Once he'd scanned me and seen I was in one piece, a scowl crossed his face. "Don't ever do that to me again, you hear?" The words were almost a growl, then he pulled me in for a rib-cracking embrace so tight I could hardly breathe.

"Hey, Derek?" Greg put a hand on Derek's arm. "Gentle, okay? She's still not a hundred percent after the wreck."

"Oh, right."

Derek loosened his grip enough that I could breathe, and I shot Greg a grateful look before hugging my brother back. "Good to see you, too." I hoped he still felt that way after everything I had to tell them.

After he'd let go, he shook Greg's hand. I let out a breath when Derek didn't bat an eyelash as Greg put his hand on the small of my back, guiding me into the apartment.

Avery hollered when she saw us together. "You two are adorable!" Then she ran at me full tilt, arms open for an exuberant hug, which I wholeheartedly returned. She had no qualms about hugging Greg as well. He almost seemed to expect it, which didn't surprise me. *That's Avery for you.*

Liam sprawled on the couch, and Gina perched on a barstool at the kitchen island. I waved to them both, unsurprised to see them there, since I hadn't specified that we needed to speak in private. Maybe it'd be good for Avery to have the extra support.

"Where's Josh?" I asked Gina.

She lifted a shoulder. "Play practice. He got a minor role in *Fiddler on the Roof*. The constable, I think."

"Nice," I said, nodding. He was a theater major, which I admired. "Let us know when the play is."

"Will do."

"Want something to drink? Or eat?" Avery asked as she took my coat, then she paused, staring at my outfit. "I'm still not used to seeing you in jeans and boots." A big smile split her face. "Rhonda Elgin, slumming it. Who knew?"

My cheeks were hot as Greg chuckled. He answered for both of us, saying, "White wine, if you have it." He led me to the free end of the couch, where he sat down, tugging me next to him. His arm wrapped around my shoulders.

Avery appeared with our drinks, then she snuggled in beside Derek in an oversized armchair. They were drinking whiskey, Liam had some sort of beer and Gina plopped onto the floor with a mixed drink in her hand.

"Okay, sis, tell us what happened," Derek said.

I took a sip of the wine, followed by a deep breath then I did exactly that.

Obviously, there were some things my brother didn't need to know, like the intimate details of what happened with me and Greg. When we got to the bit about Kevin, I couldn't look at Derek, but I felt his gaze boring into me. I explained about getting another picture at the reception, but not who was with Kevin. I needed that to be its own thing, not overshadowed by our accident.

Avery gasped when I described the car accident. And I haltingly admitted my claustrophobia, how terrified I was while Greg had left to find the cabin. Then I finished with our recovery, and how he managed to get us home.

"Oh, Rhonda, I'm so glad you're okay," Avery said sympathetically. "But stranded in a remote cabin in the middle of a snowstorm..." She let out a sappy sigh as she turned to my brother. "Sounds like something straight out of one of my romance novels."

"Avery." Derek said her name like a warning. "No. Just no, this is not the time or the place." When her lower lip jutted out, he softened. "We'll talk about it later, okay, Cupcake?"

She answered him back, just as softly. "Aye, aye, Captain."

Liam pretended to gag, so Gina threw a pillow at him. "Just because you don't have a romantic bone in your body."

He glared at her. "I'm plenty romantic when I need to be. I make sure my women are always satisfied."

She snorted. "Oh, is that why you're single right now?"

I took advantage of the distraction to perch on the arm of the chair next to Avery. I kept my voice low while Gina and Liam continued to bicker, at each other's throats as usual. "So, the picture Kevin sent on New Year's Eve..." I sighed. "Avery, it was of him and your mom. I wanted to be the one to tell you. I'm so sorry! He's such an asshole."

To my surprise, she burst out laughing.

"What?"

"Oh, Rhonda, no, it's just—" She laughed again, flopping back in the chair. "That's too funny." Sitting up straight, she grinned at me. "I got word this morning that Mother is finally divorcing my dad. I'll have full medical power of attorney over him, and I can get him the care he deserves, all because she met some young hotshot. She wouldn't tell me his name, though." She sobered. "I'm sorry he sent you that picture, but it's the best possible thing that could've happened for my dad."

I blinked in stunned silence.

She nodded. "Funny how it all works out, isn't it? Actually, Derek's family lawyers have been checking into it. Derek convinced me to take her to court for misuse of my dad's funds, and they think I've got a pretty good case. The hearing will be in a couple weeks."

"Wow, good luck with that." I glanced at Derek, my heart squeezing at his protective expression, focused solely on Avery. I'd been so jealous of the two of them just a week ago. But now, I didn't have to be. Warmth seeped through me as I settled once more next to Greg, who tucked his arm around me again.

"You know, Rhonda made me leave my sister's wedding just to come tell you about that picture." Greg arched an eyebrow at me, as if daring me to argue. Avery gasped, and Greg chuckled. "Yep, there was a raging blizzard outside, and she'd had several glasses of champagne, or she'd have driven herself. Right, Jellybean?"

I ducked my head, focusing on my wine. This was not the kind of attention I was used to, and I wasn't sure how to handle it.

Greg's voice went soft, tender. "You should have seen her, telling me off. She demanded I drive her down here, so she could tell you in person, Avery, or else she'd find someone who would. It didn't matter that it was New Year's Eve. It didn't matter that my sister's reception was still going on. It didn't matter that there was a blizzard in full force." His finger brushed my cheek.

I finally looked up at him, and I was glad I did or I'd have missed the way his eyes brimmed with love and admiration. For me.

Chapter Twenty-Three

Greg's phone rang, breaking the tender moment. He glanced at the screen, then at me. "It's Joe. I should answer this." He looked to Derek, asking permission to take it down the hallway, wandering that way when Derek nodded. Then he disappeared with a, "Hey, Joe, whaddya know?"

While he was gone, Derek turned back to me with a frown. "So, what gives, sis? You've been keeping secrets from us?"

I didn't answer right away, studying my lap instead. I hated appearing weak, and admitting what I'd been going through would be doing just that.

"I was really worried about you." Derek paused, then added, "We all were. You haven't been you for a while now."

Everyone nodded. I remembered what had prompted me to go on this trip, the wanting to belong, the void in my life. Maybe I wasn't best friends with Gina, but she'd given me solid advice before leaving with Greg. And I'd grown up with Liam.

Derek trusted these people, so did Greg. I'd watched them rally together for Avery and Derek. If I'd learned nothing else the last week, it was that I didn't want to fight alone anymore. And I had a whole group of people here, ready to be my support, if I'd just let them in. What better way to start than by being honest?

A long sigh left my lips. "I know. Greg told me how concerned you all were about me, and I appreciate it." I stood up, putting my hands behind my back as I started pacing. "I wasn't happy here. Breaking up with Kevin was only a small part of it."

I kept my gaze on the floor, not wanting to see the pity I knew I'd find in their expressions. "I wasn't upset over the breakup. It was more because of what I'd allowed my life to become." *A shell. A game.* I stopped to cross my arms over my chest, looking at the dining room table. It reminded me of mine, where I'd hosted endless parties for my fake friends. "Nothing was real, except you guys. You're my first true friends, and it made me realize how empty the rest of my life was."

Footsteps padded around the corner, and Greg reappeared.

I smiled, feeling the light come back on in my soul. "Greg's helping with that, too."

He frowned, crossing the room to loop an arm around my waist and kiss the top of my head.

"I know he won't fix everything. I'm the only one who can figure out what I want to do with my life, who I want to be. But I've wanted Greg for a long time." I felt more at peace with him there, feeling whole. "We're in this together. I hope you all can accept that." I finally surveyed my friends to find that they were smiling. Every single one of them.

Derek shook his head, a wide grin on his face. "How can I not after watching the light show you just put on?

You're like a damn Christmas tree the moment he walks in the room."

I ducked my head, unable to stop my smile. I could live with that.

"But no more secrets, okay?" my brother pleaded earnestly.

It was a promise I intended to keep. "I'll do my best."

"Good." Derek cocked his head. "So, what's next in the life of Rhonda Elgin?"

I glanced at everyone's eager expressions, buoyed by the hope they all had for me. "Well, I get to tell our parents that I'm dating our chauffeur. They're on vacation till next month, but I want to have a plan in place for when they get back in February. Any ideas on that one?"

Liam snorted. "Yeah, don't."

Gina threw another pillow at him, but this time he tossed it back at her. She caught it and stuck out her tongue before saying, "Maybe if you tell them in a public place, they'll be less likely to make a scene?"

Derek leaned forward eagerly. "We could all go out for dinner, and you guys could make your couple status known to Mom and Dad." The way he ended made it seem like there was more, and I waited. He subtly shook his head at me.

Greg nodded. "Seems like a smart move. Any suggestions on restaurants? I'd like to get this over with sooner than later." His grip tightened on my hip. "I don't plan on leaving Jellybean's side much in the near future, so the longer we wait, the more likely we'll be found out."

"Aww," Avery cooed, staring at us, "you called her Jellybean."

It was so cute when Greg blushed. We all laughed as the guys teased Greg good naturedly. Greg snorted. "Cause Cupcake is so much better." He arched an eyebrow at Derek, who looked at the floor.

Liam rolled his eyes. "You guys are both saps. I'd never give a girl a ridiculous nickname like that."

Gina piped up, "Wanna bet?"

Both Avery and Derek yelled, "No!"

I blinked at their vehement interference, wondering what that was all about. Derek changed the subject and suggested a few restaurants which Avery vetoed. Liam named one I hadn't heard of — The Gilded Lily. Avery, Gina and Derek all vetted it, while Liam grinned, smug at the unanimous support. We checked our calendars and picked a couple of dates. I'd confirm with our parents, then make the reservation.

With all the difficult stuff out of the way, I finally began to relax. Greg got up to get each of us another glass of wine, and Derek beckoned me toward the hallway. Curious, I followed him.

"Okay, I have a huge favor to ask you." He leaned down to whisper in my ear. "Can you help me?"

A huge smile spread over my face, and I had to clamp a hand over my mouth to keep from squealing. I nodded. "Of course, I will. That's so exciting!"

We picked a time to meet, then he swore me to secrecy, even from Greg. *Well, this could get interesting.* I returned to the living room. Greg studied me in a silent question, but I just smirked, shaking my head.

Two hours later, I was beyond exhausted and ready for home. Greg had kept my wine glass filled, but he'd switched to water after his second glass. We said goodnight to everyone. I hugged Derek a little more fiercely than he expected, I think, but he patted my back.

"I'm glad you came tonight, sis."

I grinned up at him. "Me, too."

We made it back to my place, my empty shell of a house that sparked no feeling in me. I walked into the dark room, flicking on lights and I felt...nothing. I missed the warmth and coziness of the cabin.

Greg plopped my bags in the entryway, drawing my attention. "You're staying, aren't you?" I blurted out, desperation underlining every word.

"As long as you want me to." He reached out to squeeze my hand. "We could go somewhere else, anywhere else. I have a roommate, though, so maybe not there."

I shook my head, loving his thoughtfulness. "No, I'll be okay, just as long as you stay with me."

"Of course, Jellybean."

* * * *

It was weird to be back in my old life. Several weeks had passed, but I just couldn't find my groove. Like trying on a pair of pants that used to fit, but now those pants bagged in all the wrong places. I'd checked in on all my charities, made sure my mom didn't need help in her absence, and tried to be happy with Greg.

Scratch that. I was happy with Greg. It was everything else I wasn't happy with.

Maybe I needed to redecorate. It might help to have a project to throw myself into, something to keep me occupied. I sighed. I'd have to keep thinking.

For today, at least, I had a distraction. A horn honked outside, and I hurried to open my front door. Derek's sleek black Mercedes waited at the base of the steps. I gave him a cheerful wave as I trotted toward him. I'd decided to forgo my usual Jimmy Choos in favor of a cute pair of dressy boots with much better traction since Greg wasn't around to escort me this time.

"Hey, Rhonda," Derek said when I slid into the passenger seat.

"Hey. No chauffeur?"

He shook his head. "One less person for Avery to interrogate. She is ruthless when it comes to knowing surprises."

I chuckled as we headed down my winding driveway. "Do you have a shop in mind?"

"Yep." A wide grin split his face. "I know just the place."

The ten-minute drive was filled with him telling me about the New Year's Eve party he and Avery had attended with Josh and Gina at Maria's. Bin had closed the restaurant for a private celebration. Although I wouldn't have missed Mandy's wedding for the world, a prick of jealousy stabbed me as he raved about the food, the dancing, and, of course, the company.

Maybe next year.

We pulled into a simple but cute looking shop at the edge of town, and I said, "I had no idea this was here."

Derek lifted a shoulder. "Bin told me about it. One of his friends owns it, so I thought I'd check the place out."

Most jewelry shops I'd been in felt cold and sterile, but this one was warm and friendly with rich, bright paintings placed strategically on the walls. A man about our age greeted us, and Derek strode up to him. The man had blond hair and dark brown eyes. He wore an infectious smile that I couldn't help returning.

My brother said, "Hi, I'm Derek Elgin, a friend of Bin's. He told me about this place."

The man's smile grew impossibly wider. "Nice to meet you, Derek. I'm Paul. How is Bin? I haven't seen him for a while."

As Derek caught Paul up, I began perusing the jewelry cases, looking for anything that screamed Avery. I wasn't sure of her preferences, but I knew Derek had given her a rose-gold tennis bracelet for her birthday. She wore it all the time.

Maybe something to match?

"What brings you in today?" Paul asked, glancing from Derek to me.

"I'm looking for an engagement ring. My sister, Rhonda, is here to help."

"Congratulations!" Paul headed my way. "Anything you want to see up close?"

I checked with Derek first. "Did you have any setting or metal in mind?"

"I thought rose-gold since Avery seems to like the bracelet I got her."

I nodded, happy that my thoughts were on the same page. I pointed to a tray of rings. "Can we see that one, please?"

Derek ambled over as Paul set the tray on top of the counter. We studied the beautiful jewelry in silence, but one with a square cut diamond in the center kept calling to me. The band was delicate, with two pieces of metal weaving through each other in an elegant design. I reached for it at the same time Derek did.

We both laughed, and I let him pick it up. "Great minds."

"Yep." He turned it over several times then handed it to me. "I really like the band on this one."

"Me, too. It's so delicate." The diamond wasn't too big either, and it would look nice on Avery's hand. "I think she'd love it."

Derek nodded and turned to Paul. "Okay, tell me about this one."

I tuned them out, going back to perusing the cases. I wondered if Derek had practiced his proposal, and my mind shifted to Greg. Marriage to Greg...it was a fantasy that had seemed unattainable for so long. We were definitely too new for a leap like that, but someday. I couldn't picture myself with anyone else.

Once Derek had the ring, we decided to go to a nearby cafe for lunch. He patted his pocket when he got out of the car and again when we sat down.

"The ring still there?" I teased.

His cheeks tinged with pink. "Yeah, I'm just nervous, I guess."

"Derek." I paused, reaching out to grab his wrist. "Never in the history of mankind has someone had a more solid chance of their girlfriend saying yes. Avery is all in."

He grinned softly. "Thanks, Rhonda."

When the server came by to take our orders, I got a water and a chicken salad. Derek chose a French dip with homemade chips. The server left, and I fiddled with my napkin, unsure what else to say.

"How are you doing?"

I looked up at him, needing clarification.

"Coming home, settling in with Greg. Is that all going well?"

A sigh escaped me before I could stop it. "I just don't fit anywhere." I explained the way I'd been feeling. "It's not Greg. I'm happy with him, beyond happy. But I don't have a purpose here, and I miss that."

He shot me a sympathetic smile. "I'm glad things are good with you and Greg, but as for a purpose? It just takes time. You'll figure it out."

I shrugged. "Hopefully."

"Have you talked to Mom and Dad at all?"

"Not since scheduling the dinner." I twisted my napkin in my hands. "I'm nervous, Derek," I admitted quietly. Only two weeks stood between us and the looming announcement to my parents.

"Hey." He waited for me to look at him before continuing. "Greg is a great guy. Mom and Dad, well, they might need some time, but they'll come around. Maybe they'll surprise us both, and you'll be worried for nothing."

I scoffed. "Yeah, right. I'm just hoping they'll give me the chance to explain." But I knew even that was unlikely.

"Well, we'll be there for you guys, no matter the outcome." Empathy rested in his gaze. "And I don't plan to propose to Avery until after you've introduced Greg. If they accept him, then they can be a part of our celebration. Otherwise..." He shrugged. "They don't deserve the chance."

Warmth spread through me as the server appeared with our food. I didn't take my eyes off my brother, thrilled to have this with him. Thrilled that he was a part of my life once more. And thrilled that he had my back, no matter what.

* * * *

That night, Greg and I met Derek, Avery, and Liam at the bar Gina worked at, called The High Five. Her boyfriend, Josh, was there too, running lines for his part while she worked, so we all crowded around a big, round table in the middle of the floor.

"Hey, guys, what are you having?" Gina looked cute in her fitted tee and tight jeans. Her short dark hair and tan skin always made me think of a young Halle Berry.

We all greeted her, rattling off our drinks as well as getting some appetizers to snack on.

After Gina left, Avery exchanged an excited grin with Derek. "Okay, so Gina already knows, and I can't wait another minute. Mother's trial was today, and they found her guilty of misappropriation of funds! I have a trust Daddy set up for me from my grandparents that I've never had access to. Plus, so much of their money was his in the first place." She beamed. "She has to pay all sorts of fees, on top of the divorce being final. I can finally get him the care he deserves."

"I'm so happy to hear that, Ave." I grinned. What a relief that must be for her, not to have to sneak around to see her father and worry about his isolation.

The others murmured their congratulations.

Gina came back with our drinks, handing them out and leaning a casual hand on Josh's shoulder. "Avery told you the good news, huh?" She stayed to chat for a bit before she was called away.

Then Derek steered the conversation to me. "How are you doing, Rhonda? Any progress?"

I froze with my wine glass at my lips, knowing he was referencing our conversation the other day. I needed to catch everyone else up. After taking a sip, I set the glass back down. "I'm all recovered from the accident, and Greg's been staying with me, but I still feel...off."

I'd promised to not hide anymore, so even though it was hard, I wanted to try. "My charities are all running themselves. I don't have any desire to jump back into the social circle I was in, with the society luncheons and committee meetings and country clubs." I shrugged. "I'm still trying to find my niche."

Greg leaned closer to place a warm hand on my back. My brother nodded thoughtfully. I knew it wasn't the answer he'd hoped for, but I could tell he appreciated my candor. Liam changed the subject to a light-hearted story about his morning at the gym.

I glanced over at the hallway where the restrooms were. The worst thing about The High Five was their little one person bathrooms. But nature called.

My chair scraped against the wood floor as I stood up. Greg glanced up, so I jerked my chin in the direction of the restrooms, not wanting to interrupt Liam. A line appeared on Greg's forehead, knowing my issues. I patted his arm to let him know I'd be fine and strode away.

I glanced back as our table erupted in laughter at whatever Liam had said. I smiled and shook my head, loving how well we meshed as a group.

The dingy bulb in the narrow hallway didn't offer much light, and I steeled myself as I pushed open the bathroom door. In and out, I told myself. I started to shut it, but someone pressed on it from the other side.

"It's occupied," I called, trying to latch the door. I stumbled backward as the person gave a violent shove. "What the hell?"

Kevin's leering grin met my stunned face. "Hey there, Rhonda."

I was too shocked to scream, and by the time I'd thought of it, he had one hand clamped over my mouth while the other locked us inside the too small bathroom. The combination of the cramped space, filled with the extra body and the pressure of his hand on my face had the panic pressing in more with every moment.

"I couldn't believe my luck when you and your friends walked in tonight. I've just been biding my time, waiting for a chance to talk to you."

The smell of alcohol hit me, even through his hand, and his eyes had a glassy quality to them. I struggled to process his words over the tightening grip of my panic. But I needed to stay in the present, and I searched for an opportunity to scream or kick as he prattled on.

He swayed as he stepped closer. "Have you been enjoying my pictures?"

I glared at him, summoning my anger to burn through panic's grip.

"Ah, there's the fight I want to see." His dark gaze raked over me, and I squirmed. His leering smile sent a shiver through me, and I struggled to get away. He tightened his grip. "That's right. I always did enjoy the spunky ones, not that you ever lived up to that."

He leaned into me, his stale breath hot against my cheek. "You took everything from me, Rhonda. I came home from a wonderful vacation with a new life all planned out. Only to be served a summons for a lawsuit on sexual harassment by my bitch of an ex-fiancée." He brushed back my hair, exposing my neck, and running his fingers down my cheek.

I yelped into his hand, jerking and trying to get away from his iron grip. I had nowhere to go, stuck between the wall at my back, the sink to my left, and the toilet on my right.

His menacing laughter was colder than the winter air. "Not only that, but your brother's lawyers saw to it that my new girlfriend just got taken for a hefty sum, leaving us practically penniless." His voice turned to steel. "Is that your new man out there?"

He must be drunk if he didn't even recognize Greg. Although he was used to seeing Greg in a uniform, and Kevin never had been one to pay hired hands much attention. Unless they were female.

"I saw him put his hands on you," Kevin growled. "I watched you lean into him. He got you all warmed up for me, huh, Rhonda?"

As he pressed against me, a new hardness against my hip had me fighting even more. I yelped against his hand, and he slammed my head back against the wall, hard enough that I saw stars.

"Shut up, you bitch. You owe me, after everything you've put me through." He fumbled with his belt, cursing under his breath when the buckle caught.

His hand dropped from my mouth, and I took full advantage of the moment. Fighting a wave of dizziness from the blow to my head, I braced myself against the wall, sucked in a full breath then screamed at the top of my lungs.

Kevin backhanded me before grabbing me by the throat. "You—"

A heavy fist pounded on the door. "Rhonda!"

Greg. I sagged with relief, even though I could hardly breathe around Kevin's tight grip.

"Rhonda, answer me!"

When I didn't, the door shuddered, once, twice, before it splintered open at the doorknob. Greg lowered his leg mid-kick. When he took in Kevin's hold on my neck and his partially undone pants, the fury on Greg's face hit me with a surge of raw gratification. He was here. His hand shot out so fast, I almost missed it, but I heard the crunch when it connected with Kevin's nose.

Kevin's head snapped backward, and his eyes rolled back into his head as he collapsed onto the toilet. I sucked in air, even as my knees gave out. But Greg was right there to catch me. I opened my mouth, then closed it, burying my face in his shoulder as the tears leaked out. He picked me up, carrying me into the hallway, where our group of friends waited.

Derek was right there. "Is she okay? Is she hur — ?"

"Kevin was in there with her." Greg nodded. "Good thing I went to check on her, or else I wouldn't have heard her scream."

Derek's jaw dropped.

"Is there an office or back room or someplace I can take her? Someone needs to call the police. And Kevin's going to need some medical attention." Greg's calm, no-nonsense tone was my anchor even as I trembled in his arms.

Chapter Twenty-Four

Gina pulled the office door shut behind us. Greg carried me over to the high-backed chair and sat down, cradling me on his lap. Great big gulping sobs erupted from me as I buried my face against him.

He rubbed my back, murmuring until I finally started to calm down. "It's okay, Jellybean. I've got you. Are you hurt? Did he…?"

I shook my head gingerly, wincing at the movement. I explained haltingly, "He slammed my head against the wall, and he backhanded me." Greg went deathly still beneath me. I knew if Kevin hadn't already been knocked out, he would be for what he'd done to me.

"He blamed me for all of it. He was going to—" I stammered over the word, "r-rape me, but he couldn't get his buckle undone." I pressed my face into Greg's soaked shoulder again, trying to hide from the fresh horror. I took a moment to compose myself then sat up once more. "He said I owed him, for pressing charges and for our family lawyers taking away his new girlfriend's money."

Greg went pale at my words. His jaw clenched, and it was a long moment before he spoke. "I'm so sorry, Jellybean."

I sniffed, frowning at the guilt in his face. "No, Greg. You saved me. Thank you."

I wrapped my arms around his neck, needing his closeness. His arms tightened around me as I sat there, just breathing him in. His cedar and peppermint scent enveloped me, calming me even more. The dark memory played out, but there was light at the end of the tunnel. I remembered Greg storming in, and I pulled back.

Staring at him, I let my awe show. "That was some pretty hot hero shit you pulled in there. A one-punch knockout. Where the hell did that come from?"

A small smile tilted up one corner of his mouth. "I've done some amateur boxing on and off since high school. That's how I keep in shape and let off steam." He sobered. "When I saw his hand on your throat, Rhonda, I lost it. I could've killed him." His mouth tightened as he swallowed. "I hope that doesn't change your opinion of me."

Needing to lighten the mood, for both our sakes, I said, "Actually, it does."

Disappointment and hurt appeared as his face fell.

"I didn't think you could get any hotter, but damn, Greg," I teased, even managing a real smile, "you might have just turned me into a boxing fan."

Sirens sounded, and Derek texted us that both the police and EMTs were here.

"You really should get checked out," Greg said.

I was loath to leave the secure space of his embrace, but I knew he was right. I clung to his arm as we walked through the bar and outside. As an EMT checked me over, an officer took my statement. Greg refused to leave my side. Once the officer was done with her questions for both me and Greg, the EMT stepped back.

He gave us his findings. "No sign of a concussion. Your cheek is already starting to bruise, and you have a small lump on the back of your head, so you'll want to be careful with that. Ice it, take an anti-inflammatory. You might also have some bruising on your throat."

I nodded, grateful it wasn't worse.

"The other thing we recommend after events like this is counseling. It can be a huge help." He extended a business card, and Greg took it. "There's a website and a hotline on here. They can find you someone who will fit your needs." He and Greg exchanged a look before Greg thanked him. "Otherwise, you're free to go."

Another EMT wheeled Kevin by on a stretcher, one of his hands cuffed to the metal bar. Kevin's glare fixed on me as they steered him through the room. I shuddered, burying my face in Greg's chest.

Greg asked a nearby officer, "What's going to happen to him?"

The officer smirked. "No need to worry, sir. Between this lady's previous pending lawsuit and the current assault charges, he'll be locked up for a long time. Plus, there was another incident involving him earlier today, filed by his girlfriend of all people."

A weight lifted off my chest, and I sagged against Greg, ready to be away from the noise and curious stares.

"You okay, Jellybean?"

I nodded. "Take me home, Greg."

We made it to my house, the events of the evening pressing in on me. I walked in the door and went right to the couch, sinking into it.

Greg sat beside me, grabbing my hand. "Tell me what you need."

But I didn't know. I looked down at my outfit, realizing under my coat were the clothes that Kevin had touched, that Kevin had tried to rape me in and panic bubbled in me. My breath came in short bursts. "He touched these clothes. He touched me, Greg. I—" I felt disgusting.

"Rhonda." He said my name calmly, tugging on my hand to ground me. I focused on him, on his touch. "Do you trust me?"

I nodded.

One hand reached up to brush the hair back from my cheek, and his focus lingered on the mark I knew was there. "Then let me take care of you."

His words were enough to help me let go of the panic, and I surrendered myself to him. He knelt before me, picking up my right foot to undo one dainty buckle of my Jimmy Choo. His hands slid down my ankle, caressing me before setting my foot back on the floor. He did the same for the left.

Then he stood up, removing my coat first. His was next.

The mirror above the mantle showed my outfit in stark detail and the memory of Kevin's hip pressing against me flashed in my mind. I shuddered. "Please, Greg. I don't ever want to see these clothes again."

"Shh, it's okay." He kissed my forehead, following my gaze to the mirror, then he turned me so I could no longer see my reflection. "We'll make sure of it." He cupped my face with both his hands. "Eyes up here, Jellybean."

I stared at his beautiful face, focusing only on him. His movements were swift, steadfast as he undressed me, moving my limbs like I was a doll.

He gave me a small smile. "Close your eyes."

And I obeyed, trusting him implicitly as I stood there in my bra and underwear. I felt the air move as he brushed past me, then I heard the rustling of a bag. My mind kept wanting to think about what he was putting in the bag, picturing it, but I shoved the images aside, bringing Greg's face back into focus.

"All set." His voice was gentle, as was his warm touch on my shoulder. "You can open your eyes now." His thumb rubbed back and forth against my bare skin.

I wanted to cringe away from his touch, feeling dirty still.

His hand dropped away. Pain laced his words, and I knew he wanted to help when he said, "Tell me. Tell me what you're thinking."

My hands came up to grip my biceps, shielding my chest as my chin dropped. "I want to take a shower."

"Of course." He hesitated. "Do you think you'll want to go to bed after that?"

A wave of exhaustion hit me then, and I nodded, feeling completely drained on every level.

"Okay. I'll meet you in the bedroom." He stepped back reluctantly. "Just holler if you need anything, all right?"

Again, I nodded, then I forced myself to climb the stairs. In the shower, I scrubbed until my skin was pink, wishing I could scrub away my memories with it. I hated Kevin, hated what he'd done to me and the fearful mess I was reduced to. *Why can't I be strong and resilient?* I didn't deserve this, especially now when things with Greg were just starting to go right. I hoped this didn't change things between us.

When I came out, my favorite pair of pajamas were sitting on the bathroom counter, and warmth spread through me at Greg's thoughtfulness. I finished getting ready for bed, then I climbed under the covers next to him.

He lay on his side, watching my every motion. "Will you let me hold you, Rhonda?" His voice was full of raw need, desperation hovering in his eyes, but he didn't move until I gave him permission. Then he crushed me to him, cradling me to his chest.

Tears leaked from me, and I started sobbing before I could stop myself. My thin hold on my self-control slipped as the events of the day caught up to me. But Greg was right there for me to lean on. He held me until my tears ran dry, not letting go even then.

* * * *

A couple of days passed in a muted blur. I didn't sleep well, had no appetite. Didn't go anywhere except from the couch to the bed and back again. I knew Greg was concerned, but I couldn't bring myself to care.

He'd brought up therapy several times, asking me to call them — for his sake, if not for my own. But it was so much work. I had to dial the number, explain the situation, make an appointment that fit in with my calendar. So many steps, and it was just…daunting. I just didn't have the energy.

My phone sounded with a message from Avery, just checking on me. Again. I told her I was fine. Again.

Greg wasn't home. He'd gone to his place to grab some things. He planned to pick up dinner on the way home and asked me to text him if anything sounded good.

I hadn't texted him. I'd just sat here. I didn't even play on my phone.

It wasn't like me to do nothing. I was constantly moving, always going, my mind switching from one task to the next. Not only did I not have anything on my to-do list, I had no ambition to put anything on it. Was this how my life was going to be from now on? A big void of meaningless days that tumbled one after another like dominoes?

The door opened and in came Greg, a smile on his face, a box under one arm, and a bag from my favorite Chinese restaurant balanced on top of the box. "Hey," he said, setting the stuff down and coming over to kiss my forehead.

I should've probably warned him I was greasy from not showering yet today. But I didn't. I tried to smile, but his face fell, and I knew I had failed.

"Hungry?" Hope lit his face as he waited for my answer.

"Not really." I hated being the one to douse the spark, but I didn't want to lie either.

He shrugged. "Okay. Maybe in a little bit. I'm going to put my stuff away."

After sticking the food in the fridge, he disappeared up the stairs. I sighed and resumed my staring.

Then our Bluetooth speaker in the living room kicked on, blaring *Pony* by Ginuwine, the iconic song from *Magic Mike*. Confused, I looked around, knowing I hadn't started any music. And it wasn't a song on Greg's usual playlist.

Movement on the stairway caught my attention. His eyes held a mischievous glint, his lips tilted up in a sexy smirk, and his hips swayed to the heavy beat of the song as he descended.

My eyebrows shot up. *What is going on?*

He came to stand in front of me, touching my chin. "I've noticed you've been doing a lot of staring, and I thought, maybe you'd like a change of scenery." His tone was all suggestion.

A spark of heat pierced the void inside me. "Are you offering to strip for me?"

His cheeks had a little extra color as he nodded. "If you think it'll help."

My smile grew wider the longer I thought about his offer. "Oh, I think it would help tremendously." I drank in his fully clothed body, anticipation building inside me. It was a welcome relief from the apathy.

"Anything for you." He started by untucking his shirt, lifting up the hem just enough that I got a tantalizing glimpse of those gorgeous abs. Then he slowly undid the top couple buttons, his heavy gaze on me the entire time.

I couldn't look away. I'd seen him naked often, but this was different. This was solely for my benefit, an acknowledgment from both of us of how pleasing I found him. The buttons were undone to his navel now, and I sucked in a breath. He smirked, turning around to take the shirt off.

Maybe he'd thought to tease me by taking away the view of his front, but he'd underestimated how gorgeous his back was. As the shirt slipped down and he tugged off the sleeves, I studied his defined shoulders, letting my gaze roam freely over that exquisite tattoo I adored.

Then he turned, tossing the shirt at me. "Souvenir for the lady?"

I inhaled deeply, his scent of peppermint and cedar turning me on even more.

He strutted over, "I won't touch you unless you want me to, Jellybean." His throat bobbed, his stormy eyes darkening with tormented emotion, and his voice growing husky. "But I've missed you these past few days."

Guilt hit me then, and I stared at the floor.

"Hey, none of that." He squatted until I looked at him. "You're working through some heavy shit. I get it. I'm just saying I'm here to help if you'll let me, and maybe we could make some new memories." A dazzling smile spread over his face. "I like making memories with you."

My cheeks heated as I thought of all the fun we'd had, all the new positions we'd tried. "I like that too, Greg."

He stood up, offering me a hand. "What do you say then? Are you in?"

I stared at his palm beckoning me, and it felt like a lifeline. I slid my fingers across his warm skin to grip his wrist, sucking in a sharp breath when he yanked me to my feet, pulling me flush against him. "Yes."

"Good. I've missed you, Jellybean." His lips brushed over mine.

"I've missed you too." I slid my hand over his collarbone, gliding until I gripped his upper arm, then I tilted my chin up for another kiss.

He groaned. "Maybe we should do an exchange?" His touch mesmerized me, and his voice dropped even lower when he asked, "How much do you like that shirt?"

The pajama shirt I wore was older, a button-down, and nothing I was in love with. I shrugged.

His mouth brushed over mine as he tugged on the buttons of my shirt, a devilish glint appearing in his gaze. "Brace yourself." Then he ripped it apart, buttons flying everywhere.

I gasped as he shoved the fabric off my shoulders. His hands came up to skim my breasts down to my stomach one more time, and I clung to his arms, so my knees didn't buckle.

"What's next?" he asked.

"Socks." I smirked, letting go of him before I stared pointedly at the black socks covering his feet. "Nothing worse than a beautiful strip tease ruined by awkwardly removing a pair of socks. There's no sexy way to get them off, so do it now." I smiled hungrily. "Then get on with the good stuff."

Resigned to my flawless logic, he bent over, pulling off his socks and tossing them to one side. "Better?"

My nod was quick as he reached for his belt. As he undid it, I had a flashback to Kevin in the bathroom, trying to undo his belt. I felt the color drain from my face.

"Rhonda?"

I whispered, "His belt got caught."

Greg's voice was low as he murmured, "Shit." The belt was gone in seconds, then his hands cupped my cheeks again. "Stay with me, Jellybean." He grabbed my wrists, placing my palms on his bare, warm chest. "I'm right here."

The feel of his smooth skin brought me back. I spread my fingers wide, unable to cover his entire pecs with the span of my hands. The small patch of chest hair beckoned, and I ran my nails through it lightly, following the trail down past his belly button. I heard him swallow, could see the evidence of his arousal pushing at the front of his pants.

"I'm waiting, Greg." I kept my tone light, teasing as I ran a finger along his waistband.

His answering smirk tinged with relief as he stepped back, hands on his fly. The zipper went down, revealing red plaid boxers and a delicious bulge begging to be touched. "The question is, how much scenery do you want?" His pants hit the floor.

"All of you, Greg. I need all of you." His eager erection sprang out as he lowered his boxers next, and I couldn't look away.

Chapter Twenty-Five

I reached for Greg. He stepped forward to meet my hand, my fingers closing around the velvety skin of his cock.

His groan echoed between us as I gripped him hard, stroking him once, twice. "Rhonda, wait."

I released my grip, realizing he needed this slow build between us, needed to go at his pace. His hands gripped my waist, sliding my pants off me. Then his lips were on mine, his hands at my waist, his cock against my stomach. I looped my arms around his neck, kissing him back.

"What's next?" I asked.

"How about a shower?" His heated words stoked the fire within me.

His expression turned tender as he bent, sliding one arm behind my knees to pick me up. Moments later, he set me down in the bathroom, undressing me the rest of the way as the water heated up.

I stepped in first, basking under the warm spray. The shower door closed behind him, and his hands slipped over my sides, his fingers splaying across my abdomen. His erection pressed into my back as he cradled me to him. I dragged my fingers over his arms, leaning back into his firm torso. I couldn't be more grateful for this amazing man.

"Now what?" I asked, tilting my head back.

He nuzzled my neck. "Can I wash you?" he asked, the husky words sending a jolt through me.

I nodded, and he slowly stepped away. Pouring shampoo into his palm, he rubbed his hands together. I stayed facing the spray, but I tipped my chin up as he smoothed the shampoo into my hair. His deft fingers kneaded my scalp in a perfect massage, and I hummed.

He nudged me forward slightly, aligning the cascade of water with my peaked nipple. Pleasure shot straight to my core, and I gasped.

His low chuckle rumbled between us. "You like that?"

"Yes," I said breathily.

"Good." He spun me around to face him. "Close your eyes."

When all the suds were gone from my hair, he spun me around again then repeated the process with the conditioner. Complete with nudging me until my other breast rested under the spray.

The teasing game had excitement coiling in me as he rinsed out the conditioner. His dick pressed between us, and I couldn't help running my hand down him. I leaned in, caging him between my hand and my abdomen. He let out a guttural groan, thrusting once, twice, then stepping back with his mouth tight. I loved how close he was to losing control.

"Turn around," he said gruffly.

I glanced back to find him lathering up a washcloth with my body wash. He started with my shoulders as he stood to one side, his eager cock grazing my hip with each movement. It was all I could do to keep my hands to myself.

His touches were gentle and light, meant to tease and awaken but not satisfy. The exquisite torture lit my nerves on fire, stoking the blaze in my core as I ached for release. He washed my back, my arms and sides, then he dragged the washcloth over my chest, just above my breasts.

"Greg," I whimpered.

He smirked, finally brushing the rough cloth over my aching nipple. He cupped, kneaded and fondled as my thighs clenched together. Then he dipped lower to my abdomen.

Anticipation coiled within me, but he made me wait as he washed my feet, ankles and knees. He pushed me gently until my back was against the shower wall, then he lifted one of my feet, propping it up on the low seat. I swallowed at the sight of his lips parting, at the desire in every inch of his face as he stared at my apex.

He slid the washcloth under my right inner thigh, coming so close to where I wanted him. Then he did the same on my left leg. My breaths were shallow, and I couldn't look away.

Finally, finally, he edged the rough cloth along my outer folds, then back, and he brushed my aching clit. I gasped when he dropped the cloth then cupped his hand, letting the water pool in his palm. He rinsed me, pressing his palm into my clit more each time.

By the fourth pass, I was ready to grab a handful of his hair and drag his mouth to me, but he did it first.

His tongue eased along my seam, then his hold on his control snapped. Grabbing my ass, he held me against his wicked mouth, fucking me with his tongue. Delving in, over and over as a delicious pressure built rapidly inside me.

I clutched his hair, taking everything he gave me. I couldn't think, could barely breathe in the face of this barrage of pleasure. My orgasm burst over me like an avalanche, and I screamed his name as I shuddered against his mouth. He held me there until I finally shoved him away, unable to take another second.

"Greg," I breathed as he stood up and turned off the water.

He cupped my cheek. "You're safe now, Rhonda. He can't hurt you anymore."

The lingering pain in his eyes dragged across my soul. "I know." I slid my hand over him, realizing this was healing for both of us, and it was my turn to take care of him.

I grabbed his towel and started with his face, followed by his muscular shoulders. He stared at me, all tenderness as I dried his arms, his abdomen. Then his legs and back. But when it came to his hair, I couldn't reach. He chuckled, bending down for me to towel him off.

I quickly dried myself, then I led him to our bed where I pushed him down. He settled on the pillow and laced his hands beneath his head, content to let me lead. I straddled him, rocking my wet pussy along his impossibly hard length.

Concern still lingered in his gaze, so I said, "I'm okay now, Greg. Really. I'll get help, but I'm done sitting on the sidelines as the world goes by."

Relief flooded his expression, and he reached for me, crushing me to his chest. "Jellybean," he murmured. "You scared me. I thought you were gone for good."

"I'm here," I whispered, and it was true.

Our lips met in a tender kiss, full of promise and hope. But desire quickly flooded back in as our movements became more frantic. I ground against him again, and he moaned in my mouth.

"I seem to remember you promising to fuck me against the wall someday," I said, my voice sultry and full of suggestion.

He raised an eyebrow. "I do remember that." I ground against him once more, and he growled, "Now?"

"Yes, please," I answered demurely.

He rolled us over, his turn to grind against me. Just once. I tipped my head back, basking in the friction before he stood. Grabbing my legs, he dragged me to the edge of the bed and picked me up. I wrapped around him, our mouths colliding hungrily as he strode toward the wall.

My back hit the cool surface, and his fingers dug into my ass seconds before he slid himself inside me. I gasped as he filled me. He stilled, dipping his head so his lips hovered before mine.

"Greg?" I asked, concerned.

"I missed you," he whispered.

I tightened my legs around him. "Show me," I demanded, knowing he was worrying about how fragile I was, knowing he was struggling to keep in control. And that wasn't what I wanted at all.

He stared at me for a long second, and I deliberately gripped him with my inner walls. It was enough to break his barriers. He slammed into me, leaving no space between our torsos, and his cheek pressed to mine as he kept up a furious pace. I clung to him, taking all of it and knowing with every second that I was safe.

Another release beckoned, and I clenched around him, making him groan. He gripped me so hard I knew his fingerprints would leave a mark. But they were from him, and I would wear them with pride.

His breathing became ragged, and mine matched. He frantically slid his hand between us, pressing his thumb against my clit. It triggered my release, and I buried my mouth against his shoulder as I dug my nails into his back.

He bit out my name, slamming into me one last time before he went rigid.

The only sound was our heavy breaths, though my heart pounded so hard, I wondered if he could feel it.

When I could finally speak, I kissed his lips, then his cheek, and said, "I think that is my new favorite way to come on your cock."

He let out a surprised laugh and shook his head. Brushing a strand of my hair back, he smiled and said, "I love you, Jellybean."

My heart was full, almost to bursting. And I knew I'd turned a corner today, because of him. I put all my feeling into my words as I answered, "I love you, too, Just Greg."

* * * *

I kept my word about getting help. Greg even booked my appointment, offering to go with me if I needed. The therapist was kind, understanding and insightful. My sessions made all the difference, and I wished I'd started sooner. I made sure to thank everyone for pushing me to go. I planned to keep going, knowing it'd be a while before the incident was truly behind me.

The night of the big dinner with my parents finally arrived. I tried not to be nervous when we walked up to the elegant restaurant. We were a little early, wanting to be seated first. I wasn't ashamed of Greg at all, but I knew my parents, knew their elitist attitude and was afraid of what they might say.

It wouldn't matter to them that Greg was the best thing that had ever happened to me, that he was a thousand times better than anyone else I'd ever chosen. All they'd see was 'former chauffeur' stamped on his forehead. But I was borrowing trouble. Maybe they'd surprise me...

And maybe pigs would fly.

Derek, Avery, Gina and Liam came in right after us, all dressed to the nines. Josh had planned to come but had an 'emergency' rehearsal at the last minute. Gina had been beyond annoyed, but he'd refused to budge. Derek ordered us appetizers and champagne, winking at me as he did so. I hid a smile, but not fast enough to escape Greg's notice.

When the hostess brought my parents over, Greg squeezed my hand. "Here we go."

I stood up to greet my parents, as did Derek and Avery. I let them say hi first, then kissed my father, followed by my mother, carefully staying between them and Greg.

"So where is this new beau?" Mom asked.

Greg stood up, taking his place next to me.

"Mom, Dad, you know Greg Peterson? We reconnected recently, and I spent New Year's with him in Marquette, meeting his family. He's —"

"The chauffeur," Dad said flatly, and my heart sank.

"Rhonda, is this some kind of joke?" Mom looked around as if trying to spy a hidden camera crew.

I protested, "No. Greg is the real deal, better than any guy I've ever met. If you just give him a chance —"

"No daughter of mine is dating the hired help." Dad practically vibrated with anger. "I forbid it."

It was an effort to keep my voice even as I met Dad's irate stare. "Fortunately, that's not your right anymore. I choose Greg. You can either accept that and have a nice dinner with us…or you can leave. But right now, you're making a scene."

There was nothing my parents abhorred more. Mom glanced at Dad, always looking to him for direction.

Dad straightened, knocking his heels together. "Come, Harriet, we'll find dinner elsewhere." And they left.

Even though I'd pictured it a hundred times in my head, the image of them walking away had me unable to stand in the wake of the pain wracking me. I took several steps after them before I even realized what I was doing. They'd chosen their image above their daughter's well-being. I'd known my father was callous, putting business and money first, but I'd thought I rated somewhere up there.

I saw Greg, and I took in his tight mouth, his downcast eyes. I wasn't the only one they'd hurt. His words echoed in my head, *"It's one of my biggest fears, that I'll be the one to hold someone back, be the thing that keeps them from reaching their potential, the brick that makes them drown."*

I strode back to my boyfriend. "Hey." He didn't look at me, so I slid my hand down his arm to entwine my fingers with his, leaning into his arm. "It doesn't matter what they say. It's their loss for not seeing how amazing you are. You're not holding me back—you're helping me through. I couldn't do this without you, Just Greg, and I love you. So very much."

His lips twitched, and he squeezed my hand before finally meeting my gaze. "I love you, too, Jellybean."

Derek appeared next to us. "Hey, they'll come around, just give them time. I know it hurts now, but it won't be like this forever. Trust me." His smile was full of empathy.

I knew I could believe him. I'd just helped my parents see his full potential a month or so before, and they were still coming to terms with it. This was my first time being on the receiving end of their snubbing, though. It would take some getting used to.

But Derek patted my hand. Then my gaze kept going, meeting Avery's caring stare and heartfelt nod. Gina looked like she'd murder my parents if she could. Even Liam seemed annoyed on our behalf. We weren't alone.

"Thanks, guys." I squeezed Derek's hand back, then leaned into Greg. "Thank you all for being here and loving us the way we are." I paused, an ironic smile forming on my lips.

"What?" Greg asked curiously.

"I didn't even get to tell them that you're the heir to the Peterson logging empire. They have no idea they just snubbed Marquette royalty." I giggled.

Greg sniffed haughtily. "They will rue the day."

We all laughed, the lighter mood returning. Then Liam pulled out his wallet, throwing a twenty at Gina who beamed.

I frowned. "What's that for?"

"I bet they'd at least sit down." Liam crossed his arms, leaning back in his chair to sulk.

Gina shrugged. "Sorry, Rhonda, but you two didn't stand a chance."

Standing up and clearing his throat, Derek said, "All right, moving on. There's another reason I wanted you all here tonight, and I was hoping our parents could be part of it, but they had their chance." His hand went in his pocket, and he walked around to stand next to Avery, moving the chair next to her so there was plenty of space. Then he knelt on one knee, taking her hand.

She gasped. "Derek!"

"Avery, you are the love of my life, the sweetest thing in it. Since the day you walked up and kissed me out of the blue, I haven't been the same. I know we haven't been together very long, but I've never been more certain of anything in my life. I want to spend the rest of it with you. Cupcake, will you make me the happiest man in the world, and do me the honor of becoming my wife?" He pulled the box from his pocket, opening it to show off the gorgeous rose-gold ring.

"Yes. Yes!" Avery flung her arms around my brother, kissing him over and over.

He finally calmed her down enough to slide the ring on her finger, a perfect fit. "Do you like it?"

She nodded, blinking away tears. "I love it."

Greg leaned over to whisper in my ear, "This is your big secret, isn't it?"

I grinned and gave him a short nod. "Surprise."

"I think you nailed it." The intensity of his gaze caught me off guard and took away my breath. "I love you." The words were a whisper meant only for me.

"I love you, too."

"Champagne, for everyone! She said yes!" My brother's happy declaration cut through our moment, but I couldn't fault him.

Especially when I got champagne out of the deal. With our glasses full, we raised them high, clinking them together and yelling, "Cheers!"

It was a fun-filled night of celebration, laughter, and joy. I couldn't have been happier for two of my favorite people.

Before we left, Avery grasped my hands. "Rhonda, after all those stories from Greg about how you saved his sister's wedding, would you help me plan mine? I have to admit, I can't think of a better person to do it."

It felt like all the pieces of my past aligned, all my niche skills and my connections had brought me to this one shining moment. My eyes were open to what I needed to do with my life. "Oh, Avery, I'd love to." I pulled her in for a hug, unable to express how her simple question had shown me my purpose.

When we got back to the dark and empty house, I looked around once again, feeling even more secure in my revelation. Then I grinned at Greg, tugging him to the sofa. "I know what I want to do."

He smiled tenderly as his hand stroked my hair. "What's that?"

"I want to start my own business, as an event planner. I'm perfect for it. I have all the connections and just the right background." I beamed. "What do you think?"

His grin widened. "I think you're right. You are perfect for it."

I bounced on the couch, then tucked one leg under me as I faced him. "I don't want to do it here, though. I want to move, Greg. To Marquette." I swallowed, nerves gripping my gut. "Will you come with me?"

"What?" He grew serious as he waited for an explanation.

"I know it seems out of the blue, and maybe it is. But I didn't just fall in love with you up there. I fell in love with the place, even in the dead of winter." I stared at him, showing him how earnest I was.

"Since I've been back, nothing feels right. This house doesn't fit. This town isn't me. I can't find my place here. But anytime I think about the little shops on Presque Isle, or Raymond's restaurant, or the rows of chocolate at Decadence, I get homesick."

He still seemed skeptical. "But you just agreed to do Avery's wedding."

"So much is done online or through email anyway. Plus, she was talking about a destination wedding, which would all be remote in the end." I grabbed his hand. "Remember when I asked you if you'd ever want to move back up there? How you said the land is just begging for someone to conquer it?" I searched his face. "The land calls to me. I've never felt more at home than up there, with you. What do you say? Will you go with me?"

Silence was my answer. The pause was long enough that my heart began to sink, making me question what I'd do if he said no.

"Rhonda, I'll go anywhere with you." A disbelieving smile split his face. "Really? You want to move to the U.P. with me? *You* want to be a yooper?"

I nodded.

His whoop echoed off my house's empty walls, and he picked me up, swinging me around. "We can go snowmobiling, skiing, hiking, swimming…"

Joy swirled in me at his exuberance. "And watch sunsets on Raymond's deck."

He nodded. "And start your business together."

"Together." That magic word made my happiness bubble over. "I love you, Just Greg."

"I love you, too, Jellybean."

As his lips met mine, I wrapped my arms around his neck, clinging to my rock, my partner, the man of my dreams who would be by my side as we started the next chapter of our lives, hand in hand. Together.

Epilogue

"Are you sure you want to do this?" Greg asked, concern written all over his face.

I squared my shoulders as I stood outside The High Five and raised my chin. "It's the only way we could all get together one more time before we move." Between Gina and Derek, it had been a bear getting all our schedules aligned.

But the last time I'd been here was when Kevin...

I shoved the thoughts aside. This was just a normal bar, nothing sinister about it, I reminded myself. Kevin couldn't hurt me since he was locked away in prison. I needed to face this.

Taking a deep breath, I laced my fingers through Greg's. "Let's go."

Together we walked inside the bar. I winced as soon as I stepped fully in, a horrendous voice assaulting my ears. No one had mentioned it was karaoke night.

The bouncer greeted us over the caterwauling, and Gina waved on her way to deliver a beer. The tension that coiled inside me eased when I saw for sure there was no Kevin. His ghost was erased by the awful singer and the enthusiastic crowd. The place had a whole different energy to it tonight. And I was oh so grateful.

As long as I avoided the bathroom, I should be fine.

"I've got them, Burt," Gina called, hurrying back to us. "Hey guys!" The singer tried and failed to hit an extremely high note making us all wince. "Sorry about the 'karaoke'." She used her fingers to make quotes around the word. "It's not usually quite this bad."

I kept my smile on my face, though it was an effort. "Hopefully she only signed up for one song."

We all laughed painfully, then Gina nodded toward the tables. "Liam already has a place back here."

Greg and I hurried after her as she led us to one of the tables in the middle of the bar. Liam grinned when he saw us, and I waved in response. Menus and silverware were all laid out, so we just claimed a spot. My phone chimed, and I pulled it out of my purse.

"Oh," I frowned. "Derek got held up at work, so they'll be twenty minutes late. He said to go ahead and order if we're hungry."

Gina frowned. "Josh is running late as usual, so no need to wait for him."

Liam didn't need to be told twice. "I'll take an order of wings with—"

"Ranch," Gina said along with him, smirking. "You'd bathe in the stuff if you could."

"How do you know I don't?" he quipped back.

I raised my eyebrows at Greg, disbelief coursing through me. They were teasing each other, in a fairly civil manner. Was the world ending? When Gina left, I leaned over to Liam. "What's going on?"

He frowned. "What do you mean?"

"I mean you didn't bite Gina's head off and you just teased her back. Are you feeling okay?"

He rolled his eyes. "I'm in a good mood, all right?" He took a sip of his beer, but his cheeks seemed flushed. And not from the alcohol.

I folded my arms, leaning back in my chair. "If you're in such a good mood, why don't you go sing for us?"

Growing up with Liam and Piper had been an amazing experience. Piper had gone on to fame because of her voice, but I'd always thought Liam could have done the same. I hadn't heard him sing in forever.

He shoved away from the table. "I think I will," he smirked before striding toward the karaoke table.

Greg draped his arm over the back of my chair. "This should be interesting."

As Liam took the stage, I glanced at Gina, wondering if she'd heard him sing before. She was busy washing glasses, preoccupied at the sink. The twanging opening notes of Garth Brooks' *Two Pina Coladas* echoed through the place, then Liam's strong, velvety voice filled the room. Diners quieted, the clink of silverware faded and people paid attention.

Including Gina.

She glanced up, then did a double take with her jaw hanging down. She straightened as she watched him, absently setting the glass down as soap dripped down her arm. As if she couldn't tear her eyes away. I nudged Greg, and he grinned when he saw Gina.

"Maybe Avery's dreams will come true after all." He chuckled.

Avery always waxed on about how perfect it would be if she could get Gina and Liam together. But I'd never thought it possible.

Gina suddenly flinched and shook her head, then returned to her work. She didn't look at Liam again, a sure sign she was trying too hard to avoid him.

To my surprise, Liam didn't come straight back to our table. He detoured by the bar and chatted with Gina. Her face lit up before she schooled her features into a neutral, friendly expression. They talked for a few and shook hands.

As soon as he came back, I pounced. "Okay, what was that all about?"

He shrugged, leaning on the table. "Just burying the hatchet. What you said made me think that there should be some truce, at least for the wedding. I mean, I'm the best man, she's the maid of honor." He took a sip of his beer. "It just seemed like the right thing to do."

"We're here!" Avery sang as she sashayed in the door, Derek on her heels.

I stood up to return her exuberant hug, then embraced my brother. Gina rushed over to get their drink orders, and I surveyed my friends, knowing I would miss them. Yeah, I was really looking forward to moving to Marquette, but leaving these wonderful people would be extremely difficult.

As if he knew what I was thinking, Greg stroked my shoulder with his large hand then gave me a squeeze. I looked up to meet his warm gaze and soft smile. There was no doubt in my mind that I was making the right decision. This man was worth it.

And so was I.

Want to see more from this author? Here's a taster for you to enjoy!

Sweet Nothings: The Red Hot Stakes
Maren Jenner

Excerpt

I stared intently at my phone as Gerard Butler appeared, the opening bars of *Music of the Night* from *The Phantom of the Opera* beginning in my left ear. My eyes didn't leave the screen as I used one hand to shovel the bland chili I called my dinner into my mouth. *At least it's free.* The bar I worked for, The High Five, had it on special tonight, though there was nothing special about it.

"Yo, Gina!"

The familiar voice overpowered Gerard's, and I sighed, hitting the pause button. Liam Davenport, the best friend of my best friend's fiancé, was here. Again. He'd recently started showing up on a weekly basis, which wouldn't be so bad if he didn't enjoy pushing my buttons so much.

"Gina Rossi!"

The use of my full name got my attention, and I turned to glare at him.

A satisfied grin spread over his face when I met his emerald-green eyes. "You on break? Where's your area?"

He's persistent. I'll give him that. I set my jaw, glancing at the three guys I didn't know who huddled near him, all their eyes on me.

His grin widened when my gaze met his. "What time do you get off?"

Oh, that's just too easy. My mind immediately jumped into the gutter, and I smirked, happy to repay the inconvenience of him interrupting my break. "For you?" I raked my eyes over him then sniffed haughtily. "Never."

His group burst into laughter when Liam shot me a dirty look. One of his friends glanced at him with sympathy. "Want some ice for that burn, man?"

Burt, the bouncer, arched an eyebrow at me. "These guys bothering you, G?"

I waved him off. "Naw, Burt. They're fine." I met Liam's exasperated stare with a smug smile. "I just have to make sure they know what they're getting themselves into. Go ahead and put 'em in my section. I'll be over in a few."

Liam and I had formed a truce a few months after Avery and Derek had gotten engaged in February. We'd agreed to put our differences aside for the sake of Avery and Derek's wedding. They were our best friends after all. Since then, he hadn't been quite so irritating. He was a decent tipper, and the caliber of our karaoke improved any time he took the stage. Plus, Avery liked him.

But that didn't change the fact that he was still Liam. Get on my every nerve, push my buttons, annoy the living shit out of me, Liam.

His gaze lingered on me as Burt checked IDs, stamped hands, and finally let them pass, directing them to a booth in my area. Liam winked at me before sitting down, as if he'd won something by getting me to cave. It set my teeth on edge.

I slid a piece of cinnamon gum in my mouth then hurried to clear my dishes. Gerard disappeared as I pushed the button to make my screen go blank.

Phantom would have to wait.

A sigh escaped me. I'd really been hoping to hear something decent before karaoke got under way. Preoccupied by the thought of the caterwauling line-up in my future, I forgot about the uneven lip between the bar and the kitchen, snagging my toe. Luckily, I managed to catch myself before face planting.

The cook, Wyatt, chuckled. "All right there, G?"

I nodded, glaring when he laughed more. We'd all complained to Mr. Weston about the hazards of that stupid lip to no avail. *What will it take to get it fixed?*

In a nook of the kitchen was a mirror I used to check my teeth for any stray bits of food, then I finger combed my pixie cut hair, applied my tinted cherry lip gloss and retied my apron. I practiced my smile until it didn't look fake before making my way to Liam's table.

All eyes were on me when I arrived. "Hey, as I'm sure you heard, I'm Gina, and I'll be your server tonight. What can I get you?"

The guy to my left clearly hadn't learned his lesson when I'd put Liam in his place earlier. He scanned my length, looking up in what I guessed was supposed to be a seductive way. "Sugar, I'll have one of you." His eyes stopped on my coworker, a willowy blonde named Sarah. "With a side of her. And we can go anywhere you want."

His friends chuckled, all except Liam.

I leaned both hands on the table, snapping my gum right in the guy's ear. I wrinkled my nose at his oily hair and the odor wafting up to me. "Sure, honey. Let's start with the shower. It's about time you got introduced."

"Ohhh!" The guy's cheeks flushed as his friends slapped his shoulders.

My eyes found Liam's, and I smiled at the approval in his gaze. "Now, to clarify, is there anything you'd like to eat or drink? I am *not* on the menu."

Liam just chuckled as his friend slumped against the booth. "How about a pitcher of Bud, a large buffalo wings, large nachos and waters all around?"

"Ranch?" I asked, already knowing the answer.

"Of course."

With one last snap of my gum, I grinned. "I'll be back with the beer as soon as I get your order in." I collected the menus, stopped at the kitchen to give Wyatt the food slip and started filling their pitcher. After I'd set the beer and glasses on the table, Liam nudged the guy who'd hit on me.

His friend cleared his throat. "Gina? I'd like to apologize for my earlier rudeness. Please accept my apology."

I glanced at Liam, who winked before I turned back to his friend. "On one condition."

Hope sprang into his gaze as he looked up. He'd do anything, and I knew it.

"Karaoke begins in ten minutes. You start the singing, and all is forgiven."

He looked to Liam whose glare had him swallowing, making his Adam's apple bob. "Okay."

"Great." I beamed. "Follow me."

Five minutes later, I was back behind my bar while the poor sap turned pages in our plastic bound book of song choices. My gaze flicked to Liam automatically, and he raised his glass in my direction before taking a sip. I dipped my chin in acknowledgment.

"He's been in here an awful lot lately." Sarah set down her empty tray, nodding the table of guys. "What's his deal?"

The last thing I needed was her thinking something was going on between the two of us. I shrugged. "He's just a guy I know. My best friend's fiancé's best friend." I looked away from her disbelieving stare.

"Yeah, right. I never see him when you're not here." She started filling a pitcher of Bud Light while I moved over to wash our never-ending stack of dirty glasses.

Several women sauntered over to slide into Liam's booth, and he slung an arm behind one of them.

I let out a triumphant, "Hah! See?" I pointed with the dripping glass. "*That's* why he's here. He comes on karaoke night to pick up some chick and take her home."

He never hung out with the same girl twice. Not since his last girlfriend, Carla, and the escape room fiasco.

Sarah snorted. "He hasn't left with a girl yet."

Wait, what? My forehead furrowed as I frowned at her.

"You haven't noticed? He flirts with one girl all night, gets her number, then leaves. Alone." She lifted a shoulder. "I think there's only one person he wants to impress, and she's behind this bar. In ten minutes, he'll be over here asking you what song he should sing, using the girl in his booth as an excuse."

My eyebrows almost shot off my face at the implication.

A grin eased over her mouth. "Five bucks says I'm right."

Unease sat within me like a brick. Everyone knew I only bet on sure things, and I rarely lost because I always listened to my gut. But that meant Sarah was right, which couldn't be true.

Liam and I were like oil and water. Like black and white. Like heads and tails. We were never on the same side of things, always betting against each other. The idea of anything happening between us was so ridiculous, I couldn't not take the bet.

I nodded firmly. "You're on."

Seven minutes later, Liam sauntered over to slide on to a bar stool. "Hey, Gina. Help me figure out what song I should sing for that girl."

Sarah strode by, nudging me with her elbow before she grabbed her food order. Her voice carried, loud enough for him to hear. "You owe me."

I glared after her, my mind racing as I turned back to Liam. "Um, you can't pick one out?"

"You haven't steered me wrong yet." His emerald eyes glittered in the neon beer lights from behind the bar.

The word no was on the tip of my tongue, but when I opened my mouth, a sigh came out instead. "What's she into?"

A brilliant grin lit his face. It totally changed him, and I blinked when he eagerly leaned forward. My stomach flipped, and my lips tilted up on their own as the sight drew me toward him like a magnet.

"She likes the old country, deep twang."

I nodded. *His teeth are so straight.* "Like Johnny Cash?"

"Perfect." He held my gaze, locking me in as if he had some strange spell over me. "Which song?"

Have his lips always been that full? I quickly gave myself a mental shake, trying to clear the daze I was in as I tried to remember what we'd been talking about. *Oh, right, Johnny Cash.* "*Ring of Fire?*" It was one of my favorites.

His voice dropped, low and husky. "Do you like that one?" When I nodded, he smacked the bar, startling me fully out of my trance. "Thanks, Gina." He winked, jumped off his barstool and strode toward the karaoke station.

I watched him walk away, wondering what the hell was wrong with me. Sarah whisked by, and I grabbed her arm, yanking her hand to my forehead. "Do I feel warm to you?"

"What? G, what's your problem?" She snatched her arm back and went to wash her hands.

No fever…maybe I have food poisoning? Maybe the chili's bad? The first strands of *Ring of Fire* started up, and Liam grabbed the microphone. He saluted me, then his eyes flicked back to the booth, to the girl we'd picked the song out for. I relaxed. *I had just been helping him out.*

But then he started singing.

I hated this part. His voice was like cashmere, and I wanted to wrap myself in it for the rest of the night. The first time it'd happened several months ago, I hadn't realized it was him singing. I'd always been a sucker for a guy with a voice. When I'd turned around to see him on stage, I hadn't known whether to cringe or stare longer.

Liam was actually kind of hot when he sang. He had a good four inches on my five-foot-seven frame and he was muscular, fit. Somehow, the stage lights made him drool-worthy. I loved hearing his deep voice belting out, seeing his corded forearms tense as he gripped the mic and those tight jeans clinging to his hips…

"Earth to Gina!" Sarah snapped her fingers in front of my face.

I jumped, blinking at her. "Holy crap, what?"

She just laughed. "Table seven wants you. And where's my five bucks?"

I reached into my pocket and threw a five-dollar bill at her. "Here." Then I stomped off to see what table seven needed as Liam finished his song.

They wanted a full round, and Liam's table flagged me down after I'd delivered it. Just as Liam slid in. The brunette plastered herself to Liam as soon as his ass hit the booth. *Not that I was staring at his ass.*

"That was amazing," she crooned, pressing her boobs against him.

I cleared my throat. "Did you guys need something?"

One guy had his arm around a skinny blonde who leaned heavily on him. "Another round, right?"

"Kitchen's closing in ten. Any last food orders before we shut her down?" I glanced at Liam only to find him staring at me.

He quickly ducked his head, his cheeks flushing before he looked around the table. "Nah, just the drinks."

Then the floodgates opened. Sarah and I had trouble keeping up after that, running drinks, tending bar, cleaning tables. It was a lot. All to the wonderful music of amateur karaoke. It was probably a good thing Liam had sung early on—I didn't have time to lose focus again.

Things were finally calming when Liam came over to where I was wiping down the bar. "I need your help. One more song, and I get her number."

I sighed, too tired to even protest let alone think of a song. "Just see what other Johnny Cash we have." I went back to washing glasses. *So many.* I even dreamt about cleaning them sometimes.

"No, you have to help me."

Sarah came by with another load of glasses and a knowing glance. "He's ba-ack."

"Relax. I'm helping out a friend." I rolled my eyes as she breezed back by with a full pitcher of beer.

Liam gaped at me. "Did you just call me your friend?"

Shit. "No."

He grinned. "Yeah, you did."

My teeth ground together. "You must have misheard me."

"No, I didn't." He shook his head. "You called me your friend." When I glared, he arched an eyebrow. "Rock, paper, scissors, best two outta three wins. I win, you're my friend."

"I win, and this never happened." I quickly dried my hands and faced him across the bar.

We held out our hands and chanted together, "Rock, paper, scissors, shoot."

His rock beat my scissors. *Dammit.* We did it again. My rock beat his scissors. I held my breath as we faced off for the third time, ending with rock once more. He grinned, covering my fist with his paper and squeezing. I growled as I yanked away from his touch.

"Sorry, *friend*. You lose." Liam put his hand to his ear. "I think you have something to say."

I pursed my lips. "Fine. You win." I gritted my teeth, wincing as I added, "Friend."

He shoved away from the counter, grinning widely. "And now I know exactly what song to sing."

If only I could hide in the back while he was on the stage, but no, the dirty glasses were seemingly endless. And here was Sarah with more, along with another knowing look. The familiar opening of *I've Got Friends in Low Places* started.

Liam scanned the room. "I'd like to dedicate this one to all my *friends*." And he raised his glass, mostly to his booth in the corner. But then his gaze landed on me, his lips tilting in a self-righteous smirk.

I bristled with anger. *This is why I don't get along with Liam. If you give him an inch, he'll take a mile. Or more.* I sniffed. *Low places, indeed.*

His voice was, unfortunately, perfect for this song. I continued scrubbing with renewed vigor as I tried to tune him out. But I lost the battle when the rest of the bar joined in, as if determined to taunt me. My anger rose while I sorted the stack of clean glasses. The song finished just as I ran out of space, and I grabbed a full crate then stomped toward the kitchen.

In my angry haze, I forgot about the uneven threshold lip. Again. My toe caught the spot just right, and I went sprawling. The entire crate of glasses flew into the air, time freezing as I waited for them to rain down around me.

The noise was deafening — glass smashing on every side, some into walls and shelves. The chaos continued for an eternity. I covered my head as best I could while I waited for it to stop. A sharp pain pierced my forearm, but otherwise I was mostly unscathed when it finally quieted once more.

"Gina? Don't move."

Of course, it's Liam. I winced as I moved my arm, pain shooting through it, something wet dripping on my nose. *How'd he even get back here? This is an employee only area.*

Liam squatted in front of me, looking me over. "I said, 'don't move'. Can't you follow directions for one second? You've got a huge shard of glass sticking out of your arm, and I need to make sure there aren't any more."

Wyatt gaped at me over Liam's shoulder. He seemed unscathed, and I was thankful he'd been out of range.

"I'm fine. My arm's the only thing that hurts." I lowered my other arm and straightened, wincing at the tinkle of glass joining the pile on the floor as it slid off me.

"Please."

The pleading note in his voice combined with an earnestness in his eyes made me pause. I sighed, reluctantly obeying. Relief shown in his gaze before he went back to circling me.

"Gina! Are you okay?" Sarah's worried words carried from the doorway to the bar.

"I'm —"

"What happened here?" Mr. Weston's furious voice sounded from the back stairs that led to his office.

Liam stood. "Sir, are you the manager?"

"Owner. And just who the hell are you?"

"Even better. Your employee is seriously injured because of workplace neglect, and I will be taking her to the emergency room as soon as I finish making sure she's capable of walking." Liam gestured to me. "Okay, Gina, go ahead and straighten your back. I need to check your legs."

"Excuse me. Sir!" Mr. Weston stormed up to Liam. "Identify yourself at once."

Liam clenched his jaw, apologizing to me with a glance before he stood to face Mr. Weston. "I'm Liam Davenport."

The pale man went even whiter at Liam's full name. The Davenports were well-known in our area for their political involvement and their obscene wealth. Even my cheap boss wouldn't go toe to toe with a billionaire.

"And Gina tripped on an uneven surface while working in your establishment. One I have heard from several employees that you were made aware of. Multiple times." Liam stepped right up to Mr. Weston's now sweating face. "So if you don't want my family's full team of lawyers suing you within an inch of your life, you *will* get your ass back up those stairs to fill out all the paperwork necessary to resolve this incident."

"Yes, sir." Mr. Weston hurried toward the stairs.

Liam called after him. "I want the paperwork sent to Gina as soon as it's done."

Maybe that stupid lip will finally get fixed.

About the Author

Maren Jenner lives in Michigan with her supportive husband and spunky daughter. She loves writing, and when she's not working on her next book, she's got her nose in a different one. Her summers are spent on any lake she can visit, but the beaches of Lake Michigan are her favorite.

The Cupcake Standard is her debut novel, though she's been writing for as long as she can remember. It's always been a dream to become a full time author. Her dreams wouldn't be possible without the love and support of her family and friends.

Maren loves to hear from readers. You can find her contact information, website details and author profile page at https://www.totallybound.com

Home of Erotic Romance

Sign up for our newsletter and find out about all our
romance book releases, eBook sales and promotions,
sneak peeks and FREE romance books!